Praise for Roy David's previous wo

Lester Piggott; Downfall of a Legend
'Compelling reading.'
Daily Express

'An absorbing and fair-minded account, spiced with a knowledge of racing's shadier side.'
Kenneth Rose, *Sunday Telegraph*

'An enthralling tale, full of pace.'
Howard Wright, *Racing Post*

The Shergar Mystery
'Stunning.'
Daily Star

'Roy David knows more about the Shergar kidnap than any man. His book is the standard work on the saga.'
Brian Vine, *Daily Mail*

Robert Sangster; Tycoon of The Turf
'Roy David's best prose is for the horses, and details of them and the money are vivid enough to make your hands smell.'
Sunday Express.

'A worthy successor to the much-acclaimed book on Lester Piggott.'
Sporting Life

About the author

Roy David has forty years experience as a journalist and has written for most of Britain's national newspapers.

On leaving school in Liverpool, he became a drummer for a Cavern-based blues band, appearing with acts including The Rolling Stones, Stevie Wonder, Sonny Boy Williamson, Howlin' Wolf, Memphis Slim and Eric Clapton and the Yardbirds.

Roy then went into journalism and was at various times a news reporter, crime reporter, sub-editor and racing correspondent.

He is the author of *Lester Piggott: Downfall of a Legend* (Heinemann, 1989), which reached No. 9 in *The Sunday Times* bestsellers list and was short-listed for the William Hill Sports Book of the Year Award. Previous books include: *Short Heads and Tall Tales, The Shergar Mystery* and *Robert Sangster: Tycoon of the Turf*. Roy was also originator and technical advisor of the major BBC drama, *Shergar*.

He lives in Cheshire and is married to an emeritus professor.

By the same author

Short Heads and Tall Tales (Stanley Paul, 1986)
The Shergar Mystery (Trainers' Record, 1986)
Lester Piggott; Downfall of a Legend (Heinemann, 1989)
Robert Sangster; Tycoon of the Turf (Heinemann, 1991)

AN ENEMY WITHIN

Roy David

Book Guild Publishing
Sussex, England

First published in Great Britain in 2014 by
The Book Guild Ltd
The Werks
45 Church Road
Hove, BN3 2BE

Typesetting in Sabon by
YHT Ltd, London

Printed and bound in Great Britain by
CPI Group (UK) Ltd, Croydon, CR0 4YY

A catalogue record for this book is available from
The British Library.

ISBN 978 1 909716 23 0

For all brave journalists and truth-tellers

Thanks to:

Everyone at The Book Guild for their professionalism, especially copy-editor Imogen Palmer for her eagle eye and designer Kieran Hood for a great jacket. Gratitude as well to my friends who read and commented on the work: fellow authors Julian Assange and David Donachie, former colleagues Fred Meachin and Michael Unger, and also to Tony Mulliken, ex-US marine Charlie Rose, Charlie Wright and rock star Bob Young. Finally to my brother Raymond for his encouragement, and, of course, to my darling wife Tricia.

1

20 April 2003

The voice inside Lieutenant Matt McDermott's head taunted him, driving him crazy, as he watched for moving figures on the screen. It sent a gnawing chill, like a hunger, to churn his gut.

'It's just like a video game, man,' it kept repeating. 'That's all... just a crazy freakin' video.'

His eyes reached straining point, fixed on the thermal viewer monitor inside the Bradley Fighting Vehicle. Ahead, he could see ghostly shapes of low-roofed buildings as the vehicle inched slowly towards the Baghdad hamlet. An insurgents' training camp, intelligence said.

'Take them by surprise if possible – and hit 'em hard,' the major had instructed back at base, dispatching two Bradleys, nine men in each, on their first engagement. A pincer movement.

And McDermott, nerves at screaming pitch since leaving HQ, was in command. His rookie operation.

He fingered the crucifix around his neck and prayed: *Dear God, help us all get through this.*

The Bradley came to a halt, now in range. He ordered his driver, Bobby-Jo, to cut the engine. Now they switched to silent watch mode, the only sound the faint hum of battery power.

Still no movement on his screen. What was he waiting for? He'd visualised coming under attack as they'd drawn closer, maybe a barrage of mortars, RPGs, Kalashnikovs. Then returning fire with the Bradley's superior force.

But he had the element of surprise. The enduring simplicity of battle throughout the ages. Invaluable. The perfect offensive action scenario – just as they'd said at the Academy.

'Wait, wait, wait,' McDermott breathed into his mouthpiece to the six infantry outside, taking cover behind the Bradley.

McDermott's master gunner, Joe Herman, also received the order in his turret. He could see the target buildings through his night sight.

Suddenly, the sound of gunfire. Although distant, McDermott was taking no chances. 'Open fire!' he yelled.

Herman's 25 mm cannon burst into life, spewing out rapid-fire rounds into the darkness – a thunderous, overpowering, metallic hammering, shaking the frame of the Bradley and sending McDermott's seat jumping. The noise seemed so much louder than on exercise.

Instantly, red tracers from the rest of the unit smashed into the huddle of ramshackle houses. On the monitor, McDermott saw them as dotted white lines, rising in a slight arc at first, then falling away.

The Bradley's grenadier, a twenty-year old acne-ridden kid they called P.J. from someplace in Iowa that none of the unit could remember, was ordered to let loose with illumination rounds from his grenade launcher.

In the eerie light from the white star clusters, McDermott spotted figures scurrying to a gap between buildings. He counted three, dark-clad. One stumbled. 'Hajiis – LEFT!' he screamed. The unit's sustained fusillade dropped them all in seconds.

A minute later, after no sign of resistance, he called for a ceasefire. Silence. 'You okay, Herman?' The words came out croaky.

McDermott had cautioned his gunner about the earplugs. He'd caught him on their last exercise without them, oblivious to the black and yellow warning sticker in the turret near his head. 'You'll be deaf by the time you're thirty,' he'd admonished.

Now he wasn't wearing them again. It was against regulations. But what could he say? He'd had no answer to Herman's retort that muffled messages can get you killed.

2

'Yeah, Lieutenant. Just fine and dandy,' Herman now replied from the turret.

'Wait some,' McDermott said.

No one flinched. Except McDermott himself. Sudden excruciating cramp in his left calf muscle. The commander's seating compartment in a Bradley, back-right of the driver, was a squeeze for anyone over 6 feet. Grimacing, he shifted posture, half-standing and flexing his foot upwards, so the spasm vanished just as quickly.

Outside, his men waited, soaked in the sweat of fear and adrenalin. Half-choked with dust and cordite, some gasped for breath in the windless calm. Somewhere in the distance, dogs barked. Then more gunfire. McDermott deduced it came from the second Bradley, realised it was the origin of the first shooting they'd all heard.

'Hit the lights and wait ten,' he said. 'And, Herman – don't forget!'

Herman's searchlight flooded the area. McDermott trusted he'd remembered to slide down behind the armoured glass window of his turret. In a briefing to young lieutenants fresh out of West Point like himself, the consequences were hammered home. Some dumb-cluck gunner who forgot ended up in the mortuary with a sniper's bullet through his right eye.

McDermott gulped hard. They were 300 metres away but, in the screen's close-up mode, he could see the shapes of several bodies in and around the alley. So this is what it's really like. The killing. This taste of war. 'Dear Lord,' he whispered under his breath.

Duty called him to survey the carnage, yet he didn't want to move.

'Fall in,' he eventually spluttered to his men who gathered behind the vehicle. 'Let's go, Bobby. Real slow,' he said to his driver.

Bobby-Jo started up, hit the accelerator and, grabbing the steering yoke with both hands, moved the Bradley forward on its tracks. Closing in, McDermott called a halt. Lowering the rear ramp, he picked up his rifle and dismounted. On his first few steps, his legs felt unsteady – not just because of the rocky terrain.

He left Bobby-Jo sitting rigid in the driver's seat, Herman on cover, now with the machine gun. Leading the rest of his men towards the buildings, he made sure they fanned out, just like the infantry manual said. Closer, he could see some of the buildings were rough breeze-block affairs with corrugated iron roofing, other structures crudely assembled.

'Semi-auto,' he ordered, activating the night light on the barrel of his gun. A one-pull burst of three rounds was enough to take anyone down. The pencil beam lit up a doorway.

He gestured for two of his men to go round the back, his forward obs man and another to check the alley. With the other two, he ran to the only entrance in sight.

McDermott kicked the flimsy wooden door so hard it came off its top hinge. 'More light,' he hissed.

P.J. switched on a flashlight, quickly scanning the room. 'Dear God... holy fucking Mary,' he shouted. McDermott constantly reprimanded his men for swearing. This time he didn't flinch.

Two women were slumped in a corner, obviously dead. 'Sweet Lord,' McDermott said, slowly kneeling down beside them. 'Oh, no... no,' he wailed, spotting the shoeless feet of a baby, half-hidden beneath one of the women, whom he guessed was its mother.

He ran his finger down the baby's face, a smear of blood still wet. Probing further, no injury was apparent. Reasoning the crimson slash came from the mother's wounds, he let out a long, laboured sigh and, with trembling hands, picked up the little body which slumped in his arms as lifeless as a doll.

Herman's high-explosive bullets had punched holes through the building's façade like it was papier mâché and the woman had tried to do what all mothers did – protect her baby.

'She must have fallen on it, smothered it,' he said, devastated, hugging the baby as if the embrace could restore life.

The spectre of their ordeal burst into his head. Huddled together in a hopeless battle for existence. Inconceivable terror as bullets pulverised the building. He felt so grateful he'd been too far away to hear the screams.

But the poor child... 'Suffer the little children to come unto me and forbid them not, for such is the kingdom of Heaven.'

Gazing into the baby's eyes almost overwhelmed him. Still open, the deepest brown, staring at him kindly, nearly a smile.

He remembered the photograph of himself, on the mantle-piece back home. The same look in the eyes, the same colour.

For a moment, this was him. Bouncing on his father's knee, all chuckles, after Pop came home from the timber yard, the smell of fresh pine on his rough workclothes. Mom scurrying from the kitchen, wiping her hands on that red apron, con-stantly praising the Lord for giving them this gift, their only one. A boy who was so cherished they cried when he told them he was joining up.

'But why?' they pleaded.

It was a question he had been trying to answer to himself ever since.

His earpiece suddenly crackled to life, his forward obs man from the alley. 'We've just got several old dudes down, Lieutenant.'

'All meet up outside,' he barked, carefully laying the baby down next to its mother, jumping to his feet. He felt flustered, aware his men were watching him. He wanted to reach out, touch the wall to steady himself. God, he wanted to be some-where else, anywhere but here.

He pressed a button on his radio. 'B unit, come in.'

'Yes, Lieutenant.'

'Got anything, Sergeant?'

'All clear and secure. No casualties. Body count fifteen, sir. All male, look like Hajiis to me – loads of weapons, too.'

'Thank Chri... meet up. You stay put. Someone your end shine one.'

Outside, lifting the rifle to his eyes, he peered through the night-sight into the distance, saw a flashing light.

'You got a fix, Lieutenant?' the sergeant said.

'Yeah,' he said, exhaling loudly. 'Yeah, I see you.'

It was only a video, the voice had teased him. But, for the love of Jesus, this was no game.

* * *

A heavy silence hung, pall-like, inside the Bradley as it rumbled back to base.

McDermott dimmed the light, but the pale orange glow still caught faces frozen in sombre reflection.

P.J. began to cough, desperately trying to clear his throat. The noise grated, even above the clanking of the twin turbo diesel engine. McDermott turned his head to look. P.J. raised his hand to cover his mouth, pressing back hard. The lieutenant could see he was starting to retch.

'Halt,' McDermott shouted, the Bradley coming to a quick stop. 'Outside,' he gestured to the grenadier.

Others sat, unmoved, until they heard P.J. throwing up. Two more dived for the rear door, just making it in time. McDermott swallowed hard, could feel the bile rising in his throat. He reached for a water bottle, taking a long gulping drink.

He mustn't be sick, not in front of his men. Stooping, he worked his way to the open ramp. Deep, measured lungfuls of the night air quelled the feeling. He gazed up into the starless sky, a shudder running through him. Rubbing tired eyes, he felt them moist on his fingers.

'Let's hit the road,' he finally urged, handing water bottles to those in need.

Just before starting off, Bobby-Jo fingered a CD he'd picked up at the base, a thumping, heavy metal band he thought would rock them all the way home after the operation. The guys liked his choice of music. He glanced at the cover but put the CD back in his rack, figuring it would have to wait for another day.

Halfway back to base, Joe Herman broke the silence, suddenly exclaiming that intelligence had screwed up big time. 'No women and no children,' they'd assured.

It was true, McDermott thought. He'd read the intel briefing many times, practically knew every word off by heart. They would claim mitigation, of course. Impossible to get everything right.

But where did that leave him? What would everyone say?

Numb, and lost in his own world, visions of the baby flooded his mind, setting his hands trembling. Rubbing sweaty palms down his trousers, he glanced out of his forward periscope, only a mile to base. Sudden fear screwed up his insides. What sort of charge would he be on? His unit had wiped out harmless civilians – under his command. It wasn't his men's fault. Only he would carry the can. He'd step forward, take full responsibility and accept whatever they threw at him. A court martial? He'd be disgraced, annihilated, his whole life in ruins. The thought churned his stomach.

Just before they parked up, McDermott reflected that during the attack, he'd also called them 'Hajiis'. Back in Kuwait, preparing for the invasion, he promised himself he'd be different. He shook his head, disgusted with himself that he hadn't even stuck to that simple vow.

McDermott ordered each of the team to say nothing to anyone. The major would instruct them further after debrief.

Finally dismissing his men, he waited for everyone to disperse then headed for a quiet spot, which he found in the shadow of a palm tree. For several minutes he knelt on a patch of damp turf, seeking God's guidance and offering a prayer for the dead. He wondered what the baby was called, but knew he would never find out.

He strode purposefully towards the major's office, his mind set.

There, he believed he would be in the deepest trouble a soldier could ever imagine.

* * *

'Come in.' McDermott's CO was an experienced tough-nut major named Walter Douglas, early forties, from a good Boston family. He rose from behind his desk.

McDermott stood nervously to attention. He'd tuned himself for the onslaught he thought was coming, his body braced. Would the major shout and bawl, flay his very soul with a terrifying, barbed attack, and suspend him from duty there and then?

'At ease, Lieutenant, take a seat.'

McDermott gulped, licked his lips, his mind at once in turmoil. Was he hearing correctly? He took a faltering step backwards as the major approached.

Smiling, the major extended his hand. McDermott shook it limply. 'I... I don't understand, sir.'

Gesturing McDermott to sit, the major pulled up a chair beside him.

'I bumped into your staff sergeant in the corridor earlier – a damn good result, Lieutenant.'

The words hit him like a Force 10. For a moment, they took his breath away. His jaw dropped, rendering him speechless.

'Lost for something to say, Lieutenant?'

McDermott puffed out his cheeks, ran a hand over his cropped head. 'Well, I just don't know. A good result, sir? But the dead civilians – a baby, women, old men. Intelligence said... '

The major waved his hand dismissively and leant forward, elbows on his knees. He studied McDermott, this tall, lean figure, the hair cut so close he could hardly tell its colour. Rarely had he seen a smile on the boyish features. Come to that, many of his men were still only boys. McDermott was another of those thoughtful, serious young guys the Academy seemed to

8

be turning out these days. Maybe a touch too sensitive for this job. Sometimes it didn't do to think too deeply.

'Never mind intel – they don't always get it right. We don't live in a perfect world.' The major stood up, walked towards his desk. 'How old are you, Lieutenant?'

'Twenty-five, sir.'

'First real action?'

'Kind of.'

'Look, son. The units under your command took out a bagful of terrorists – fifteen less insurgents to worry about. Who knows how many of us they might have killed if you hadn't gone in there. Sure, it's mighty upsetting to see the innocents caught up in this – but this is war, Lieutenant. I've seen it all; Kuwait, Afghanistan, now Iraq, and I can tell you it'll only get dirtier and uglier no matter what they say back home in Washington. They wouldn't know shit from gold. You struck gold tonight – I'll be informing divisional HQ.'

'I... I just can't get that baby's eyes out of my mind, just staring at me, helpless.'

The major pulled out a half bottle of bourbon from a drawer, poured them both a slug. Alcohol, taken by any of the troops, was strictly off-limits. Even so, an illicit market flourished in the locally-produced whisky and the clear moonshine the soldiers called 'Hajii juice'.

'Knock this back, son – purely medicinal.'

McDermott downed it with a grimace.

'Trooper, you go and get some chow. It's just collateral damage, that's all. It happens. Tomorrow it'll be different. I'll speak to every member of the team personally – we all say nothing about the side damage.'

McDermott stood up, wiping his mouth with the back of his hand. He managed a half-hearted salute, wheeled about, and left the office.

His appetite non-existent, he went straight to his room, taking great care not to disturb his sleeping fellow officers.

Without bothering to undress, he took his Bible from the top drawer of his bedside cabinet, and began reading by the light of a small torch, searching frantically for solace.

It was open at the Old Testament, Leviticus, chapter five. His eyes came to rest at verse 17: 'And if anyone doth sin and does any of the things the Lord has commanded not to be done, though he was unaware, still he is guilty and shall bear his punishment.'

He read the verse repeatedly, staring vacantly at the ceiling. Unable to sob, unable to sleep.

A pair of brown eyes haunting him.

2

Just after sunrise in Baghdad. And on the type of cloudless morning that greeted Matt McDermott, it wasn't hard to forget there was a war going on.

A few moments of peace before the construction contractors started up, before the night patrols came rumbling in, before the next rota moved out after only six hours off. Relaxation? Forget it.

Now the sun peeped tantalisingly over the skyline, merely temperate before its 100-degree heat of early spring.

For the next hour or so it would be what his folks back home in Parkersburg, West Virginia called 'fair weather'. McDermott lifted his head to the warmth and tried hard to capture the boyhood essence of mornings such as this with Pop; a fishing spot up the Ohio River where they would stop with the camper and clamber down a steep slope through the trees to the water's edge.

Mom would always tell them to 'watch for those bears' before they set off. But the boy, to his great disappointment, never once clapped eyes on a black bear, although Pop often enchanted him with tales of their habits. Now, he knew that throughout their long winter hibernation, the black bear never eats, drinks, urinates or defecates.

The snarling growl of a nearby bulldozer starting up broke his concentration. He closed his eyes tighter, desperate to remain wrapped in his memory's comforting embrace. But thick acrid diesel fumes assailed him from all directions, forcing him back to the stark reality of a country in chaos.

His shoulders were stiff from last night's concentration at the Bradley's monitor screen. Flexing his head from side to side, little clicks cracked from his neck as he crossed the parade square to the officers' mess. The baby's face peered at him. Several times he shook his head sharply to rid himself of the vision.

A mass of feelings fooled with his mind. Was the major right, that it was just collateral damage? Innocents were bound to die, he knew. They'd talked about it at the Academy. But had they ever seen the repercussions? Had any of them picked up a dead baby and seen those blissful eyes?

And what would Mom and Pop say if they ever found out? It would destroy them, then he in turn.

Right now, he felt hibernation would be a wonderful gift from God.

As he neared the mess, he could see a newly-arrived detachment being put through its paces before it got too hot. He glanced their way. Kids, most of them. Blameless so far. Clean hands. Would they soon have blood on them? Like him? So engrossed in his thoughts, he almost missed their sergeant's salute, recovering just in time to return it.

The door to the mess was closed when he reached it. With a trembling hand, he turned the handle, taking a deep breath before going inside.

The place was packed. The clatter of cutlery on plates sounded its own discordant symphony. Soldiers eating was always a noisy affair. Panic immediately rose in his stomach as he glanced around. Any second now he felt their eyes would be upon him. It would go deathly quiet. Someone would shout out. What would they say? *Murderer*. No, *child murderer*. They'd point his way; accusatory fingers like darts at his soul. All hell would let loose. They were bound to know what happened by now. Someone would have talked.

But, as he stood transfixed, the only reaction was a gentle chiding to 'move along the line'. A sudden feeling of relief swept over him.

Scouring the breakfast menu and surprising himself, he chose a huge rib-eye steak, mashed potatoes, and gravy. A fellow lieutenant beckoned him to join his table. They had been at the Academy together.

'Hey, Matt. You outside the wire today?'

'Later. Me and the boys got ourselves a stand-down for the morning – had a late night.'

'Yeah, I heard something. Sounds like a top result, con-gratulations. I'd like to hear about it.'

McDermott shot him a suspicious look. Deducing the remark held no trace of the sarcasm, the derision, he felt would have been justified, McDermott simply said, 'Maybe... we'll have a coffee sometime.'

Then his fellow officer shook his friend by the hand and saluted him, striding off purposefully into the unbearable heat and the dust.

McDermott idled over his coffee. Would the major be able to keep a lid on it, like he said? If so, for how long? And how would McDermott be able to recount the raid to anyone without lying? And with God as his witness? His heart grew heavy at the very thought.

Closing his eyes, he said a silent prayer for himself and his men for later when he would be out commanding a foot patrol, dodging the bullets and the rats in the raw-sewage-filled gutters, piled high with mountains of stinking garbage in every hell-hole of a street.

And, all the time, not knowing which pile hid the bomb.

* * *

The heavily fortified Green Zone covered some four square miles, a vast area of tree-lined grand boulevards housing the private villas of Saddam's Ba'athist cohorts and his half dozen bombed-out palaces.

McDermott's unit had been hurriedly installed within this myriad of avenues, primarily as part of the protection force guarding the hundreds of civilians arriving daily to help set up the headquarters of the new Coalition Provisional Authority which would run the country.

Leaving the mess hall and turning left into a road that had not yet been cleared, McDermott made his way along a pathway between the rusting wrecks of two Mercedes cars. His gunner, Joe Herman and driver, Bobby-Jo, appeared from the opposite direction.

A motor cavalcade passed by, a Bradley front and rear.

'And still they come,' said McDermott, nodding at the new arrivals.

'They say there's going to be five thousand of them, sir,' Bobby-Jo chimed in.

Joe Herman spat out a piece of gum he'd been chewing. 'From the White House to the shite house, if you'll pardon the expression, sir. These pencil pushers will have to shit in buckets – all the bathrooms have been looted.'

McDermott frowned. 'Yeah, well, let them squabble among themselves as to who gets billeted in which palace. We got a modified shipping container if they're not happy with a villa.'

For a second McDermott sensed an awkwardness between the three of them. Bobby-Jo stared at the ground. Herman was about to speak when a Black Hawk helicopter passed overhead drowning out any attempt.

The lieutenant eased their misery, saluting them both, and marching off. He was sure they'd wanted to talk about last night but he would have discouraged it. Better for him to discuss things with his sergeant, get a feel for the atmosphere, inform the men of his feelings via the sergeant.

He reflected on the mission, his unit's first 'kill'. Sure, they'd let loose with plenty of ammo from their M16s on their big drive north from Kuwait a month ago after the countless waves of precision bombing had softened their way into Baghdad.

The antics of some guys had troubled him, though. So hyped up they shot at anything that moved; dogs, cats, the odd donkey or goat, even their own shadows as the convoy trundled through the Baghdad slums.

'Let them know we're coming, boys,' the major had said. And so they fired, and fired some more. But, when they set up camp in the chaotic days that followed, no one threatened so much as a warning shot at the looters as they ransacked palaces, schools, and hospitals. It was not their concern, they were told. So they stood by, pitifully, and watched.

Like many others, McDermott was amazed no one appeared to have planned for such an event.

* * *

He was relieved to find his room empty when he returned. He closed the door to the muffled 7 a.m. call to prayer from the nearby mosque. Its chants fought a daily losing battle with the lion's roar from the bulldozers and earth movers outside, constantly hungry for more detritus.

A copy of the *Washington Post* lay on a table. The war coverage was front page, several more inside. His eye caught a latest poll showing forty-five per cent of Americans believed Saddam was behind the 911 attack on New York. They also believed his regime was a base for al-Qaeda.

McDermott pondered the findings. Surely it should have been ninety per cent – give or take the doubters. Wasn't this why they were all here? That, and Iraq's weapons of mass destruction which, they'd been told, were just waiting to be found.

A loud rap on the door made him jump. Staff sergeant Dan Rath saluted crisply when McDermott swung open the heavy metal door with a clang. 'Sir!'

'At ease, Sergeant. I thought for a minute it was Saddam come to give himself up.'

'Now that would be a result and a half.'

'Pull up a chair – what's the skinny?'

McDermott had the utmost respect for this man; his honesty, his experience, the discipline he commanded among the men.

He knew they feared a tongue-lashing if they fouled up. 'The wrath of God' was how he'd heard it called.

Wide-shouldered and a few inches shorter than McDermott, Rath was a solid family man, dependable. Just what a young lieutenant not long out of West Point leaned on.

'About last night, sir. We never really got chance to talk about the civilian casualties...'

'Yeah, well. It happens. We gotta keep sight of the main game.' McDermott heard the words tumble from his mouth almost like an out-of-body experience. At the same time, a voice in his head asked him if he was really saying this. 'You did well, Sergeant. The whole unit's happy, the major's happy...'

'Yeah... maybe,' Rath said, hesitant, rubbing his chin. 'You heard the major sent word up the line?'

'So he said.'

'I wanted to say... well, it was your command, Lieutenant. You know I'm no glory seeker.'

McDermott smiled, a melancholy look. If he had been able to see his expression, he would hardly have recognised himself from only a few weeks ago.

The sudden brutal hard-ball of this conflict had already created a stranger within him.

* * *

In his office at the Pentagon overlooking the Potomac River, Gene Kowolski opened the file that had landed on his desk from Command Headquarters in Qatar. It was marked 'highly confidential'.

Richard Northwood, the new director of the CIA's Iraq Bureau, had instructed him to search for a hero, someone who could become the President's golden boy. He hoped the contents he was about to read could provide one.

He took out a pair of reading glasses from his desk. They were new and he still felt ill at ease putting them on. But, since using them, the blinding headaches that often drove him to distraction had mercifully stopped.

At the age of forty-two, he told himself he had done well to get this far without them. It wasn't as if he really needed them, either. They just helped magnify the words enough to lessen the strain. And that was the way he liked to operate these days. No more beating himself up over some issue or another. Stress was what gave guys his age a heart attack.

His doctor had told him a couple of years ago that working at the frantic pace at which he did would end in a one-way street. 'Anyway, you should be married with kids, snot and chicken-pox to worry about – it's a great counterbalance.'

'God forbid,' he'd replied with a shudder.

Ostensibly known as Senior Special Advisor at the Pentagon, his talents reached much further. Some people believed he commanded the ear of the President himself, though no one dared ask him if it were true.

As architect of the media's strict rules of reporting on the invasion and its aftermath, an office and staff awaited him in Baghdad. From there he would monitor events at first hand – a loaded broadside on hand for anyone transgressing his stringent controls.

He opened the thick folder, a profile of Cavalry Officer Matthew John McDermott, Second Lieutenant, attached to US Army Infantry.

Starting with McDermott's early education, Kowolski noted it ticked all the right boxes; reports from each of his years in elementary school, 'a serious, thoughtful boy who applied himself diligently'. That was a theme that ran through junior high and high school. The definitive clincher for what Kowolski had in mind came later.

It was a real gem; three years at the Joshua William Christian Brotherhood College in Pennsylvania, culminating in a general degree. 'Hallelujah,' he exclaimed.

Privately, Kowolski found it loathingly irksome that most of the present White House administration came from such places. But the Joshua William ethos was perfect for this scheme: 'From where Christian men and women will lead our nation and shape our culture with timeless biblical values and all due deference to our Lord's decree.'

McDermott was another product of the boom of the last decade of religious zealotry throughout the country. Rightist colleges like the Joshua William, Virginia's Patrick Henry, Boston's Gordon College and many others, had been encouraged by the present government in word, deed, and financial aid.

The place was full of them. Fundamentalists to the fore, Kowolski called them.

It reminded him of when he'd first become aware of the growing influence of such religious fervour. At a White House meeting several years earlier, to his astonishment, the group was invited to pray and 'seek the Lord's guidance' in what they were about to commence.

He had stood with his eyes open, watching to see if anyone else in the assembly of bowed heads was of the same persuasion as himself. He had caught the eye of a particularly curvaceous brunette secretary who, he noted enthusiastically, was smiling at him.

Later, in bed with her after an afternoon of energetic sex, she admitted that working with a heap of 'geeks' and 'Bible freaks' was getting her down. Though she did not know it, a word from Kowolski to her boss got her transferred out of state and he never saw her again.

Kowolski might not have held the same beliefs as many of his fellow workers but he never let his own personal beliefs obstruct his work. He was a professional, unconcerned with the ideology, the policies, the foibles, of his masters. The irony of his life so far; the more he learned of politics, the more of a turn-off it became.

The cynicism was now almost complete; he simply followed orders with disregard for the morality of it all.

McDermott, he read, then applied to join West Point. Four years at the esteemed military academy, before joining his battalion less than six months ago after finishing among the top of his intake. In Iraq only a few weeks and he had already led a unit that took out fifteen of the enemy. Kowolski almost smacked his lips when he got to the company CO's description of the action and the recommendation for honours.

'You're a hero, son. A goddam hero,' he muttered to himself, closing the file.

* * *

That same day, working on a rush of adrenalin late into the night, Kowolski formulated his ideas, re-writing and editing it several times. He ended by typing, 'All the world loves a hero. We will mould this man into a household name and ensure the ensuing hero-worship rubs off on the President.'

Then he entered an email address few people possessed. When he pressed the send key he knew his message would automatically encrypt. Kowolski sincerely hoped for a response from CIA headquarters at Langley before he left for Iraq. Organising the visit of his country's Defense Secretary, Donald Rumsfeld, had taken up most of his time recently. Now, it was up to him to make sure Richard Northwood's idea actually worked. A successful outcome would provide a massive boost to the President's popularity. In turn, that would attract the tens of millions of dollars in donations so necessary as lifeblood of the re-election campaign.

The reply from Northwood came the following afternoon. It entered Kowolski's inbox as a series of jumbled letters and punctuation marks. He held down the control button of his keyboard, pressed a sequence of numbers, then opened the message.

It read: 'Looks perfect, well done. Better if not seen to have come from you. Get someone within the ranks to suggest it (as his idea) to DR. Take it from there. Regards – Richard.'

Kowolski sank back in his chair. So the CIA's new Iraq chief liked his plan. Good. This would call for all Kowolski's guile, his political experience, so he should have been feeling pleased. When Northwood had come up with the idea of finding a hero, Kowolski could have justifiably protested he wouldn't have space to develop it due to his already considerable workload. But, carried away with the junkie-like fix of the sophistry, the temptation proved too great.

His mind in top gear, he envisaged a strategy where the benefits outweighed the drawbacks. Or did they? Putting the hero McDermott alongside the President would bring the big bucks rolling in for the re-election campaign – that was a certainty. Kowolski had only seen McDermott's service photograph. The kid looked the part, but you couldn't tell a person's character from a picture. Would he be up to what Kowolski contemplated? Could he cope with the adulation that would follow him everywhere? In Kowolski's book, playing the hero in public called for far greater reserves of courage than the bravery they'd shown in action.

Rarely did Kowolski question his own judgement but, for a reason he couldn't fathom, a disturbing unease began gnawing at him. The more he reflected, the more the cloud of doubt hovered, dark and heavy.

With a sigh, he opened McDermott's file again. The young face below the closely-cropped head gazed out at him, the lively brown eyes encapsulating the keenness of youth, the lips slightly parted in something of a self-conscious half-smile.

Kowolski's head was suddenly flooded with the famous Rumsfeld words from a press briefing on Iraq twelve months earlier. Commentators had scoffed, but Kowolski saw a lot of sense in his proclamation.

'There are known knowns – things we know we know. Then there are known unknowns – things we know we don't know.

20

But there are also unknown unknowns – things we do not know we don't know.'

Kowolski figured his most disturbing 'known unknown' was the extent to which the Iraq conflict could affect any man. How would he himself handle it? He had no experience of a war zone, so how would he react? Would they come under fire? He'd been assured they'd be safe within the heavily-fortified Green Zone. But how many 'unknown unknowns' lay lurking?

His mouth dry, he poured himself a glass of water. He figured his subconscious was playing tricks, slightly off-beam with the big trip imminent.

Still, with such high stakes in play, could he afford the consequences if things went wrong? He knew he couldn't. But it was too late to turn back now. The engine had been fired.

Strange for him, the sudden urge to murmur a prayer entered his head. But he felt awkward with himself, not sure what to say. It had been that long.

Failure in this mission would be catastrophic. His career and his reputation were all he had in life.

And without them, he was nothing.

* * *

Richard Northwood gazed out of the expansive window of his new, larger office at CIA headquarters in the Langley district of McLean, a town of 40,000 mostly affluent souls in northern Virginia.

Staring eastwards, he searched for inspiration beyond the vast neat-hedged lawn, hardly registering the dense forest beyond where black oak, dogwood, persimmon and ash buffered the constant roar from the George Washington Parkway.

He turned, catching his reflection in the bookcase against the far wall. The dark hair, greying at the sides, was trim, just short of military style. Although the onset of middle age had initially caused him a degree of consternation, he was now resigned to it in a begrudging sort of manner. Pushing his chin downwards as

21

he did most mornings in front of the bathroom mirror, he was pleased to see no sign of a jowl that might have detracted from the fine jaw line he knew still attracted admiring glances.

Smiling at his reflection, he felt pleased with himself. He hadn't expected such a successful start to his grand plan. The intelligence for the raid on the insurgents' camp had been relatively easy to collate and pass on to the major. The Predator UAV had hovered undetected, its spotter camera recording the encampment's activities in fine detail. The joyous outcome was he'd bagged himself a hero in double-quick time. If he could pull off this trick, he was confident his career would be fast-tracked further. He'd already heard from the White House that his efforts would not go unrewarded if the endgame was judged a success.

Focussing on the contents of the bookcase, he ran his eye along the titles of a neatly-stacked row of hard-backs, mainly classics. He reached out for one, Tom Paine's *Rights of Man*, a work he had never read.

The slim volume, light in his hands, was the same as all the other books on the shelf, a dummy. Its gold-coloured inner edging had been lined to look like pages, but was merely a vacuous piece of cheap plastic designed purely for show.

3

Alexandra Stead pulled her international travelling bag from under the bed and unlocked the clasp.

It was a present from her parents five years ago – her twenty-fifth birthday. But it had lain unused for months and dust billowed into the air causing her to sneeze. She reached for a handkerchief already damp with tears. Hesitant, she began to pack, her sniffs drowned by the cacophony of honking yellow cabs in the Manhattan street below her apartment.

Should she go to Iraq? She knew she must. What little work she'd taken on these past weeks hardly paid the bills. And with another large mortgage payment to make soon, her overdraft was in danger of meltdown. But the concept still filled her with dread.

This guy, Kowolski, wanted only one photographer to cover the Donald Rumsfeld trip to Basra and Baghdad, a top freelance like her who could, as he put it, 'operate under pressure'. So she should have felt flattered to be chosen.

'Your pictures will be syndicated across America – just think of that,' Kowolski said when booking her on the high-praise recommendation of a magazine editor he knew.

In truth, Alex's war pictures had gained coast-to-coast coverage many times, so accepting Kowolski's offer was a case of needs be; money first, fame later. Besides, although the US Defense Secretary was flying into a war zone, the job itself would be straightforward enough. And that was just about as much as she could cope with right now.

Alex had never felt so low. In the months since the end of an affair with a married man, she'd been full of self-recrimination and it had dragged her down as surely as a dead-weight on a

23

body in a river. Things might have been a little easier had there been someone else to blame. But there was only herself.

Pity had turned to loathing, frustration to anger. A whole mix of feelings magnified to manic proportions, usually by the first glass of wine from the second bottle she was drinking most nights. Taking the best part of the day to try and figure out why she felt so down, the cycle would begin again each evening. She knew it had to stop – but it was getting harder. The sides of a pit seemed all the more slippery when you dug it yourself.

Her sleep was being disrupted with frightening regularity, too. The disturbing legacy of her last job abroad in Afghanistan left her with decisions she couldn't find the courage to face.

Letting out a deep, shuddering, sigh, she opened a drawer, took out a couple of shirts and folded them neatly into the bag. She picked up the black beret she'd worn on that fateful day in Kandahar, which brought memories flooding back. She'd been one of the first photographers to land in the province after the defeat of the Taliban. Even the most liberated media outlets had baulked at some of her pictures. To see how the Afghan tribal fighters had treated their Taliban enemy was triple X-rated stuff.

It also raised the question of what she was trying to achieve by recording such hardcore scenes. Her answer always used to be the same; to portray the truth – however horrific. Her passionate, obsessive fight against war seemed to know no bounds.

Her best friend once asked her, 'Why do you do it, Alex? Being so anti-war and all?'

'Everyone's got a voice. Some don't use it. I just hope my work shouts a lot louder,' she said.

But Alex had come to realise the cost of such high principle was now proving emotionally expensive. Doubts about her future as a war photographer surfaced uppermost in her mind.

Once, it had seemed so simple. Inspired by the countless books of iconic photographs on her bookshelf, the transition from staffer on a New York glossy to freelance war photographer proved seamless. She packed her bags – and off she went. No thought of danger, her belief in the pictures she produced and the shows she got outweighed everything else. Her own personal crusade.

Now, she faced the ultimate impasse that many of her battle-hardened colleagues had warned about: the loss of nerve. A contributory factor lay in that very honesty she aimed to portray. Writers, she knew, often stretched the truth and got away with it. Alex wondered if stretching the acceptability of the truth had reached snapping point with the magazines and newspapers she worked for.

She knew she must come to the junction before much longer: to turn left or right?

As her mind wandered, she found herself gripping the beret tightly and when she looked down, her hands were shaking.

Flavours of her bad dream flashed by like a familiar taste. Shivering, she let the beret drop to the floor. Memory rampant, it overruled her attempts to shut them out. She was drowning in a sea of corpses, frantic for air. Pinned down by grotesque lifeless arms and legs, the same suffocating scenario replayed – a bloodied arm splayed across her throat, heavy and choking. Relief only ever came at the last minute – a sudden petrified consciousness that always left her drained, sitting up in bed, bathed in sweat and gasping for breath.

Her phone rang. She went into the living room, quickly trying to compose herself. Answering it, she tried to sound as bright as possible. But the voice of her ex-lover, Richard Northwood, destroyed her calm in an instant.

'Richard,' she croaked. 'I thought we agreed we wouldn't...'

'We did, so I'm sorry for the call. This is business,' he said without trace of emotion. 'I hear you're off to Iraq with Mr Rumsfeld. There's something you could do for me and the department – for old time's sake.'

A growing sense of shock consumed her. Her hand reached for the top button of her shirt. He was asking her to do *what?*

Twisting the button hard, it soon fell off in her trembling fingers.

'I don't believe it – you're asking me to spy for the CIA?'

'We prefer to call it intelligence gathering, Alex. The situation out there is fast-changing. It's only weeks since we dropped the first bomb and the rats and mice have scurried off to their little hidey holes. We need to know where they are – and when they're likely to come out to play.'

'But you've got your agents out there?'

'Of course. We've got a fully-staffed bureau in Baghdad reporting to me here at Langley.'

'So you've been promoted? Well, congratulations.' Then, through clenched teeth, 'I'm sure your wife will be very pleased – you always said she wanted you to go far.'

Although Alex had never met his wife, it was clear she was the driving force behind his ambition. Pregnant with their third child, she'd turned him off. Alex turned him on, he'd said. Her off-beat way, such an opposite to his conventional lifestyle, had enthralled him. And, like a fool, she'd fallen for all of it.

He ignored the jibe. 'Listen, Alex, you know damn well journalists can find themselves picking up bits and pieces – sometimes it's all we need to complete the jigsaw.'

Alex desperately wanted to ask him if he knew how much heartbreak he'd caused her, tell him how much she'd wanted to hear his voice again. She'd rehearsed the scenario a hundred times since they'd split. But not like this. The words just wouldn't come.

'I... I don't know,' she said, lying to him that there was somebody at the door, and hanging up.

Traipsing over to the seat near the window, she gazed up into a cool grey sky. Confusion reigned. She'd spent the last several months hoping he'd call. Now he had, and she hated him – and for what he'd asked. But if he'd turned up at her door and told her he still wanted her, would she have loved him for it?

Winner or loser? Which side of that fine divide was she on?

Angry now, she flung a few more things in her bag hoping Iraq could straighten her out, get her back on track.

All the time, fearing it wouldn't.

* * *

Kowolski noted the change in the drone of the engines of the MC-130 Combat Talon aircraft, guessed they were almost in Basra.

He shifted, mightily relieved the flight from Kuwait was a relatively short one. How the troops managed for hours in these claustrophobic double-facing rows of canvas-webbed seats was anybody's guess. He supposed comfort never figured on the agenda for their normal occupants, Special Operations Forces. Some of them were acting as minders now, dressed in black and sitting silently, knee to knee, hardly moving.

He wondered how their prize cargo was faring. This was a million miles away from a soft office chair in Washington. He glanced along the row. Donald Rumsfeld, co-architect of the invasion, sat at the front end, gesticulating and talking loudly to be heard above the deep resounding roar of the four turbo props. His aides hung on every word.

Kowolski thought the man sitting opposite the Secretary must be feeling pretty pleased, too. Flying a senior politician into the battle zone only six weeks after the first strike was quite an accomplishment for Lt General David McKiernan, commander of the allied ground-force invasion.

He tried to catch the eye of the woman opposite, Alex Stead. Just my type, he said to himself. Just his type? If he were honest with himself, they were all his type.

Slim, Kowolski saw a flash of liveliness about her. Athletic, she looked more springbok than gazelle. Okay, she didn't have model looks, and her fair hair, pulled back and half-hidden under a black beret, was too short for him and quite plain. With her khaki combat trousers and boots, he thought she could almost pass for one of their special-ops minders. But there was

27

something about her eyes, a penetrating grey-green, the sort a man noticed.

He stretched. *Damn seats.* Leaning his squat frame as far forward as he dared, their knees touched.

'In or out?'

'Pardon me?' she asked, feigning innocence, but drawing back.

Damn, he thought. Did I leer just then? 'Your legs, my knees,' he whispered.

'I usually keep my legs closed,' she clipped, those eyes flashing.

He felt the cold shoulder with a vengeance. For the next few minutes he could tell she was pretending to be interested in a geeky White House guy sitting next to her who, he overheard saying, built model aeroplanes. *Model aeroplanes, for Christ's sake!*

The captain's voice over the tannoy told them they would be landing at Basra in five minutes. It was a calm, matter-of-fact, drawl of a Texan. Yet it made Kowolski immediately stiffen.

He knew the captain and his augmented crew – co-pilot, two navigators, two flight engineers and two loadsmen – would now be on full alert. The thought of it made him feel quite ill.

Despite its high-tech missile and radar warning systems, this lumbering giant was at its most susceptible when coming in to land at a 150 knots. That was why he felt beads of sweat suddenly break out on his forehead, caught himself swallowing hard, gripping his seat until his knuckles turned white.

He visualised the pilot pointing the big beast downwards while a flight engineer's hands hovered over the control that would activate a chaff and flare dispenser to send a shooting-star barrage of diverting flak. Just in case anyone down there happened be pointing a SAM missile their way.

For several minutes Kowolski's stomach matched the gyration of the aircraft. His self-preservation sensors screamed full alert. Alex watched him, curious. The brashness had suddenly vanished. Now he wore a strange mask with darting eyes and a set jaw. Had she been a touch closer to him, she would have heard him grinding his teeth.

Alex took pride that her profession had honed her observational skills to a fine degree. Being acutely aware of a subject's demeanour was now almost second nature. Responding to it quickly meant the difference between a good picture and a great one. Studying Kowolski at this moment, she wished she'd had a camera in her hands.

Eventually, they touched down to an almost perfect landing. Kowolski felt a lightness sweep over him as he unbuckled his seatbelt, giving Alex a baleful glare. He was not used to the brush-off. If not for him, she wouldn't even be on this goddam trip, he thought.

He told himself to remind her of that fact before long. Not too sternly because he had another job for her after this. One that would be far more important.

Yawning, he stretched his arms in the air, an act of nonchalance so overplayed it didn't fool Alex as she returned his gaze. What a jerk, she thought. A few seconds ago she was ready to feel sorry for him, watching him squirm in his seat. Everyone had a monkey on their back of one sort or another.

Consulting his clipboard for the umpteenth time, Kowolski squinted at it, hesitant of taking out his new glasses. Alex peered over his shoulder.

'What have we got?' she said.

He briskly put the clipboard under his arm. 'A meeting with the British top brass – Seventh Brigade, First Armoured Division. They've got Basra under control now and our esteemed visitor wants to relay his thanks. You're allowed into the briefings to capture the mood so you'll have to be on your best – no getting in the way.'

Alex offered him her camera case. 'Maybe you'd like to do the job yourself?'

'Okay, okay,' he said impatiently, his hands up in surrender. While waiting for the plane to unload, he considered Baghdad, their next destination. If all went well, he would seize the opportunity to implement the next step of Northwood's grand plan for Lieutenant Matt McDermott, soon to be feted as his country's latest hero.

It was imperative the President got a flying start to one of the most crucial periods of his tenure. The election proper might be some way off, but the want of substantial donations was insatiable. A daunting target for campaign funds had already been set at 130 million dollars by the end of the year. Kowolski's role was crucial. He would remain in Iraq, monitoring the vast outflow of news, ready to pounce on anything that would reflect badly on the White House and, in turn, hamper the inflow of those glorious greenbacks.

And Kowolski knew there could be no slacking. An election vehicle couldn't run without gas. His task was to make sure there was going to be plenty in reserve. McDermott, the hero, was going to help him achieve it.

With this in mind, his strategy was now well formulated. He would casually mention a 'rough idea' to a Rumsfeld aide with whom he was friendly. Ostensibly, the aide would take the credit. This was how Kowolski operated. Word of it would eventually get back to the White House.

And the circle would be almost complete.

* * *

Kowolski waited while Rumsfeld got out of his seat, heard General McKiernan's words: 'Welcome back to Iraq, sir.'

It was twenty years earlier, as President Reagan's Middle East envoy, that the plain Mr Rumsfeld clasped Saddam in a warm embrace to signal the renewal of diplomatic relations following a sixteen-year freeze between the two countries.

Kowolski was then a high-flying politics student at Harvard, studying the Middle East and particularly intrigued by the show of US neutrality to both sides in the ongoing Iran-Iraq war.

Through his subsequent work at the Pentagon, however, he'd

seen a stack of classified documents that revealed the true outcome of that Rumsfeld diplomatic mission.

Although the world assumed America was non-partisan, Kowolski discovered the US was secretly supplying Iraq with military and logistical intelligence soon after the war started. Such aid continued despite Washington being aware Saddam was using chemical weapons against Iran – even on his own people, the Kurds in the north of Iraq.

Kowolski stood stiffly, watched Rumsfeld descending the aircraft's steps for the red carpet treatment on the tarmac below. He wondered if the Defense Secretary ever reflected that some US companies supplied the ingredients for those chemical weapons.

But what could he do to change history?

He was never quite sure whether the discovery of such duplicity proved the turning point in his own sceptical philosophy. Or was his cynicism a gradual progression, like a leaking tap?

That the US knew Saddam was also harbouring various Palestinian terrorist groups in Baghdad, notably the Black June and May 15 gangs, was another irrelevance at the time. 'Political expediency,' Kowolski bluffed whenever anyone raised the subject.

As he left the plane, he mused that the Reagan administration's number one priority those two decades ago differed little from the US objective now: to preserve America's access to oil, to project its military power in the region, and to protect its local allies from internal and external threats.

Kowolski permitted himself a wry smile at this piece of déjà vu some twenty years on. It was important, in the sordid world in which he worked, to keep a semblance of humour.

Even if it was sardonic.

4

Gene Kowolski counted forty-one people in the room besides himself.

Honey-coloured wooden oriental arches, set against veined marble walls, matched the tan leather chairs and sofas of the airport's VIP suite. Secretary Rumsfeld, dressed in a navy blue blazer and grey slacks, listened intently as Brigadier Graham Binns, head of the British First Armoured Division's Seventh Brigade, outlined the Desert Rats' march into Basra and the extent of the resistance they had encountered.

'In some cases it was hand-to-hand combat with bayonets,' the Brigadier noted.

Alex moved with a professional air around the seated group, concentrating on her work and trying to remain unobtrusive. Her mind was solely focussed on the best composition to reflect the mood of the meeting.

Had she dared tune in to the talk of the dead and the injured, the battles and the strategies, she would have been repulsed. So she worked with the cool detachment of a nurse cutting away the bloodied clothes of yet another hopeless casualty.

She glided to the far side of several large coffee tables, chose one of the two cameras around her neck to capture a wide-angled shot. *Oh good*, she said inwardly as Rumsfeld crossed his legs, leant back in the seat, then pressed his fingers together, raising his hands to his lips in contemplative fashion.

By capturing the two plates of uneaten biscuits in the fore-ground, she hoped it would convey the seriousness of the talks. Relaxed as the meeting was, closer inspection of her pictures would reveal there had been no time for cookies.

Kowolski watched her intently. A British officer began an

assessment of the current situation in Basra, a baton pointing to a large map of the city on an easel at the front of the room. She was good, Kowolski thought, just like they'd told him. Fast, efficient, nimble. No fuss.

Alex checked her watch. The meeting had twenty minutes to run, giving her time to send the first batch of photographs over to New York. But, to her horror, she realised they were winding up now.

She swore under her breath. Quickly leaving the room, she hurried along the corridor to a small office, almost slipping on the polished marble floor.

The world was waiting for her pictures. Missing her deadline would be a disaster. And what if they wouldn't wait for her when they left for Baghdad? If Rumsfeld said jump – everybody jumped. Kowolski would be powerless to delay the plane, she was sure.

'Ah, there you are, Miss,' a British army corporal said. 'But I'm afraid the lines are down at the minute.'

'Oh, no!' she gasped, putting her gear down on a desk with a clatter.

Kowolski put his head round the door. 'We gotta go – now!'

'No chance,' Alex said. 'I need more time.'

'Fuck,' he shouted storming off.

Retrieving a USB connector from her camera case, she plugged one end into a camera, the other into her laptop. Her pictures downloaded in seconds, flashing up on screen as thumbnails. Then, satisfied, she repeated the exercise with the other camera.

She typed in an email address, pressed the send button. Nothing.

The corporal watched the screen over her shoulder. 'It can be down for minutes – or hours. Pot luck mostly.'

Flipping open her mobile phone, she checked for a signal, pressed a fast-dial key and waited. 'Phil, hi... it's Alex in Iraq. The first batch of stuff from Basra will be on its way shortly.'

'Shortly?' the agency's picture editor demanded.

'Lines are down.'

'Shit.'

She could hear Phil's agitated voice booming out across his office, imagined the wheels of consternation starting to spin. The agency prided itself on a slick service to the nation's media. Everyone would be awaiting Alex's pictures – they'd have been scheduled in editorial conferences up and down the country.

Voices in the corridor outside grew louder, someone arguing. *Damn*, they were on the move. Her eyes returned to the screen. The waiting was agony. She could feel the perspiration running down the sides of her body, her face on fire. It shot through her mind that she needed a drink.

Phil came back to her. 'This ain't gonna look good, Alex.'

'Tell me about it,' she said, a note of defeat in her voice.

Her mind in turmoil, she tried to think of the best plan of action. It was possible to transfer her picture file to the corporal's computer and ask him if he would send it. Then she could still catch the flight to Baghdad. But it would be torture being airborne not knowing if the agency had received them or not. And if she reached Baghdad to find the pictures had still not got through, what then? She could file them from there herself but she'd have well and truly missed her deadline. Her name would be mud.

'Are you all right, Miss?' the corporal said. He poured her a glass of water.

Alex mopped her brow. 'Thanks,' she whispered. She slumped forward, elbows on the desk, head in her hands. Her first step back into action and it was all going wrong. She'd feared as much.

'Hey, we're back on,' the corporal shouted, excited, rushing to his screen. 'Try it.'

Alex pressed the send key. This time it worked, sending her pictures 6,000 miles in seconds. Her eyes filled with tears of relief.

A minute later, her mobile rang. 'We got them, Alex. Well done,' Phil said. 'Captions?'

'Sorry, not much time. The Brit sitting on the left is Brigadier... wait a sec.' She checked her notebook. 'Graham Binns, commander of the Seventh Brigade, the guy in civvies I think you'll know. The meeting was at Basra Airport – all British top brass. Gotta dash, man. Ciao.'

She hurriedly packed her gear, gave the corporal a hug, and dashed out of the corridor.

When she reached the airport apron, Kowolski was waiting for her at the bottom of the aircraft steps. He escorted her to her seat.

'That was a close one,' Kowolski said, fumbling with his seatbelt.

'Thanks for waiting. Don't know how you managed it.'

'I told them I'd been charged with looking after you and I wasn't shifting.'

She nodded her appreciation. Maybe she'd got this guy figured wrongly. It wasn't every day she'd be able to keep someone like Rumsfeld waiting. Perhaps Kowolski did have a streak of humanity in him.

Alex took the beret out of her pocket, ran a hand through her hair, and put it on.

Kowolski watched. 'I like the way you moved back there,' he murmured. 'You do know you were my choice to come on this assignment?'

'To take pictures – nothing else.'

'Whatever gave you the idea that... ?'

'Just call it a girl's intuition.' She looked him straight in the eye, half expecting a blast.

Instead, he chuckled. 'Okay, I surrender. I guess I'm not as smart as I think I am.'

'No, I guess you're pretty smart.' Then she made an extravagant show of patting her camera case. 'Just remember, though, I'm also pretty smart at capturing someone's bad side as well as their good. You wouldn't like a nice negative piece in *Newsweek* by any chance?'

His face reddened. 'You wouldn't dare,' he spluttered.

'We could headline it on the high-flyer who's scared of aeroplanes – that's a great angle,' she said, smiling mischievously.

'I'd hoped it wouldn't be that obvious,' he said, defeated. 'Between you and me, okay?'

She nodded, watching him grip the arms of his seat once more. Realising her guard had been lowered, she resolved to watch her step. She was sure he hadn't got where he was by being a regular Joe.

Until recently, she'd thought Richard Northwood a nice guy.

* * *

A little over six weeks earlier, traffic on the road from the airport north of Baghdad city looked like any major route of four lanes – cars, lorries, vans, petrol tankers. The only ostensible hazard was the large number of vehicles loaded to bursting, crammed with as many people as possible.

But all moved reasonably smoothly – unless Saddam was on his way. Then, chaos reigned. Policemen suddenly turned into monsters, commanding major junctions with frightening ferocity, halting and haranguing, fearful of being singled out for incompetence. Saddam and his Republican Guards demanded smooth passage and stopped for no one.

Now, it was one of the most dangerous roads in the country. Pockets of resistance were appearing with alarming frequency, each time bolder in their resurgence. Roadside bombs, snipers, the occasional rocket-propelled grenade, all serving to remind whoever dared travel the highway that this was no Route 66.

Kowolski descended the steps of the plane at Baghdad airport, scouring the aerodrome. The pungent smell of kerosene assailed his senses. A vast assortment of military aircraft jostled for space on the site; jet fighters, bombers, transport planes, helicopters. Far off, engineers were still filling in bomb craters on a runway.

Rumsfeld's cavalcade of limousines and armoured Humvees sped towards them along the tarmac, a couple of Bradleys bringing up the rear. Kowolski let his shoulders relax. He wouldn't fancy a solo trip along this highway, but even this short journey was preferable to any plane ride. Besides, the military had assured him there'd be plenty of hardware in support. 'Attack would be peashooters against an elephant,' a colonel said.

The entourage came to a stop near a giant aircraft hangar. Rumsfeld walked briskly inside to address the troops who'd done his bidding. Alex nipped in first, firing away as he made his entrance to a rousing reception.

* * *

'Better put this on, sir.' One of Rumsfeld's aides handed him a flak jacket, putting one on himself, as they approached their convoy.

Kowolski did the same. 'Take the hint,' he said, passing one to Alex, helping her to fasten it.

'It's going to be okay, isn't it?' Alex needed reassurance. She'd heard about this road.

'Sure. Don't worry. I said I'd look after you, didn't I?'

He ushered her into a black sedan, hesitating outside the car for a few seconds while gazing skyward as if trying to pierce the apparent limitless blue of the upper atmosphere. He knew a U-2C spy plane from Saudi Arabia's Prince Sultan Air Base was monitoring their route.

Some 12 miles up on the edge of space, the pilot would be wearing an astronaut's spacesuit, drinking and feeding through tubes, scrutinising the terrain below through the aircraft's bank of powerful cameras. Watching, listening, waiting. Their guardian on high.

The motorcade swept through the desolate mud-brown vista

of the airport grounds. Bombed-out bunkers, deep craters, wrecked radar fixtures, stood in stark remembrance of the initial attack. A vast, stinking, rubbish dump smouldered from the base's own garbage, an ongoing reminder of the occupying force. When the column moved out on to the highway, two Bell OH-58D Kiowa attack helicopters fluttered in escort.

Kowolski glanced at Alex. Flicking the fingers of her right hand against her thumb in a steady silent rhythm, he guessed it was her turn to test the nerves. He felt like putting a comforting hand on her knee but was sure it would be taken the wrong way.

They reached the main avenue of the Abu Ghraib complex. Kowolski checked his watch; the journey from the airport took twelve minutes. His budget was fifteen. Part of Saddam's two-billion dollar display of profligacy lay in this sprawl of three palaces. Palm trees lined the wide boulevard like a guard of honour, some shading the 65-ton, uranium-armoured Abrams tanks lurking among them.

Alex gazed at the metal monsters. She wondered if the tank that fired on the Palestine Hotel a couple of weeks back was among them. Two journalists were killed in the attack on the media centre, several injured. She did not know the cameramen from Reuters and Spanish television who were killed. But she reckoned it must have been unbearable for their families to know they had died by the purposeful hand of their own allies.

Outside the main palace, Kowolski took Alex by the arm, surprising her. 'Shall we do the grand tour together?' he smiled.

She glanced across at him. He was difficult to work out. One minute the cold apparatchik, the next exuding a paradoxical degree of warmth.

They walked on into the main reception area. Alex disengaged from him on the pretext of wanting to take some pictures. Strolling arm in arm didn't figure on her agenda. More that she wanted him at arm's length. Snakes always felt smooth to the touch – but they could strike in an instant and some had a deadly bite.

38

Saddam Hussein's ostentatious influence lay in every corner of the palace. His embossed initials stood stark on the black and gold jalousies of each ornate window in the building, sculpted on its many grand entrance columns.

'Talk about obsessive grandeur,' Kowolski said, running his fingers over the carvings. 'And look at all this.' He gestured at a couple of chandeliers, ripped from the ceiling by looters, then discarded.

He bent down to pick up a fragment. 'You know, Alex,' he said, handing it to her. 'What you see is not what you get with Saddam.'

'Plastic!'

Kowolski smiled. It was the same in all of Saddam's palaces – tat and bling that would run Las Vegas close.

'We launched cruise missiles on this palace when Operation Iraqi Freedom began – a pity Saddam wasn't at home,' Kowolski said.

Alex rattled off several shots of the substantial damage, one whole wing blasted to ruin. They made their way through a myriad of rooms, stepping over mounds of rubble. Lumps of pre-cast concrete hung at crazy drunken angles from the ceilings, their mangled steel rod innards hideously exposed like the intestines of a giant beast. Glass from shattered windows covered the floors, crunching like gravel underfoot.

'Some place, huh?' Alex said.

'They're all the same,' Kowolski countered. 'Most of them built while the UN sanctions were operative – oil for food, oil for medicine. He turned it into an oil-for-palaces charade for himself and his buddies. There are lots of places like this, dozens of square miles of one man's vulgar obsession with himself – each one with a complex of underground bunkers.'

Kowolski felt a well of anger rise within him and kicked out at a piece of the plastic junk, sending it crashing across the floor.

'The State Department did a survey three years ago that

reckoned he had as many as four dozen palaces. Can you imagine that? They came up with a count of twelve hundred buildings on these sites – mansions, villas, you name it. The ordinary Iraqi Joe Shmoe could kiss his ass.'

'Not too loud,' Alex whispered, 'he might still have the rooms bugged.'

'Yeah? Well we're coming for you – you sonovabitch,' he shouted, his words echoing eerily on the sad bare walls.

Returning to the main reception area, they were told Rumsfeld was now 'off limits' in a closed meeting with army commanders, so they gratefully accepted a coffee and wandered outside.

Kowolski closed his eyes and lifted his face up to the sun, taking a deep breath as if to cleanse himself of the depressing atmosphere of inside. 'Say, do you fancy sticking around for a little while? There's a little job that's cropped up.'

'I. . . don't know,' Alex said, suddenly nervous.

'I'll personally make sure the money's good – top rates. That is, if you don't have anything or anyone to rush back to.'

She found herself thinking of a raft of excuses why she couldn't stay in Iraq. Each reason abruptly countered by her inner self. What was facing her at home? She had no work lined up. Only the dreary state she'd slid into. And the endless lonely nights.

Kowolski could see he'd struck a hopeful chord – she hadn't refused outright. But could he trust her not to blab if she did turn him down? 'Look, can I tell you something in complete confidence?'

She shot him a hesitant glance and let out a sigh. 'Okay,' she said, feeling her resistance crumbling. 'Shoot.'

Kowolski eyed her seriously. 'This is not for publication, right?'

'What? You caught Saddam and you want me to capture his best side?'

'Cut the bullshit, Alex.'

Kowolski outlined the job. She would be embedded with the crew of a Bradley Fighting Vehicle, recording their daily duties in and around the Green Zone, going out with them on patrol.

'I want you to focus on one man in particular – a young lieutenant, Matt McDermott, a great kid, totally committed to this cause.'

'Why him?'

'Because, before much longer, he's going to be the biggest thing since buttered bagels.'

'Really?' She could not help but notice the sudden look of fierce determination in Kowolski's eyes.

'Really,' he said emphatically. 'There won't be anyone back home who won't know the name of one Lieutenant Matt McDermott.'

* * *

Carl Whittingham, a senior aide at the Defense Department, leant against the huge sandstone pillar outside Abu Ghraib palace, watching Kowolski approach. They had attended the same university and that intimacy had added an extra layer to their working relationship.

'I got two minutes, Gene. The boss is due out soon. What gives?'

'Just an idea I've been running through my head. But I don't want it to look as though it's come from me, so if you're game… '

Whittingham was not slow on the uptake, immediately realising there could be something in it for him, the chance of a Brownie point or two. 'Fire away.'

'We've got this kid, right here in Baghdad, a young lieutenant. First assignment, he goes out and bags fifteen Hajiis, a haul of AK-47s, RPGs, the lot. Now imagine this. We bring him home, turn on the lights, he meets the President, front page of *Time Magazine*, every goddam magazine, television… you name it. What's that going to do to the President's popularity?'

'Sends it skywards.'

'And, boy don't he need it right now. I mean, the Columbia space shuttle tragedy, all this shit here. This lieutenant fits the bill, too – Joshua William College, West Point.'

'Joshua William?' Whittingham whistled softly. 'Wow.'

Kowolski extracted a sheet of paper from his briefcase. 'It's all in here,' he said, handing it over. 'And it's your idea, Carl. One hundred per cent, okay?'

'Sure. Thanks, buddy. I'll have to wait for the right moment to float it.'

'Right. Attaboy.' Kowolski gave him a slap on the back, then watched him saunter off with a noticeable spring in his step.

* * *

Later, Alex said she'd accept the job. Despite initially trying to argue herself out of the commitment, deep down she hoped it made sense. Keeping busy might help her forget her troubles and, of course, she needed the money. But it had been a close-run thing.

Because she was afraid of what she might be letting herself in for.

5

Their car snaked through heavy traffic, heading east of the city for the al-Jumhuriya Bridge over the Tigris. Kowolski let out a sigh of relief. The day had gone as well as planned.

'I would have put you up in the Al Rashid Hotel in the Green Zone but our boys threw the press out when they took it over a couple of weeks ago. So you're in the Palestine with the rest of the world's media.'

Kowolski was saying something Alex already knew. Greg Spencer, an Australian writer pal who was based at the El Rashid, called her at the time grumbling about the move.

Alex studied the set-square haircut of the driver's fat neck in front of her. Army precision down to the last hair. 'Is it safe now at the Palestine?'

'Sure, we've set up a buffer zone between the Palestine and the Sheraton.'

'I didn't mean from the opposition.'

He shot her a glance. *Feisty, jeez.* Was she spoiling for a fight? 'That was an unfortunate event – deeply regrettable.'

'Yeah, the tank commander didn't know this eighteen-storey building, standing out like a sore thumb against the landscape, was home to the world's press. You telling me he didn't have the co-ordinates and that someone looking at them through binoculars from a fifteenth floor could have simply been a journalist?'

'They thought he was a forward obs man for the enemy. The military said shots came from the direction of the hotel.'

'And a hundred journalists at the hotel flatly refuted that,' she said, studying his deepening frown. 'You saying that the attack on the al-Jazeera Baghdad office that killed another journalist and the one on the Abhu Dhabi television station were also accidents? All on the same day? Jesus.'

'You seem well versed with events.'

'What? For a photographer? Think I'm some dumb-ass happy snapper?'

'I didn't say that.'

She felt like sounding off on feminism, the rights of women, how men could be total pricks. But, knowing what little she did of him, she was pretty sure it would be a waste of time.

'It's laughable,' she said derisively. 'The US Army kills three journalists, so the Pentagon says news organisations should pull their reporters from the city – probably because some of their stories were not to America's liking.'

'But they haven't.'

'Damn right.'

An awkward silence prevailed as the car entered Firdos Square. Alex could see the Palestine Hotel overlooking the square's giant roundabout. She gazed at the empty plinth which featured in that iconic picture of the war – the toppling of Saddam's statue.

She couldn't help but think how convenient it all was that the spectacular 'image of freedom', so quickly broadcast around the globe, happened right in front of the world's media. Just two days after they had all been moved there from the Al Rashid Hotel.

Back in New York, she'd seen the wide-angled pictures of the same event. Most outlets chose to ignore them, preferring to use the medium shots and the close-ups of the statue falling.

The wide-angled pictures showed the square sealed off by tanks and only a hundred people or so in what the media called 'this spontaneous outburst of support for America.'

She also knew many of the crowd celebrating the statue's removal were from Ahmed Chalabi's rag-tag 'Free Iraqi Force', a group of about 700 men who the Pentagon had flown into Kurdish-controlled Iraq only a day or two earlier.

Chalabi, one of the more prominent Iraqi exiles living in the US, wanted his men to lead the way into the country in the initial onslaught but, unarmed as they were, such aspirations were quickly dismissed by the military.

Alex thought she might ask Kowolski about it all sometime. It would not have surprised her to know he had had a hand in it.

Kowolski, too, had been thinking about the statue. Its removal had been the perfect piece of psy-ops, or what some colleagues at the Pentagon referred to as PPR, 'political public relations'. The term was so much better than 'propaganda'.

It had all gone smoothly until some schmuck had draped the head of Saddam with the Stars and Stripes, evoking an immediate image of an American occupation. Was it any wonder it did not go down at all well with 27 million Iraqis?

That one act, while it might have puffed out a few feathers at home, certainly did a lot to foster the current feelings of unrest here. Kowolski thought it was like many things in life; if you wanted a good job doing, you had to do it yourself.

Left entirely to him, it would have been an Iraqi flag.

Their driver stopped at a checkpoint. A soldier sauntered over to the car from the other side of a barrage of razor wire, a camouflaged tank behind him. Kowolski showed him his ID, told the guy they were on Pentagon business. The car was allowed through, stopping outside the hotel next to a row of Chevy SUVs.

Alex let the driver carry her bag, declining his offer to take her camera case and laptop. Before entering the reception, she glanced up at the façade of what was one of the country's tallest buildings, saw its name emblazoned in large letters.

Yep, she said to herself, it sure was mighty hard not to spot.

* * *

The foyer was heaving.

It reminded Alex of a convention of shoe salesmen she'd once covered in Oklahoma City in her early days. The same sort of squabbling noise. Not as many suits.

Instead, jeans and t-shirts, combat trousers, some people wearing scarves draped loosely low around their necks but which would be pulled up to their faces when driving downtown into the dust and sand of the city and its 5 million souls. A couple of guys, still wearing dark glasses, loafed around with macho machine gun belts slung across their shoulders.

A frenetic throng of journalists, TV and radio people, contractors, armed private security minders, soldiers, and home-based hustlers and fixers. One such of the latter group was holding court at the far end of the room, bearded and robed, but with a tailored Western jacket thrown over the shoulder of his long white thoub. A foot in both camps.

'Here's your key, Alex.' Kowolski handed her the fob. 'Don't lose this – it cost a small fortune.'

'Where are you staying?'

'In the next room. Just in case you get lonely.' He laughed loudly, disappearing into the crowd.

She waited outside an elevator to take her up to the tenth floor. A weary-looking man joined her. He mopped his ruddy brow with a polka-dot handkerchief that he stuffed back into the top pocket of his safari jacket. She guessed he was a Brit.

'These things work?'

'Ah, sometimes not, young lady. You just arrived?'

He introduced himself as Charles Toller, from a London newspaper.

Alex shook his hand. 'You embedded?'

'I don't know anyone who isn't,' he said. 'The only way to get around, I'm afraid. Pot luck if you see any action and then you've got to be damn careful what you say otherwise they'll pull the accreditation... You?'

'Yeah,' she said as the elevator doors opened.

The lift was packed and she had to squeeze in. There was an overpowering stench of stale sweat that caused her to hold her breath, lest she gagged. Relieved when the elevator stopped at her floor, she spilled out into a gloomy corridor. Quickly locating her room, she closed the door, dumping her things on the bed when the telephone rang.

'If you fancy a pre-dinner drink, I'll be in the bar in half an hour,' Kowolski said.

She was under a lukewarm shower when it rang again. 'What now for Chrissake?' she demanded.

'That sounds like the good old Sheila I remember.'

'Greg! How lovely to hear your voice. Where the hell are...'

'Oh, about three floors down. Wondered if you fancy eating out – you won't get much more than a boiled egg here and I know a great little place.'

She'd been resigned to grabbing a quick bite and having an early night. Greg, she discovered, was only in Baghdad for thirty-six hours. She couldn't turn down a friend.

'But how did you know I...'

'News travels fast in this village of ours – see you later.'

She knew that Greg Spencer, a stringer for a host of Australian outlets, was still in Iraq because they'd spoken before she left New York. Usually in Basra with the British Army, he was due back there the following day. His good company and deprecating sense of humour dovetailed with her own take on events. Plus he was a damn good journalist who kept her up to speed.

She dried herself on an almost threadbare towel, took out a simple black jersey number from her backpack. The dress was rolled up as usual because it didn't crease and took up so little room. It was her favourite; a half-price sixty-five dollar bargain eighteen months ago at Macy's in Herald Square, just before she'd set off for Kabul on an assignment for *Newsweek* after the Taliban fled the Afghan capital.

When she thought about it, that three-week period seemed an age ago. She smiled to herself as she smoothed it down with her hands, remembering how the dress had helped her wheedle her way on to a Black Hawk helicopter, taking soldiers up to the White Mountains of Tora Bora in search of Osama bin Laden.

After flirting with its commander the night before in a Kabul bar, she had bagged the flight to the al-Qaeda caves that had just been obliterated in a massive bombardment. Her only disappointment: that they hadn't found bin Laden, the exclusive of all exclusives.

Although she considered herself a moderate feminist and would normally have disapproved of such tactics, her view was that using those alluring eyes once in a while was no bad thing. Especially for the great set of aerial shots she was able to sell from the trip.

Hurrying to the bar, she spotted Kowolski talking to a pretty blonde. She seemed to be hanging on his every word. He waved to Alex, who joined them.

'This is Francine, a colleague from the Pentagon. Francine's with our lot in the Green Zone.'

Alex shook her hand. 'I hear the admin people are piling in thick and fast, Francine, that there's trouble with billeting.'

Francine looked surprised that Alex would have heard such news already. 'Oh, we're doing pretty good – we got a villa.' She returned to gaze at Kowolski. 'Gene, you must come and see us there,' she cooed.

Kowolski nodded almost absent-mindedly. He leaned towards Alex, took in the subtle waft of her perfume. 'You want to join us for dinner?'

'Thanks, but I'm already booked,' she said. 'Besides. . . ' she nodded in Francine's direction.

'Well, maybe some other time,' he said, with a tinge of disappointment. 'At least let me get you a drink.'

Just then, the tall figure of Greg Spencer appeared weaving his way through the crowd. 'Hiya, babe.' He handed her a glass. 'White wine spritzer, right?' With his free arm, he hugged her tightly, kissing her on both cheeks.

Alex introduced him. 'One of the best writers out here,' she said, much to Greg's embarrassment.

'So, what's new?' Kowolski chipped in, eyeing him coolly.

Greg took a gulp of his beer from the bottle. 'Well, we got a whole crock of shit going down here, I know that for sure – people fighting among themselves, terrible brutality going on, hardship on a grand scale, some taking bribes and kickbacks, and that's just the US army I'm talking about. As for the Iraqis, only God, or should I say Allah, knows what hell it is for them.'

They all seemed quite taken aback by the sarcasm. Kowolski drained his glass. 'Yeah, war's a right bastard – for everyone.' He turned to Francine who had not finished her drink. 'We gotta go. So long.' He ushered her off before she could protest.

Greg watched them go. 'I think I might have upset him,' he said, pleased.

'Good. They're both with the Pentagon – it'll give them something to think about,' Alex smiled.

* * *

They took a taxi, heading south along Abu Nawas Street, running alongside the river. Several army patrols eyed them suspiciously. The remnants of burned-out trucks and buses clogged the side of the road. Palm trees, blasted by shells, lay at forlorn angles, some only stumps. Across the Tigris in the fading light, it was still possible to see the bomb damage to buildings in the distance, stark against the sinking orange sun.

'You okay?' Greg noticed Alex had closed her eyes.

'A little tired – been a long day so far. And all this... ' she waved her arm in a sweeping gesture, '... is wearisome.'

Greg directed the driver to the al-Karradah district. Entering a residential area, Alex was struck by the houses, attractive two and three-storey villas with neat gardens. They turned into a street of smart offices and commercial buildings. 'Seems a different world from the waste and despair only a few hundred yards back,' she sighed.

'I hope you don't mind but we're meeting company for dinner, people I owe a favour.'

He paid off the driver, took Alex by the hand and guided her to the entrance of a restaurant. The decor was up-market, welcoming. Starched white napkins lay on classic red and white checked tablecloths, twenty or so diners, mostly American.

Greg waved to a couple sitting at the back and made to join them. 'Alex, this is Dr Aban al-Tikriti and his good wife, Farrah. Both have been very good to me.'

'Hello Alex. It is nice to meet any friend of Mr Greg. He has been very good to us, also.'

Alex saw a man in his mid-forties, kind eyes that seemed to hold a tinge of sadness, dark hair beginning to go grey at the sides. A sober blue business suit over a lemon open-necked shirt made for such a modern appearance that Alex felt she could be on Broadway – supper after the show. His wife, her dark hair in elaborate ringlets, wore a black shawl, tastefully embroidered in red and gold, over a white silk trouser suit.

'That's a beautiful wrap, Farrah,' Alex said touching it.

'Yes. An anniversary present from my husband – from Syria. Say one thing about Saddam, we can... we could wear what we like. For how much longer, I don't know.'

Her husband took a bread stick from a holder on the table, snapped it in two, and began chewing, waving the other half in the air. 'There is a feeling, particularly among women, that the religious zealots might now come to the fore... people are afraid.'

Alex needed another drink. Clenching her hands under the table, she braced herself and ordered fizzy water instead. Taking several sips in quick succession, the bubbles burst at the back of her throat, helping ease the cloying grime of the day.

Her heart went out to the couple when she learned Aban was out of a job, having held a senior position in the Ministry of Commerce. They had two sons and were now living off their savings.

'But surely they'll ask you back,' Alex said. 'The new administration here must desperately need men of your experience to carry on where you left off. I mean, the country's in a terrible mess.'

'Maybe. Who knows? Perhaps the Americans think they can run Iraq better than we did.'

They found Aban in talkative mood. Alex was happy at first, allowing herself to be the sponge of his anxiety. It deflected her own problems for a while. But, as he unloaded his fears for the future of the country, she could feel the tension rising within her.

A waiter came to the table. Greg pointed to the menu. 'Masgouf.'

'A very nice river fish, Alex,' Aban said. 'I have forgotten what it is called in English.'

'River carp,' Greg replied. 'Okay for all?' Everyone nodded in agreement.

'Tell me,' Alex said, 'what was Saddam really like?'

Aban lowered his voice, looking about him. Old habits died hard. 'You could say good and bad, but mostly bad. I believe he operated on two levels, fear and greed. A complex man, paranoid certainly, breathtakingly ruthless. But, under his reign Iraq made good progress. Infant mortality was down, literacy up – the highest school enrolment of any developing nation – healthcare improved enormously.'

He broke off to take a sip of water. 'But it was a dictatorship all the same, one that must be measured against the worst human rights record in the world. That was until the sanctions took effect after the Gulf War and the country headed into serious decline. Can you imagine your child with cancer and no drugs other than paracetamol to treat the pain? A few weeks ago I could not speak like this. I dared not even think it, never.'

'A few weeks ago, Aban, you were Aban Mohammed Ali,' Greg said.

'Yes, it is true. Saddam forbade any of us in high positions from using our tribal names. Instead we had to use our own first name, then of our father, and that of our grandfather. So many of us Sunnis in government, you see – but no one could identify us as such by our name.'

The waiter brought the fish, filleted it at the table.

'And how long are you in Baghdad, Alex?' Farrah said.

Alex hesitated. 'Perhaps rather stupidly, I've just accepted a stint for a few weeks embedded with an infantry unit – in a Bradley Fighting Vehicle.' Her face suddenly turned serious. 'I was due to go back home tomorrow... I'm not sure I've made the right decision. From what you say, things are going to get a lot worse.'

The table fell silent for a moment. Alex felt everyone's eyes on her. She gulped and bit her bottom lip, unaware her fingers had begun twisting the napkin in her hand. Farrah sensed the unease and patted her hand.

Their meal finished, they went outside. The air was thick, stultifying, the smell of American cigarettes hung heavily. 'It would be lovely if you had time to take tea with us before you leave, Alex,' Farrah said, kissing her lightly.

'Thank you, Farrah. I... I do hope things improve for everyone.'

In the taxi back to the hotel, Alex found her parting words inadequate for what she really felt. She was sure that for every family like the al-Tikritis, thankfully untouched by personal tragedy so far, there were tens of thousands of other Iraqi families already forced to bear the unimaginable tortured misery of the death and destruction within their midst.

The immediate future wasn't something Alex wanted to contemplate. She now realised going on patrol was not going to be easy for her whatever lay in store.

And she cursed herself for letting Kowolski twist her arm.

* * *

Gene Kowolski sucked on the swollen nipple of the girl's right breast as she moaned, writhing beneath him, pleading with him to enter her.

'Do it, Kowolski. Do it to her,' Francine urged frantically as she lay naked next to him, her hand holding him tightly at his base so that he was now fully erect again.

Kowolski had accepted Francine's invitation to see her room at the villa rather sooner than he imagined, prompted by a couple of bottles of a Meursault Premier Cru from one of his favourite growers, Louis Jadot, which he knew was American-owned. War-torn Iraq it might be, but getting hold of a decent bottle of white burgundy seemed to be no problem. It was expensive, sure. Hell, that was sometimes the price of patriotism.

When Francine's room-mate poured them all a generous brandy, then, after a large gulp, declared that being in such a dangerous country made her feel 'hot and horny', he knew he had struck home. 'Yeah, me too – war can make you feel like that,' he said only seconds before both girls leapt on him, practically stripping him and themselves in double-quick time while he lay there smiling.

He satisfied Francine and himself first while the other girl stroked his buttocks with one hand, gently kneading his scrotum with the other. When she felt him starting to come, she straddled him, rubbing herself up and down on his backside and yelping like an animal.

Francine now guided him into her room-mate, laughing lustfully as she whimpered with pleasure. 'Oh, yes, yes, fuck me, please,' the girl cried working her body hard and fast against him, reaching her orgasm within minutes to a tirade of expletives, sobs and moanful sighs. Kowolski reached his second climax of the night shortly afterwards.

As he did, he thought of Alex.

* * *

For a change, Matt McDermott slept soundly that night. He awoke to the comforting lumpiness of the Bible under his pillow. Although he felt closer to our Lord with the Good Book beneath his head, the recent habit was no more than a subconscious form of penance.

Now the morning was one of domestic chores; washing socks, shirts and underclothes, kit that took only a few minutes to dry when hanging from strategic points of the billet. Washing strung from open windows was a soldier's constant lot.

He took coffee with some of his men, checking the Bradley was clean, fit and fuelled ready to go. He reminded them they were to be on their best behaviour later when a photographer called Alex Stead was joining them as an embed. No one appeared happy about a stranger in the camp.

'What do he do, sir?' P.J. the grenadier had asked.

'He takes pictures, dumb-ass,' Sergeant Rath replied shaking his head in disbelief while some of the others sniggered.

'No, I mean who do he take pictures FOR?'

'Yeah, are we gonna be famous, Lieutenant?' The Bradley's driver, Bobby-Jo, turned to look at McDermott expectantly.

The lieutenant plucked up courage and allowed himself a rare smile. 'Be on your best and I'll personally see that colour pictures of your asses are shown in Starbucks window, Times Square.'

Their laughs rang in his ears as he walked away. It was unlike the lieutenant to crack a joke. They all thought he was something of a strange one, a bit of a homey character. And there was talk that, if not the army, he might have gone into the ministry which is why they tried very hard not to cuss when he was around. But, on the whole, he was an okay sort of guy. They knew he would do his best for them.

In his barracks, McDermott wrote a letter home:

'Dear Mom and Dad, Having a good time out here. Safe inside the Green Zone. Nothing much happening. Not seen any black bears yet... God be with you.'

He didn't want to mention anything of the event that was causing him increasing anxiety. They would learn something of it in due course, he was sure. He had never lied to them in his life. And he didn't know if he could refrain from telling them the whole truth if they sought it.

Slumping on his bed, he put his hands behind his head and closed his eyes. He felt weary. Since the incident, he sensed the energy being drained from his body, little by little. He had hoped everything would quieten down. But now, a photographer was on the prowl and the unit was under orders to fully co-operate.

His life seemed to be twisting out of control, shooting along in an inescapable vicious circle, a dilemma that was torturing him every waking hour.

6

The sound of nearby gunfire woke Alex with a start. She checked the time. It was almost 6.15. She groaned.

Her plan was to have had a lie-in, seeing she was not meeting McDermott's CO until mid-morning. She tried to re-enter that warm, floating, solace of drowsiness, but flashes of her Kandahar nightmare surfaced causing her to start.

The shooting had stirred her brain anyway. It was now wide awake and urged her body to catch up. As she flung on her clothes, half of her wanted to ignore whatever had happened. The other half needed to know – a journalist's instinct.

Checking the batteries in the Canon, she ran to the lift, sliding a spare pack into the knee pocket of her combat trousers and hiding the camera beneath her blouson.

She approached the reception desk, about to hand over her room key when she changed her mind, putting it in her pocket. She saw Kowolski's room key still in its box. He was either up earlier than her – or had not been back to the hotel yet.

'I heard shooting,' she said to the clerk.

'Yes, Miss – at the end of the street,' he gestured.

Turning right out of the hotel and jogging along the sidewalk, she reached the road junction where a large crowd had gathered. A gut-wrenching sensation suddenly stopped her. Did she really want to witness this? Only half awake, she'd been operating on auto pilot so far, old instincts. But indecision always missed the picture, she reasoned. Steeling herself, she took a deep breath and joined the throng.

A group of soldiers stood nonchalantly around a bullet-ridden car. The bloodied body of the young driver lay motionless in his seat, the engine still running. An army paramedic truck screeched to a halt. A soldier wearing sunglasses, chewing gum and keeping the onlookers at bay, diverted his attention to the medics. The crowd shuffled forward. Alex took out her camera and, over the shoulder of the man in front of her, began shooting.

Music blared from the car stereo; a Beatles number: 'All You Need Is Love'.

The medics pulled the driver from the car, laid him out on the pavement and began attempting resuscitation. After a few minutes they gave up. Suddenly, a woman in a black abayah pushed her way through, shouting, hysterical. A soldier stepped in her way but she pushed him aside. Letting out an uncontrollable wail, she knelt by the young man's body, cradling his head in her lap, screaming at the soldiers who backed away. Alex rattled off several more shots.

She looked about her. 'Anybody tell me what she's saying?'

A man in a striped dishdashah stepped forward. 'She is saying that they have killed her only son.'

An Iraqi translator with the soldiers began shouting at the woman. She screamed back at him, spitting venom in her words, tears flooding her face.

'The Americans say they saw him acting suspiciously, that he was driving around the block many times like he was watching them. She says he was giving a lift to a friend to the university where both are students – but the friend was late. She says she told her son never to stop and wait near an army patrol and that is why he was driving round – waiting for his friend to appear.'

'Shit,' Alex said, shocked, backing away. She'd seen enough. She headed towards the hotel, her stomach churning. Glancing round just once, she caught sight of the body being loaded into the ambulance. The tormented mother sank to her knees, crying woefully to the sky.

Alex trembled, sending a shiver through to her knees, her eyes filling up. She hadn't signed up for this. Walking slower, now, her breathing heavy, nausea finally forced her to stop. She put a hand out against a wall – and threw up all over it.

A film crew scurried past towards the scene, closely followed by an army press liaison man. No one gave her a second glance. They would be too late to capture the scene – she possessed the only picture that mattered.

She called Greg's mobile – he was at breakfast. She asked him to meet in her room and to bring her a strong sweet coffee.

An envelope had been pushed under her door; a list of ground rules for embedded journalists to be signed and handed to the major. She noted it was fifty paragraphs long. Tossing it aside, she went to the bathroom and splashed water on her face.

Greg tapped on her door just as she was downloading the pictures to her laptop. He waltzed into the room imitating a room-service waiter. 'Good morning, Madam. Coffee, as requested, khubz – flatbread to you – and jam. Sorry, there is no butter in the whole of Baghdad.'

She could only manage a thin smile.

'What's wrong?' he asked.

Taking a sip of the drink, she pointed to the screen.

'Wow, what the...'

'The shooting.'

'I slept through it, I'm afraid – you sort of get used to it. I did hear the guys on the barrier outside say they'd bagged themselves another baddie.'

'Bullshit,' she said, shaking with anger, going into detail.

Greg let out a low whistle. 'We've got to get a piece out to go with the pics – the bastards are shooting anything that moves out there.' He thought for a moment. 'Send them to me and I'll bang a piece over to the agency in Oz – they have worldwide syndication. Keep your name out of the frame, no byline – don't want to compromise your work here.'

'And what about you?'

'I'll take my chance – no byline, either.'

'But what if someone blabs and word gets back here? That'd be the end of your embeds.'

'Fuck them. We've got to tell it how it is for Christ's sake, laugh or cry.'

Alex considered the options for a few seconds. 'I'm with you, let's do it!' she said emphatically.

He unscrewed a bottle of water, offered it. She took a long gulp.

Resting an arm round her shoulder, he pulled her closer, sighing. 'Call me naïve, but I just can't believe someone didn't plan for all this. It's total bedlam out there, good people like this kid. . . ' His voice broke away.

'That poor mother,' she whispered.

For a few moments, there was silence between them.

'Hardly anything's working,' Greg continued. 'People are queuing four or five hours for a gallon of petrol, risking death stuck in a traffic jam. Aban was saying he thinks it's going to get an awful lot worse, too, once the various tribal factions start pulling for power.'

'I was sick just now,' Alex said. 'I wonder if I'm not cut out for all this any more.' She slumped on the edge of the bed, defeat in her shoulders.

Greg eyed her for a while. 'How long have we known each other – five years?'

'Guess so.'

'I'll tell you what I think you need – a loving man and a couple of kids.'

Her response surprised both of them. She broke down and began crying uncontrollably.

'Hey, don't start or you'll get me going, too,' he said, handing her a tissue and sitting beside her.

Dabbing her nose, she let out a shuddering sigh. 'Are you offering or something?'

He hugged her. 'I would, kid. But it's against the law to marry a sister.'

Drying her eyes, she gave him a resigned smile. 'Sorry about that – things are a bit rocky right now.'

Greg kissed her on the forehead and sprang to his feet. 'I've got to go. You back here later?'

'Need an early night. I was thinking of catching the President's speech. I could always give you a call at five tomorrow morning if you want to join me.'

'No thanks – you can tell me about it. And take your laptop with you. The military have been searching the rooms of late, some guys have had stuff confiscated.'

After he left, Alex started putting together things she'd need for the rest of the day. In a few hours, she was due to hit the Baghdad streets with Lieutenant McDermott and his men. In previous times, the prospect would have charged her very being, a frisson at the unexpected, all thoughts of personal danger suspended.

Now, her nerves taking over, the thought of it sent her rushing to the bathroom. Over the handbowl, she retched again until her throat and stomach hurt.

* * *

The journey from the hotel to the entrance to the Green Zone at Checkpoint 12 on Yafa Street, just across the river, was only a few kilometers. But it was taking Alex and her security driver longer than they envisaged. A slow-moving convoy of Humvees, tanks and army personnel carriers also happened to be heading west.

At first, her driver, emotionless behind dark glasses, had tagged on to the end of the convoy, seemingly oblivious to the large painted sign stuck on the rear of the last vehicle, a Bradley, which warned: 'Stay back 100 yards – or we fire'. It was only when the rear door of the armoured car opened and a soldier pointed a rifle at them that the driver hurriedly braked and backed off.

Alex gave the soldier the finger. He appeared shocked. Almost immediately, she reflected on the absurdity of a finger versus an M16.

A long line of assorted vehicles greeted them at the checkpoint. Dozens of people on foot joined the melee in the torrid heat, grudgingly acquiescent to the daily ritual of sniffer dogs, body searches and hand-swabbing just to go about their daily business.

It was then Alex discovered she had left her phone in her room. She cursed herself, imagining a dishonest maid racking up a series of calls across the Middle East.

Finally getting to show her privileged yellow pass, they were allowed through. The car meandered down the wide boulevard. They passed dozens of shirt-sleeved office people, carrying briefcases and walking to their workplaces as if they had just come out of Grand Central Station. Except, in Manhattan, no one had to be mindful of a careless trip into a mortar hole in the sidewalk. Here, it could send them sprawling headfirst into a deadly jumble of stainless steel razor wire. Alex could see its glistening barbs, concertinaed into the distance like smoke rings, separating the pavement from the road and its monotonous verges of high, pre-cast concrete T-walls.

They found Major Walter Douglas' office behind the massive blancmange-shaped Council of Ministers building, which had been heavily bombed and set alight in the initial bombardment. Alex remembered seeing it on television, glowing against the night sky as it was hit repeatedly. Surreal, then, in 36-inch widescreen colour, the ugly reality proved a sickening testimony to the deadly brute force of that opening bombardment.

The major's command post had been set up in a villa at the edge of a stretch of lush parkland, now dotted with the shipping-container homes of his troops.

A sentry scanned her pass and ID, pointing the way to the door at the far end of a corridor. She knocked and, without waiting for a reply, marched in carrying her gear, which she put down at the foot of the major's desk.

He looked surprised. 'Yes, Ma'am. What can I do for... '

ROY DAVID

She offered her hand. 'Alex Stead reporting for duty – the photographer?'

'Well, goddam. We all thought you were... '

'A he?' She sighed.

'Let me get you a coffee,' he blustered.

Presently there was a rap on the door. 'Enter,' the major barked.

Lieutenant Matt McDermott hesitated at the doorway. 'Sorry, sir. I didn't know you had company.'

'Come in, Lieutenant. This is your embed, Alex Stead.'

McDermott's jaw dropped. 'But I thought... '

'Okay, soldier, we've been through all that. Why don't you take Miss... Alex... and show her the set-up.' He turned to Alex. 'The boys are going on patrol. I guess you'd want to join them?'

She felt like telling him it was the last thing she wanted. Instead, she swallowed hard. 'Sure,' she murmured, gathering her gear. 'Oh, and this is for you, I believe, Major.' She handed him the ground rules document, duly signed. 'I'm afraid I only got as far as point thirty-seven.' With that, she turned on her heel, and left the room.

* * *

'Excuse me, Ma'am, but didn't you give me the finger just a little while ago?' P.J. gave Alex a suspicious look as she climbed aboard from the rear-loading ramp.

'I don't take too kindly to having a gun aimed at my face,' Alex snapped.

'That was you, was it, Ma'am,' McDermott said. 'Gave young P.J. here quite a surprise – him being a country boy an' all. That right, P.J.?'

'Yes, sir.'

'Seriously, though. It's bordering on plain foolish to follow a convoy too close. An Iraqi got himself killed doing that only last week, got two warnings to pull back, the third time they shot him. Could have been a suicide bomber.'

'I'll tell it to the driver – if he hasn't been shot already,' she said haughtily, checking her camera. Bobby-Jo revved up the engine and clanked his way forward. Behind them followed the second Bradley, commanded by Sergeant Dan Rath.

It was soon unbearably hot inside the vehicle once the doors were closed; Alex felt it getting worse by the minute. She glanced up to see P.J. studying her, a mix of curiosity and indignation. He turned away from her gaze, a youthful act of self-consciousness that belied his ability to fire a rifle.

Banging his M16 on the side of the Bradley, it vibrated with a hollow clang. 'Crank the A/C up a little, Bobby boy,' he shouted to the driver. Everyone laughed except Alex who felt she was reaching boiling point. It didn't help that she'd hardly eaten and her stomach still squirmed.

Determined not to react, it crossed her mind this machine might well have air conditioning and they had it switched off to test her mettle. It didn't. The only relief came from a small ineffective fan.

Some twenty minutes later, she was thankful when they stopped and took up position on a wide, dusty street where a few of the locals had set up stalls. McDermott ordered his men out of the vehicle except for Bobby-Jo and Joe Herman, on observation. Both Bradleys then began following them at a pre-ordained distance, not so close as to be intrusive. But only a glance away from being called to action.

Sgt Rath led out the patrol from his vehicle, the units joining as one platoon, fanned out at 5-yard intervals. His voice boomed to the men. 'Hardware pointing to the ground – and don't forget to smile, folks.'

Alex waited until the soldiers were some way off, then rattled off a few shots of McDermott, as if he were pointing to something in the distance. His men, in the background, gave the pictures a nice perspective.

A gang of children, curious, eager, some old enough to be at school, congregated around McDermott's men.

The translator in Sgt Rath's group addressed several of the older children. They said their classrooms had been bombed and they did not know when school would re-open. Soon, packets of sweets and chewing gum were handed out, drawing an even bigger crowd, hands outstretched, clamoring for a piece of the action.

A little further up the street she asked McDermott to stop by a stallholder who was offering flour and containers of drinking water for sale and snapped him shaking hands with the toothless purveyor. The man said something to him. McDermott called over the translator.

'He asks if we know when the electricity is going to be back to normal, Lieutenant.'

'Tell him, with God's will, very soon. Ask how business is going.'

'He says there is already a shortage of flour and water but trade is slow. Most of the people are hanging on to what little money they have because they are without jobs.'

Further along, in the flattened ruins of a bombed-out building, soldiers joined in a kids' football game, kicking the ball to one another until, finally, passing it back. Two of the older children, apprehensive at first as if fearing they wouldn't see their ball again, shrieked when it was returned. 'Americano, Americano,' they shouted, running off.

The lieutenant became aware of a young woman with a toddler making her way up the street towards them. She was holding the boy by the hand but he was crying, gesturing that he wanted to be carried. Eventually, the child stumbled. McDermott moved forward and swiftly picked him up.

'Hey, hey, hey, what's all this hollering about?' He smiled at the mother reassuringly and quickly withdrew a lollipop from his pocket. The toddler immediately stopped crying and snatched at the brightly-coloured wrapper.

McDermott held him gently, looked into the boy's eyes and, for a moment, saw the eyes of a dead baby, deep brown, innocent, smiling at him, felt the still-warm body. He saw, again, the cute little chubby legs. Just like the ones Mom used to tell him she could eat.

In a temperature of over 110 degrees, he went cold.

Some yards away, Alex was firing away on motor mode. She could not help but see the change in McDermott's expression. His whole demeanor had suddenly altered. It puzzled her how visibly upset he had become, the colour quickly draining from his face. She continued firing and, within seconds, he had gone a deathly white.

He slowly handed the child back. 'Take... take good care of him, Ma'am,' he stammered, his voice croaking.

The mother smiled bashfully and continued on her way, the child looking back over her shoulder. McDermott stared after them.

'Brilliant,' Alex whispered to herself.

There was nothing better than to capture a natural action like this, one when the subject was unaware of the camera, not inhibited by its presence. All the same, she found the lieutenant's reaction mystifying.

McDermott suddenly became aware of Alex and her camera and quickly composed himself. 'Right, let's move on,' he ordered with a wave of his arm.

* * *

It was several days later when Gene Kowolski decoded the email on his laptop within the Palestine Hotel, a smile spreading across his face as he quickly devoured its contents. It was from a senior assistant at the Defense Department, instructing him to 'seek out, interview and prepare' one Lieutenant Matt McDermott for military honours. It stated that the issue had top-level clearance and included a list of recommendations and suggestions, all of which, of course, Kowolski already had covered.

He sat back in his chair, lazily putting both hands behind his head, allowing himself a sly chuckle. The CIA's idea had nearly come full circle, having traversed the corridors of power in the White House, the Pentagon, too, then back to the man charged with carrying it out for Northwood.

If only they knew, he thought. But, in reality, it was the subterfuge, the intrigue, the machinations his position allowed that gave him the greatest pleasure. He replied to the sender, making a mental note to print a copy of the email for his file at the earliest opportunity. He was always careful to do that. In his job, you needed backup if the fire ever got out of control.

He took a car to the Green Zone, calling Major Douglas on the way. In the major's office, he got straight to the point. 'We need your boy back home. There'll be quite a welcoming party.'

'I'll have to clear it with CENTCOM, of course. Their wish is... well, you know how it is.'

'It'll look good for the division, reflected glory all round. This lieutenant, he's a good kid?'

'Sure. I have his file.' The major handed it over. Kowolski could almost recite the contents off by heart, but still made a show of reading it.

'He still look like his photo?'

'Yeah, good-looking guy.'

'You realise, Major, that the President himself is likely to take a great personal interest in this lieutenant?'

'That's very gratifying. How long will you need him and when?'

'Well, things are pretty hectic back home right now so we wouldn't need your boy for a little while. I guess the military honours committee don't work too fast and we'd want to tie it all up so the President himself is free to present whatever medal they give him.'

Kowolski handed the file back. 'How long will we need him?

We'd have to monitor it all closely, of course, but, hey, we're in the hands of the media. I mean, we can't say no to front page of *Newsweek* if it comes up. Exactly what is your boy's tour of duty?'

The major swept a hand over his crew cut, glanced at some notes on his desk. 'He's due back home next March – will have done his twelve months, counting his few weeks in Kuwait. Wouldn't be good for morale if he only served a couple of months here then went back home for an easy spell – medal or no medal.'

Kowolski took out his Filofax diary. 'What say we settle sometime in August? He will have gotten six months in here – practically a veteran. We have him for a month or so back in Washington, do the rounds and send him back to complete his tour.'

'A month?'

'Should wrap it.'

'Will leave us short.'

'I'm sure Central Command will come up with something. There must be a young lieutenant scratching his fanny down in Dofa just itching to get to the frontline.'

Kowolski got up. As far as he was concerned, his business with the major was over. This was all mere protocol. CENT-COM would soon be made aware of the request from Washington. And their co-operation was guaranteed – right up to the top if need be.

All publicity was a matter of timing. And he would choose the occasion himself no matter what the major said.

The thought struck him as he left the Green Zone that these soldier boys loved their guns and their tanks, the bombs and the missiles. But the political clout of Washington was infinitely more powerful than all the army's weaponry put together.

He had learned from bitter experience never to slap his own back on a job well done until he'd seen it through to the end. Even so, he still felt a certain measure of gratification.

After all, he asked himself, what could possibly go wrong?

* * *

When Kowolski left, Major Douglas locked his office door, returned to the desk and put in a call to CIA headquarters in Virginia.

'Northwood,' the voice answered, stern.

'Okay, we're one down, sixteen seconds to play. I'm throwing the ball now – a great lateral pass across field. Northwood collects, he's got a seventy-five yard run to win the game. He sprints. The opposition close. They're not going to catch him. My God, it's a touchdown. Hoo-hah, we just won the cup, buddy-boy.'

'Walter, how you doing?'

'Just great, Richard. I wanted to let you know Kowolski was here. He'll no doubt tell you everything's progressing concerning young McDermott.'

'Good, good,' Northwood murmured.

'You asked me for a hero, Richard.'

'And you did good, Walter, real good. It won't be forgotten.'

The major put his feet up on the desk and lit a cigar. Favours made the world go round. If his old college pal ever made it to the top as was expected, who knew how it would be repaid in the future.

7

The President was due to make his speech to the nation from the flight deck of the USS *Abraham Lincoln* off the coast of San Diego.

Kowolski turned on the radio. The news anchor, a woman, was interviewing a military expert on the occasion. Both were gushing in their praise of the President who had landed on the aircraft carrier earlier in the day.

'I thought he looked real, well... manly as he stepped from the plane in that flying suit,' the anchor swooned.

'Well, of course, it was just amazing, landing like that at one hundred fifty miles an hour on the deck of the aircraft carrier. The President is no stranger to airplanes, of course. Don't forget he was in the Texas Air National Guard... '

The anchor interjected, 'We must point out to listeners that, on this occasion, the President was in the co-pilot's seat and did not land the plane himself. But he was loudly cheered by the crew of the *Abraham Lincoln* when he got out of the cockpit... it was a scene straight from the film *Top Gun*.'

Having snatched a few hours' sleep on a camp bed in the corner of his office, Kowolski put in a call to a White House press assistant who was on the *Abraham Lincoln*, having landed there several days earlier on one of the helicopters ferrying in the many members of the media.

'How's life on the high seas, old buddy?'

'Everything's primed – the President's landing went great today.'

'Yeah, I heard and I just saw the pictures on CNN. Fantastic. The weather okay?'

'Perfect.'

'Told you the coast of San Diego would be a helluva lot better than the original idea up there in Everett. The North Pacific in Washington State can be unpredictably windy at this time of year – you'd have the TV cameras rolling all over the place to say nothing of the President's hair. You see land from the viewpoint?'

'Not from the angle of the ship – we're only thirty miles from shore, though. We broadcast in less than an hour. What time do you have over there?'

'Just after four in the morning the next day to you, my friend.'

Kowolski knew the President could simply have jumped a chopper from the California coast to the vessel. But it was so much more dramatic to have him flown in on the four-seater S-3B Viking for a tail-hook landing – all captured by live television and replayed throughout the day on every news programme in the country.

No one would know the plane made the ten-minute journey without retracting its wheels. Undercarriage problems? No sirree.

Kowolski had been delighted to see the paint-stencilled markings on the plane caught on camera: 'Navy 1' on the jet's fuselage, the words 'Commander-in-Chief' just below the cockpit window.

The President had definitely looked the flying ace, just as planned, as he stepped from the cockpit in his tailored olive-green flying suit, a white helmet tucked under his left arm, leaving his right arm free for the handshakes and backslapping that went down so well with all and sundry.

And all that paraphernalia around his neck with the oxygen mask. Folks would think he'd just flown in from a sortie dropping bombs on Saddam himself, even though the man had never seen combat duty in his life.

Kowolski's only reservation; the two rows of flight-deck crew forming the guard of honour and saluting the President as he sauntered between them. They looked straight from Holly-wood, dressed in brightly-coloured bibs and t-shirts, co-ordinated in yellow, purple, blue, red, and green. But, what the hell, he thought. It looked dazzling on screen; the work, no doubt, of one of the former TV producers, now on the White House staff, who choreographed such occasions.

The President's speech would go out live at peak viewing, 9 p.m. Eastern Daylight Time. That meant it would be six in the evening in California, the golden hour before sunset when the light was at its flattering best. Other than send the White House several observations and suggestions on how the show should proceed, Kowolski had left it to the people in Washington. He was impressed with the results so far.

So he had his fingers crossed on his free hand, a coffee in the other, as he pressed the remote to raise the volume ready for the live broadcast. Then the President appeared, walking con-fidently to the dais on the flight deck.

Now in a plain dark suit, white shirt, red tie, he strode past the tiered rows of sailors standing attentively. Kowolski noted that those with the coloured bibs were now carefully positioned at strategically-spaced intervals, once more adding colour to the occasion. 'Great theatre, boys, keep it up,' he said to the tele-vision screen.

The President mounted the step to the platform. Suddenly, Kowolski's mouth dropped. His eyes focussed on the banner behind the President, plainly visible and hanging pristinely from the vessel's giant superstructure.

He guessed it must have been 30-feet wide and several feet deep. Two words of giant white capital letters, the first word on a blue-starred background of the American flag, the second word set against the red and white of the stripes.

MISSION ACCOMPLISHED.

'What the hell...' he blurted at the screen. 'Goddam mission accomplished? Who the fuck came up with that piece of bullshit?'

71

The President spoke: 'Major combat operations in Iraq have ended. In the battle of Iraq, the United States and our allies have prevailed... '

* * *

Thirty minutes later Kowolski was still tormenting himself over the spectacle. He was furious, convinced it would have wide-spread negative repercussions. He called his colleague again. 'Well, my friend, you and your bunch certainly shot themselves in the goddam foot with that stupid fuckin' banner.'

'Pardon me?'

'Listen, you can tell those jumped-up White House press people of yours to get their big fat asses out of Washington and down to Baghdad – and then you can ask them if it is "Mission Accomplished". It's a fuckin' hell-hole down here and it'll be that way for a long time to come.'

He slammed down the phone so violently he almost broke the cradle. And his hands were still shaking when he switched on his computer and opened the first of many emails.

He stared at the screen after opening the attachment. His blood pressure went up another two points. Before him was a picture, with a lengthy caption, from an Australian daily. His eyes devoured every word.

The headline screamed:

GRIEF OF AN IRAQI MOTHER
A heartbroken mother cradles her dead son's head in her lap on a Baghdad street after the young man was shot dead by US troops who accused him of 'suspicious surveillance' of an army patrol. It seems they mistook him as a 'spotter' for insurgents as he drove his car around the same street several times. Witnesses claimed the man was a student at Baghdad University and was merely waiting to pick up a fellow student who was late for the ride. A US Army spokesman said he was unable to confirm the incident.

72

The picture told a whole lot more; the mother's eyes, deep buckets of sorrow, the angle of her head as she looked out accusingly towards the camera, the drained, helpless posture of her shoulders. It was in colour, too, so that the blood on her outstretched hand, which gestured palm outwards in appeal, heightened the dramatic impact full pitch.

'Shit,' he shouted, reaching for the telephone. 'This is all we need right now.' He punched in a number to the army's Baghdad Press Office, got through to the assistant chief, a guy he knew well and who sounded tired.

'I've just sent over a piece with picture from the wonderful land of Oz. Put out a denial on it straight away, beef up the suspicious line – make it that the guy was acting extremely suspiciously, wouldn't stop when challenged, that sort of thing. Send out a memo everywhere that anyone using it without this new official army quote will have their people taken off the embed programme immediately.'

Still seething, he fired off a round robin email to all the editors on his list, which was extensive, reiterating the rules of embedded journalists to clear anything of a contentious nature with the Press Office before being sent for publication.

There was absolutely no room in his book for the alternative view, and definitely no place for nuance.

Next, he set to work in an effort to trace the source of the picture and the words. He knew it might be difficult to go directly to a foreign publication. The Aussies could be bolshie customers and he had little clout with them. But he had contacts worldwide and the piece would very quickly be offered for syndication around the globe. A flick of a switch, the press of a key, was all it took. Sooner or later he would find out.

And there would be hell to pay.

8

Alex watched the broadcast from the media centre at the Palestine Hotel among a scattering of journalists.

Angered by the President's vacuous speech, she sat stunned, repeatedly turning her phone in her hand, an absent-minded worry bead. She'd been relieved to find her mobile unused, where she'd left it in her room. To an unseen honest maid, Alex uttered an apology.

'I wondered if you'd like a coffee,' the man said, offering a polystyrene cup. 'It's black and hot – that's about all you can say for it.'

Alex looked up. It was the reporter she'd met while waiting for the lift when she first arrived.

'Charles Toller, London.'

'Oh, hi. I guess I never introduced myself before. Alex Stead, freelance photographer, New York.'

He sat down beside her, somewhat wearily, mopping his brow with the same polka-dot handkerchief. Alex guessed he was late fifties, overweight, unfit.

'So, what d'you think of your President's spectacular?'

'Bullshit – and it's got me more worried about everything than before.'

'Mission accomplished – that was a good one!' he laughed. 'Have them all back home thinking that some five or six weeks later it's all over bar the shouting. Marvellous. What do they say? History tells us that we never learn from history. Bloody good PR for the masses – they'd soak it up, I'm sure.'

He waved his coffee cup in the air, spilling drops on his trousers. 'But you mark my words, young lady, this is another Vietnam, and that was America's longest war. The generals predicted then that it wouldn't last more than a few months – Harkin, Westmoreland, all hot-air merchants who didn't have a clue about guerrilla warfare.'

Alex felt her shoulders stiffen as he spoke. Another Vietnam? Surely to God not.

'Your government seriously underestimated the vagaries of human nature then – the assassinations, regime changes, the chaos, the political power struggle. D'you know, Kennedy sent in over sixteen thousand military advisers to help the Vietnamese Army overcome the guerrilla insurgents – that was a couple of years before the US even entered the war and started the bombing in 1965. Soon had over half a million soldiers there, half of them on dope.'

She wanted to hear more, at the same time feeling her anxiety rising. This was becoming a horror story, like watching one of those films through the gaps in your fingers and with your hands covering your face in futile protection.

'Lyndon Johnson misled the public, too, just like this clown. Got Congress to back him on military operations in SE Asia without actually declaring war – all based on selective evidence from the available intelligence. No different to this.'

He spread his arms in a gesture of futility then looked at her, a trace of apology in his face at the outburst. 'You wouldn't be around then, of course.'

'And you were?'

'A young, impressionable and somewhat naïve twenty-two year old reporter back in 1968 when I first went out. I must admit, compared to this, it was a bloody holiday camp the way we were allowed to operate.'

Alex gulped at her coffee. 'How come?'

'Well, try as they might to keep a lid on things – I do believe that was a direct order from LBJ himself – there were very few restrictions on the press. You could visit a CIA post, hang out with the guys, move on to an aid agency or mix with different branches of the military – the sort of stuff that would give you a real down-to-earth overview of the situation. You could even arrange a short spell with the VC army.'

Alex shook her head, amazed. It shocked her to compare eras. Kowolski and his cohorts wouldn't allow journalists that sort of freedom now.

'This lot here, they learned their lesson from 'Nam. Now, well it's just a one-sided take on events, isn't it? Most of the editors and the news desks have been conditioned to accept the status quo so they don't bother asking for the sort of copy they would have done in those days... still, less pressure for the likes of us, I suppose.'

'But in 'Nam, it still took eighteen months or so for the Mai Lai massacre story to break – so that was a pretty good lid,' Alex said.

He eyed her, taken aback. He was unused to young people knowing such facts. He'd once brought up the subject at a party back home when the pretty young thing he was trying to impress had asked him if the Mai Lai massacre was a pop group.

'Extenuating circumstance, methinks. Band of brothers and all that crap. Only one or two good guys among the whole damn bunch. Hats off to Seymour Hersh, though, a Pulitzer prize for eventually breaking the story.'

'Why aren't you back in England anyway, sort of taking life a mite easier?'

'Ah, don't ask. Three broken marriages, a couple of spells with the bottle – all the right qualifications for a war correspondent.'

Alex got up to go. He touched her arm, leaning close, shot her a quick, nervous, smile. 'I don't want to worry you but you really must watch your step. You're most unlikely to read it in any newspaper, but, take it from me, the streets are definitely getting meaner out there – in fact, pretty bloody.'

She watched him shamble out of the room towards the lobby, a sinking feeling in her heart. If he was right, the future was too depressing to contemplate.

* * *

The patrol entered al-Mutanabi Street. Hordes of booksellers fussed over their colourful volumes, neatly laid out on rugs and mats and old blankets on the broken sidewalks. On edge, Alex went to work.

Some people among this mass of Baghdad intelligentsia gave them a curt nod, the occasional smile. Others avoided their gaze. Suddenly, a bearded trader stepped forward, straight into Alex's path as she lined up a shot.

'Pardon me,' she said, sidestepping the robed figure.

Each time she moved, he positioned himself in the way. Without warning, he lunged at her, his hand outstretched to grab the camera, shouting in Arabic at the top of his voice. Alex screamed and stepped back.

P.J. dashed forward and pulled the man away. 'Fuck you, A-rab,' he yelled into the man's face, yanking him back to his stall.

Continuing his non-stop jabbering, the man appeared to be appealing to his fellow traders. One or two replied to him, others bowed their heads.

McDermott appeared with the interpreter. 'What's happening here?' He turned to Alex. 'You okay?' Only shaken, but not far from tears, she nodded.

'The guy thinks they should be paid for having their picture taken,' the interpreter said.

'Tell him the US budget doesn't stretch that far,' McDermott said. 'And tell him to mind his manners or we'll be back to press charges.'

Checking Alex was indeed okay, he ordered his men to move on.

They turned into al-Rasheed Street and on to a narrow stretch of unmade road, tall paint-flaked buildings either side. Some façades flaunted pock-marked masks of crumbling stucco. Alex stepped in behind the sporadic line of the lieutenant's group, rattling off a few pictures of the backs of the men, the shutter speed set to take in the whole of the vista to give the frames more depth.

'I don't like the look of this, too quiet. Stay close,' McDermott half-whispered to her, scanning the vicinity.

Suddenly, a shot rang out, ear-splitting in the confines of the street. Then another two in quick succession. The rounds whistled off nearby walls, creating splintered puffs of cement dust. Alex froze. Engulfed in panic, she stood stock-still not knowing what to do, where to turn.

McDermott glanced back, saw her. A standing target. Taking half a dozen measured running strides, he launched himself at her, grabbing her jacket and dragging her backwards into a doorway. A second later, another two rounds hit the ground where she'd been standing. She saw the mud dancing where they hit the earth.

'Stay here, don't move,' he said firmly, shielding her.

'A fix, anyone,' he shouted.

Fear choking her, she gasped for breath in short bursts, pressing backwards into the opening. He was up against her, so close she could smell the faint musk of his deodorant, could see the droplets of sweat that ran down his shirt from the nape of his neck. Squinting with one eye closed, she was able to follow the line of sight of his rifle as he scanned the buildings opposite. Now, she hardly dared breathe.

Suddenly, she was aware of his hand reaching behind him. It touched her. Jesus, what was he doing? She shrieked.

'Alex, I'm searching for a door knob – see if you can open this door.'

'I've tried already – there's nothing there,' she said.

Over his shoulder she could see the men had fanned out, two of them crouching against a wall, several more in doorways, another lying prone behind a refuse bin. Bunching together would have given the perpetrator the best chance of a hit. Worse still, a grenade would have taken several of them out.

Her knees began to tremble at the vision of the dust flying off the ground. McDermott had saved her life.

He took several steps forward, glanced back at her. She gave him a thin, nervous half-smile as he radioed Bobby-Jo to bring the Bradley round to the far end of the street. And to 'stop at nothing'.

'Anyone hit?'

'Negative, Lieutenant,' came back several replies in ragged succession.

Sgt Rath jogged backwards from his forward position to join McDermott. Alex noticed the consternation in the sergeant's face. *What a picture.*

'I'd say the source was over there, Lieutenant,' he said, pointing to an old building with a brown door, a shop front now boarded up.

McDermott gestured to three of the men closest to the building to rush it, two others to mount a covering position. Leading the way, P.J. barged into the door, lunging with a hefty shoulder charge to finally force it open. Alex just caught sight of him disappearing through the doorway followed by the rest.

Several minutes passed. She could feel her heart thumping as she tried to suck in air. She braced herself. There could be more shots any second. Was she still a sitting duck?

'Stay here,' McDermott said, making a dash for the building.

She tried to protest, but only a weak, cracked mumble came out of a throat seared dry with terror. Now facing the open street, a dull, aching dread took over. A feeling of desolation grabbed at her, tormenting her insides. For a moment, she had never felt so alone, so vulnerable.

Closing her eyes only exacerbated her alarm, for she could feel the blood coursing through her head, pounding her ears.

McDermott reached the building's entrance and she watched him lean his shoulder against the doorway, his rifle pointing inside.

Impulse gripped her. She ran after him. Gripping her camera

close to her midriff to stop it swinging, she hurtled forwards, catching up with him. He turned round, annoyed to see her at his shoulder.

'Couldn't bear it on my own any longer,' she heaved.

'You'd have been okay back there,' he snapped.

Sergeant Rath bounded down the stairs. 'All clear, Lieutenant – empty.'

McDermott surveyed the street, pressed the button on his radio. 'You got anything, Herman?'

'All quiet this end, sir.'

He turned to Alex. 'In the Bradley, quick,' he demanded.

The vehicle was still a distance away, blocking the end of the street. Should she run to it? The rear hatch opened. She could see Joe Herman beckoning her forward. McDermott urged her, 'Go, go.'

She sprinted towards the Bradley, any second expecting the sound of a shot. Just feet away from the open hatch and Herman's outstretched hands, she felt her legs starting to give way. Gritting her teeth and with a final surge, she managed to scramble aboard.

On the floor of the Bradley, shaking and bathed in sweat, she refused Herman's offer to help her up.

'Please, just leave me for a minute,' she pleaded.

'It's okay, now – you're safe in here,' he whispered gently.

She looked into his eyes, searching for reassurance. He offered his hand. Letting out a deep, shuddering, sigh, she sat up and allowed him to guide her to a seat.

A minute later, McDermott's all-clear message crackled on Herman's radio. If she trusted the lieutenant's judgement, it meant she was safe to go back out. Totally shattered, she couldn't summon up the nerve.

The safety of the Bradley cocooned her. Eyes closed, she leant back, exhausted, eventually curling up into a self-protecting ball. When she eventually came round, she realised she'd been sucking her thumb like a baby.

It was at this moment she decided she must leave Iraq.

* * *

Alex phoned the major the next day saying she was unwell. She wasn't lying, she felt wretched. The attack on the patrol had left its mark and, in the night, the Kandahar dream's severed arm tried to choke her.

Running a bath – hot water at last – she sank down in the tub to think. She wanted out of Iraq. Not because of the people or the country itself, but what it had become, a maelstrom. As sympathetic as she felt about the shambolic state of the nation, she had to leave for her own sanity.

Whether Kowolski liked it or not, there was no other choice.

* * *

He put the press cuttings down on the table of the Palestine Hotel lounge area with a bang that startled her. 'And what the hell is this, Alex?'

She looked at the picture, her picture, of the shooting incident. 'Ooh, you've even printed it off in colour – you shouldn't have,' she countered sarcastically.

'Listen, sweetheart, I'll have you off this case and back home chasing ambulances or whatever you do. There'll be no more embeds, no more Iraq, *nada*. This is bullshit, entirely against the rules and you know it… no clearance, no confirmation, no official spokesman line.'

'It's what I do, remember?'

He leaned forward, towering over her. Several people sitting nearby cast their eyes towards the raised voices. 'And who did write this piece of shit – your boyfriend?'

'Everything's a true reflection of the incident. The truth bother you?'

'Let me ask you something, Alex. You a bleeding heart liberal or something – or are you just so way left of the Democrats it clouds your thinking?'

81

She stared at him, a look of indignation, her eyes narrowing. What did he really know about her? Was he goading her into something else than this? 'I simply happen to believe in democracy – and in my book, that means the truth. I'll leave the ugly politics and the scheming to the likes of you.'

He turned on her again. 'You just don't get it do you? It's only a game to you guys. You breeze in here, report any old stuff like it's the definitive version of events, then you're gone. It's the likes of me who has to pick up the pieces, try and repair the damage.'

'Damage! That's a laugh. It wasn't the media who shot this poor mother's son. I saw it, I recorded it, it's what damn-well happened – with or without your permission.'

He slumped into the seat beside her.

'Anyway, I'm going home.'

'What? But you haven't finished.'

'I've had enough, ten days, it'll have to do. I'll email you the picture file when I get back to my room.'

She got up to leave. He reached out and held her arm. His voice was lower, almost a whisper, a hint of pleading.

'You'll be letting me down. This is really important.' His tone was no longer combative. 'Listen, let's talk again in the morning after you've slept on it – okay?'

He watched her leave the room, his eyes returning to Alex's picture. Studying it, he was drawn to the blood on the mother's hands, the last traces of her only son's life. He felt his face flush and, for a second, a lump rose in his throat.

* * *

Kowolski beamed a wide smile as Alex approached his breakfast table, standing up and pulling out a chair. He couldn't help but notice the dark shadows under her eyes as if she'd hardly slept.

'Coffee?'

She nodded, grim-faced.

'I have to admit, I was all set to twist your arm about staying – until I saw the portfolio of photographs you sent me. They're fantastic, really good work.'

'Thanks,' she said, a little brighter. 'I could have stayed another two weeks and not really improved on anything.'

'So you're going home?'

'Yep,' she said resignedly.

'Listen,' he said, lowering his voice a notch, looking around him. 'Personally, I don't blame you. I never figured things would be this bad out here – but I've taken on the job so I'll have to see it through.'

Kowolski's admission and his conciliatory nature caught her unawares. She'd been expecting another row; a scene; people staring.

In reality, he felt relatively relaxed about Alex's picture of the shooting incident. None of the major US papers had used it. The newspapers were full of the President's speech, simply lapping up the 'mission accomplished' line, devoting pages to the occasion.

Tossing a packet on the table, he leant back in his chair. 'Three weeks' work in cash – and there's more.'

'But I... '

He raised his hand, halting her. 'I'll need some of your pictures blown up big, real big. You work with a good lab?'

Alex nodded, twisting the package in her hands.

Kowolski pointed to it. 'If you did find you needed to come back here, there's a ticket in there to Kuwait and a pass that will get you on to any military aircraft coming up this way.'

She managed a half-smile. 'Sorry, but I very much doubt I'll have reason to set foot in Iraq ever again.'

But she couldn't have been more wrong.

9

Alex had the rest of the day to say her farewells, Kowolski having bagged her a ride to Kuwait on a C5 cargo plane that was leaving late afternoon. She wanted to visit Aban and Farrah al-Tikriti but they said they had no electricity. Instead, she invited them to the Palestine.

The couple greeted Alex like old friends.

'I have an interview this afternoon with the Coalition Provisional Authority,' Aban beamed.

'That's great news, Aban,' Alex said, ordering coffee. 'I'm sure you can help the country's recovery. And how is everything else?'

Aban paused until the waiter was out of earshot. 'There is great unrest in the community. We have no electricity, no water, no gas, the infrastructure is in ruins.'

Alex nodded her head in sympathy. 'I can see things are getting tighter and I've only been here a short time. I can't imagine what it's like actually living amongst it.'

Aban continued in full flow, his voice occasionally cracking with emotion. Farrah's eyes darted between them like she was watching a tennis match, hanging on his every word and anxious to endorse his take on the situation at the slightest hint of hesitation.

'The Americans think Iraqis will be grateful to them for deposing Saddam, but we do not take kindly to any invasion. It is historic – the Ottoman Empire. The Turks ruled our country for almost four hundred years and it has never been forgotten. I fear there are many problems to come.'

'What about this guy Muqtada al-Sadr and his followers?' Alex said.

'Your government would be wise to pay him full attention. He is not strong at this moment – maybe he has a few hundred followers of his extremist Shi'ite views. But only six weeks have past since the Americans invaded. In a few months, the people's growing discontent could easily turn those hundreds into thousands.'

He leaned forward in his chair, speaking more quietly. 'You remember I said that Iraq, under Saddam, at least was a secular country. Shi'ites and Sunnis worked together, married into each other's families. No one cared about such things. You were just Muslim – or maybe Christian like Saddam's deputy Tariq Aziz, who was Catholic. Our tribes were mixed – the al-Janabi tribe was Sunni and Shia, so too the Dulaimis. An Iraqi's first loyalty was to his family, to the neighbourhood, then to the tribe. Religion came lower. I think it is not dissimilar to how it is in many Western countries. But, now...'

He waved his hands in the air in a gesture of helplessness. 'It might not always be so. The al-Sadrs, the Sistanis, threaten to create their own kingdoms based on their religious extremism. Intolerance and bigotry will come to the fore.'

'Jeez – it's extremely depressing, Aban.'

He slowly shook his head, a look of defeat on his face. 'Once the lid is off the box who knows what will crawl out?'

* * *

On checking out of the Palestine, Alex took a ride to the Green Zone in a Chevy SUV with armed guards from a private security firm riding shotgun. Each minder was tall, laconic. Lazy gum-chewing jaws suggested everything was cool. Black impenetrable shades refused to reveal otherwise.

She'd been sorry not to have seen the British journalist, Charles Toller, whose alarming take on events opened her eyes to the daunting uphill task facing Iraq. She left him a note.

McDermott, on a morning off, had agreed to their rendezvous. She told him she just wanted to say goodbye. In reality, a burning desire had consumed her since the last patrol. She felt she needed to excuse her behaviour after freaking out. Curiosity about McDermott also played a part. Although he'd declined to talk about his exploits, she was interested in hearing why he thought he was fighting in Iraq. If McDermott was representative of the young men and women laying down their lives for America, Alex felt it important to know his reasoning.

One of her minders, a Brit, who'd been silent, suddenly turned to her. 'I hear your buddies shot a family to pieces at a checkpoint last night,' he said. 'Serves them fuckin'-well right.'

'You've gotta stop, man,' the driver rowed in, shaking his head. 'Could be friggin' insurgents with an RPG or something.'

Toller was right; the streets were getting bloodier.

Alex's anger suddenly took over. 'For crying out loud, you guys. Someone in the distance shines a flashlight – how the fuck does an ordinary Iraqi know who it is? Could be a sectarian death squad who'd kill you for having the wrong name. Get real for Chrissake, you've got no idea.'

The Brit looked at her with disdain. He raised his submachine gun from his lap, pointed it at the window and laughed coarsely. 'Pow, pow, pow,' he mimicked, while shooting his own imaginary Iraqi family.

Alex looked at him, disgusted. 'Yeah, very clever – it figures.' She pressed back in her seat with an exaggerated sigh.

Death from US troops, death from insurgents, death from extremists. The threat was omnipresent. And dead was dead in any language and for whatever reason.

Outside, the atmosphere looked normal enough at first glance; plenty of traffic, people walking, shopping – even if consumer goods were growing ever more scarce. Except that, these days, normality in Baghdad was a commodity in short supply.

The SUV picked up speed, just clearing a junction on a new red light. 'Stopping's a mug's game in this town,' the driver said.

'Unless you're an Iraqi family at a checkpoint?' Alex replied, hoping they'd be half intelligent enough to see the irony.

* * *

Alex spotted McDermott sitting alone at the far end of the officers' mess. Giving her a wave, he pulled out a chair.

'You okay now, Ma'am?' McDermott sat upright, running a hand over his head self-consciously.

'Thankfully,' she said, glancing about her, shifting.

He followed her gaze. 'You'll have to excuse some of my fellow officers – they haven't seen a civilian woman this close in a while. The local girls are covering up, much to the guys' displeasure. Headscarves and cloaks seem to be growing in popularity.'

'Religious clampdown. I hear a girl was threatened in the street recently – acid in her face if she didn't conform,' Alex said, shuddering. 'Listen, about the other day, I... '

'Forget it, Ma'am. Even we so-called tough guys get scared.'

'I guess – just that I'm not always like that. I mean, I've been in situations that'd make your hair curl and thought nothing of it.'

Alex immediately regretted saying that. Kandahar was a prime example and she'd done nothing but think of it since.

'That's cool,' he said.

She studied him for a few moments. Here was a clean-cut sort of guy who wouldn't look out of place in a business setting, an accountant maybe, banking, or perhaps in real estate.

'You're... a religious type of guy aren't you, Matt?'

It was the first time she'd used his first name. Her directness caught him off-guard. She looked straight into his eyes, too, which many people found disconcerting but which she used to great effect. As a journalist, she found she had to venture places others found off-limits.

'I believe in the Bible if that's what you mean,' he said, taking

87

a gulp of his orange juice. 'I try to follow the Lord's command in most that I do.'

'Successfully?'

'Only the Lord God knows that – but I try. We're all sinners, everyone. You can only ask the Lord's forgiveness, keep trying to do better.'

She recalled the expression on his face on patrol when he had picked up the child in the street. It was an image she had captured perfectly and which had haunted her ever since. For a second, he had looked so... helpless.

'And you admit to getting pretty scared out there. Where's it all going?'

'Well, I can only speak for myself. But, if it is the Lord's wish that I take a hit, then so be it.' He smiled then, a self-confident look she had not seen before, one that, paradoxically, dispelled any hint of boyishness about him. 'But I'm sure He is watching over me and all the others I pray for.'

'So, would you, say, believe in the Book of Revelation, the plague and pestilence and the second coming?'

'I do,' he said solemnly. 'You?'

'I'm afraid we'd have to agree to differ on the whole subject, Lieutenant.'

For a few moments there was an awkward silence between them. It was not every day she would have shown the slightest interest in anyone's religion. But, intrigued, she wanted to know why a young man like him could be doing this – fighting, maiming – when required. Killing to order. Plenty of others like him, too, doing their tour, serving their country. Following Jesus. But where was their conscience?

And back home, in the corridors of power, the decision-makers, the planners. How on earth did they all reconcile this mess of their own creation with their love of God and devotion to the Bible?

Taking a deep breath, she pressed on. 'Take this,' she said with a sweep of the hand. 'What are you fighting for?'

He thought for a few seconds. 'Freedom. Justice – and against al-Qaeda,' he said resignedly. 'We've got God on our side, too.'

His answer, so stoic, immediately enraged her. Was there some grand plan, some overwhelming intellect, she was missing? Or was she just too cynical to get a grip on the unswerving devotion to a cause, no matter what its ramifications?

'What if I told you al-Qaeda is not an issue in Iraq – nor are you likely to find any WMD?'

His mouth dropped as surely as if she'd told him the moon was made of green cheese.

'It's a figment of their imagination back home, the President's bogeyman – what Cheney, Rumsfeld, Wolfowitz and the other clowns need to have the public believe,' she said, her voice rising in exasperation. 'Don't you see that? Don't you realise? They had to tell you something, give you a cause. The President admitted as far back as last July that the government's policy was regime change. They invented al-Qaeda and WMD when world opinion didn't like what he'd said.'

He got up, about to leave. 'Sorry, I can't listen to this.'

'Stop a minute, Lieutenant,' she said, her voice firm.

Much to her surprise, he did as she ordered, standing with his hands on the back of the chair, deliberating whether to stay or go.

Alex gestured palm outwards, an invitation to return to his seat. He hesitated. She smiled at him.

'What's so important that you need to know why?' he said, a look of anguish spreading. 'Who's told you all this trash?'

'Did you ever see our ever-so convincing assistant defense secretary Paul Wolfowitz telling Congress the troops would be welcomed with open arms? Well, how many open arms have you seen?'

Alex could see she'd struck a chord. McDermott slumped down in his chair.

She lowered her voice. 'The only thing worse than someone lying is the person who believes his own lies.'

McDermott looked crestfallen. He'd had an indefatigable belief in the President, his government. 'He's been lying to us?' the lieutenant asked, incredulous, his face contorted in puzzlement.

Alex took on a more conciliatory stance. 'All I'm saying is that we've got a couple of hundred thousand troops swarming all over the country and we've found zilch. So you believe what you want and I'll do likewise. A truce, okay?'

He nodded, blinking several times with both eyes. She'd never seen him do that before. He looked so vulnerable, a little like his expression with the baby boy and his mother that she'd captured so well. A quirk of his when under pressure? No, she thought, they'd had a ton of it and he always appeared in control.

'Okay,' she said lighter, switching tack, leaning back on two legs of her chair. 'What about this – if you could be anywhere in the world right now, away from all this, where would that be?'

It was a question she loved asking people because their replies could be illuminating, so character-defining.

He studied her for a moment, his expression querulous, as if, suddenly, he didn't want to play this game. She watched him intently. There was something boyish about the man again.

Here was a highly-trained soldier, what the red-necks back home called a 'killing machine'. But this was no unthinking, robotic pastiche of a military assembly line. She knew this from the embed, had observed him more closely off-camera than through the lens. She could tell that beneath the rather cool façade was a sensitive, perhaps troubled soul. Despite their differences and his stubborn unsophisticated belief, it was difficult not to like him. And besides, she owed him her life.

'Oh, I don't know,' he finally said.

'Come on,' she goaded. 'Back home, or on a beach someplace? In the mountains maybe searching for those black bears you said you've never seen?'

'I guess... ' he rubbed his chin rather self-consciously,

looking vaguely into the distance. 'I think I'd just like to be with my Bible, you know – somewhere quiet, someplace I could call my... '

'Garden of Eden?'

'Yeah, that's the place,' he smiled exultantly. 'Exactly that. The Garden of Eden.'

* * *

Kowolski pushed his glasses back from the end of his nose and began studying Alex's work in more detail on his computer screen. He couldn't have wished for better. Convinced they were just what he wanted for the launching of McDermott in New York, he leant back, satisfied, putting his hands behind his head.

Despite their differences, he couldn't help but admit he had a soft spot for Alex. Not sexually – he'd got over that initial blunder. He saw some of his own dogged qualities in her; a spirited contempt for protocol, a lively independence. Moody? She could turn on a dime. A pity they weren't both on the same political side – but he could handle that.

He felt a tinge of regret he hadn't been completely honest with her about New York. He'd promised her an exhibition of her photographs in the Manhattan hotel he'd already sounded out for the grand occasion. He envisaged the moment the President pinned the medal on McDermott's chest. She'd be mad, of course, when she discovered the whole aim of the show was to boost the President's standing. But he had a job to do, however duplicitous.

He turned his attention to the latest polls from back home, at once frowning. One survey asked whether now the Iraq war was over, would the public support an attack on Syria? A majority said they would.

'The war over?' he muttered to himself. 'Yeah, of course, mission accomplished.'

How he'd love to say his own mission had been

accomplished. But it was only just beginning. There were so many opinion polls, surveys and samplings to monitor, a never-ending multitude of events he hoped he could influence if deemed important to the cause. The election was in next year's calendar but it was the rest of this year that mattered. The long hard drive for campaign donations stretched on and on. A simple equation faced the President: popularity equalled money equalled victory. And his boy, McDermott, was going to play a big part in the whole show.

Kowolski had given himself a month to establish the lieutenant's celebrity in a media onslaught. From then on, he would milk it for the rest of the campaign. He'd already thought of arranging for McDermott to make an appearance at the Iowa Primaries in January when the Republicans clicked into overdrive. Folks would love to see the President's Golden Boy on the platform, helping kick off the proceedings.

The Primaries would be a piece of cake for the President. Who would dare challenge him? So the Republicans would just sit back and watch the Democrats squabble among themselves.

Schmucks, he thought. They wouldn't know what hit them.

Planning was such an ordinary, boring word, Kowolski mused. But he loved it.

* * *

After a decent lunch, Kowolski found himself in a good mood. He was upbeat about the President's approval rating. Down to fifty-five per cent pre-war, but now riding high at seventy-two per cent.

His masters were content. For now. But he was constantly urging himself and those around him against complacency. Bad news had a habit of appearing, like the magician's rabbit. That was why he'd been anxious to lay down the law to Alex and her Australian friend. He would not be taken for a ride. The more people who knew it, the better.

The Brits in Basra had disappointed him. Try as he might to

have the Australian taken off the embed, they would not accede to his complaint. Okay, so the jerk was a mere fly in the scheme of things. But Kowolski would still like to swat him given half the chance.

A secretary came into the room carrying a sheaf of papers, which she put on his desk. Kowolski's eyes followed her out of the room.

'You getting much ass out here?' he said, turning to a young man assigned as an assistant.

The guy, a postgraduate on a Pentagon internship, blushed. 'I... er... '

Kowolski laughed. 'They all want it, son – just some more than others.'

He began reading an overview of a recent briefing by senior army officers to Rumsfeld. The generals were optimistic of a rapid pull-out of US troops to around the 30,000 mark. After several minutes, he swore softly, shaking his head. Tossing the paper to the assistant, he took off his glasses. 'What d'you make of this?'

The young man studied it. 'Well, sir, if the estimates and projections are correct, it will surely ratchet up the President's popularity.'

'You're learning, son. Yep, there's nothing like seeing our boys safely back home to the fanfares of victory.' He paused. 'And longer term – where does that leave us?'

The young man hesitated.

'I'll tell you,' Kowolski thundered. 'We'll be up shit creek without the fucking paddle. A quarter of a million of our boys vanish from Iraq and we're left with the Iraqi army, a bunch of ill-trained motherfuckers bereft of leadership and direction. It'd be a fucking nightmare.'

With that, he stormed out of the office, slamming the door. His mood was black.

10

Aban al-Tikriti regretted choosing to put on a tie.

Like many others entering the Green Zone, he'd been forced to wait over an hour in the merciless heat. Those in front had their papers checked, their identities determined, their pockets, robes and bags searched. He witnessed endless arguments. Tempers were short these days. Fear and loathing was the new common currency. Now, even with his jacket over his arm, his shirt was sodden, the trickles of sweat down his neck and his arms adding to his discomfort.

He thought of Farrah and the boys. Every ounce of his love was invested in his family. They'd discussed the prospect of joining the mass exodus to Syria or Jordan but decided to stay. The boys would continue their schooling, albeit with likely interruptions.

'We cannot leave now – what would happen to our home if we left? I will get a new job, help rebuild our country,' he told her. 'Everything will be fine. The Americans will leave shortly and let us get on with things. The future is bright.'

He always gave her a reassuring hug or patted her hand when he made such pronouncements. But his reassurances were hollow. Worse, he knew they were. Without work, their future in Iraq looked bleak.

Even so, he was glad they did not have daughters. Religious extremism was becoming rife. A neighbour's daughter, accustomed to the popular fashion of jeans and t-shirt, was recently accosted and bawled at by several men in the street who accused her of being immodest. The teenager now wore a burqa with a niquab, with only her eyes on show.

Where would it all end, he asked himself. At least under

Saddam's rule there were women engineers, scientists, doctors, teachers. And they could wear what they liked. The universities were full of women and many of the professions had equal pay.

But if the men could not now find work, what hope for women?

He glanced at the letter giving him instructions for the interview. No specific job but, as a former senior civil servant in the Ministry of Commerce, he was going into the meeting with a degree of confidence. His CV was first class, as was his PhD.

He reached the building, showed his letter to one of the two marines on guard, and was led to a door, which he opened himself. Two-dozen pairs of eyes from the packed, stuffy waiting room assailed him. Men, already here looking for work, regarded him suspiciously, a competitor. He sat down in the last vacant seat.

Many of them dressed as manual workers, ties non-existent. Some stared at their shoes, shuffled their feet in embarrassment. Others, churlish, fixed their gaze on a creaking ceiling fan that stuttered anti-clockwise, barely raising more than a breath in the silent, fetid atmosphere.

It was a further debilitating two hours before his hopes were raised. A fresh-faced young man opened the door. 'Al-Tikriti?'

Aban stood up, stiff from the waiting. Pushing his shoulders back, he strode after his interviewer with a degree of confidence he hoped would not be taken for arrogance. But the young man never turned round, simply marching on, pushing through several sets of doors leaving Aban in his wake. Aban took a wrong turn and found himself on a fire stairs landing. Hurrying now for fear of looking stupid, he had to double back. When he reached the correct doorway, his interviewer was already lolling in a chair, a leg resting on the edge of his desk.

Aban felt his insides twisting. A dark foreboding shivered through him as a pokey side room greeted him with a scowl from its bare walls and a smell of stale cigarette smoke.

The interviewer, exactly half Aban's age of forty-eight, had recently just scraped through a protracted degree course in business management. His wealthy parents, generous donors to the Republican Party, had pulled several strings to get him the posting with the Provisional Coalition. They'd managed to persuade their son that potential employers would be delighted to see he'd stuck his neck out for his country. No one would know, however, that he had not yet set foot out of the safe zone – nor did he intend to for the whole of his six-month attachment.

He had a brash, almost cocky aura, flipping through the pages of the CV in a scant manner that only endorsed his disinterest.

'So, Mr… ' he glanced at the notes, '… al-Tikriti.'

'It's Doctor, actually,' Aban said quietly. 'You will see I have an MBA and a PhD.'

'Right,' he said without a trace of apology. 'And what do you think you can do for the United States of America?'

Aban was taken aback. He wanted to respond immediately that he was not offering his services to America but for his own beloved country. He felt like asking this 'boy' what HE could do for Iraq. He was tempted to tell him that if he were in his Ministry, he would be shuffling papers as an office junior with such an attitude.

Instead, he bit his tongue. 'Well, you will see my experience is in many areas of commerce. Most of it in an executive capacity – I had over two hundred staff working for me, many departments.'

His words appeared to float over the young man's head who had now fixed his gaze on a second sheet of Aban's CV. 'It says here you are a Sunni… Ba'athist, perhaps?'

'My friend, everyone who worked for the government was a member of the Ba'athist party. It was a requirement. I thought you would have known that.'

'Wait here,' he said imperiously, quickening out of the room.

It was a further ten minutes before he returned, not even

bothering to sit. 'I have to say that we do not have any vacancies in any of our departments at this time. I hear they're looking for people at the morgue – you might like to enquire of some of your fellow countrymen down there. Good day... sir.' He quickly disappeared through another door leaving no time for a response.

Aban sat completely stunned for a moment. He was mild-mannered enough to forgive the man's rudeness, his incompetence. But the audacity had been simply breathtaking. No vacancies, no job, even for a man of his qualifications. Surely not.

The country needed rebuilding. He was desperate to help.

His mind began racing, firing off a raft of questions and emotions; self-doubts, fears for his family, for himself. Finally, the stark reality suddenly struck home like a hard, sickening blow.

So this was their game. He ran his thoughts back to recent murmurings among his friends about the Coalition.

'Don't be surprised if we Sunnis are frozen out of any meaningful position within government and the military,' one former colleague had said.

He'd read the stories in the US media; the power-holding Sunnis under Saddam were a twenty per cent minority of the population. The pendulum was about to swing in favour of the majority Shi'ites.

He knew the Sunni-Shi'ite split in Iraq was more evenly spread than that. Enclaves of one sect or the other abounded within Baghdad and the other big cities. But they were all Muslims. Little attention had ever been paid to people's persuasion. As long as it was not anti-Saddam.

Aban left the base in turmoil; angry, hurt, confused. If this was a sign of the times, his worst fears would be realised. Iraq had its own dark forces to turn the fear of a Sunni-Shia schism into the nightmare of reality.

As to his own dire situation: a job at the morgue? Farrah had a cousin, a well-meaning, likeable young man named Abu Khamsin, who worked there. He had not long returned from the US, where he'd completed his master's degree – yet could find no other work. The families had been regaled with the most gruesome of details. Aban shuddered at the memory.

'It is only a job,' the cousin told his aghast audience. 'To starve like a dog on the street is a fate far worse.'

Aban stared blankly at the numbing landscape on the journey home. He recalled an article he'd read in *Time* magazine as a young man. It had evoked a feeling of pity to hear of the dozens of highly-qualified NASA scientists thrown out of work at a stroke in America when the US space budget was slashed. Some had resorted to becoming taxi drivers.

It had struck him as incongruous that a country supposedly as advanced as the United States could do that to its cognoscenti. That he was now in the same position was a truly frightening prospect. The family had some savings, but how long would they last? And who would pity him?

Glad the house was empty, he needed time to be alone, to think. But the tight knot in his stomach made this almost impossible. He stumbled into his study and flopped into his chair, staring doggedly at the wall.

'A hundred thousand curses on America,' he wailed before breaking down, crying loudly, his head in his hands.

* * *

Alex fastened her seatbelt and braced herself as the C-5 Galaxy rumbled along the runway, rapidly picking up speed. Facing backwards and with no windows on the upper deck, it made for a disconcerting take off.

'Some power in those engines, huh?'

She glanced sideways. A man who'd been the last onboard, sitting two empty seats away, smiled at her. Unlike the military passengers on the half-empty flight, he was casually dressed in jeans and sneakers. She noted his light blue short-sleeved shirt in stylish linen.

Suddenly airborne, climbing steeply, they hit turbulence. 'Whooah,' Alex shouted, steadying herself, and giving him a startled look.

When the Galaxy levelled off, he undid his seatbelt and moved a seat closer. 'Steve Lewis,' he said, leaning over and offering his hand. 'Where you headed?'

Was he trying to hit on her – or just being friendly? She couldn't tell. He seemed fairly laid back, though. And, she had to admit, it was good to see someone smile at last – an uninhibited lightness notably absent in Baghdad.

'Home,' she said. 'New York – I'm Alex Stead, freelance photographer, by the way.'

'Lucky you,' he said, running a hand through his dark hair and fastening his seatbelt.

Alex shifted position. Her feet touched her cabin bag under her seat. She pulled it out and undid the zip. Finding her laptop, she placed it on her knee. She'd planned to start a reluctant memo to Richard Northwood from the notes on her laptop. She intended to keep things brief and to not name her source. But Aban's alarming views on the situation in Iraq, now and future, would surely be of some use to him – even if only endorsing intelligence they already possessed. Then she would put Richard Northwood out of her mind for good.

'Hope I'm not disturbing you,' Steve said. 'I'm very good at sitting quietly. In fact, I've often thought I'd make a good dog – sitting by my master with the occasional pat on the head to keep me happy.'

He had light blue eyes and when he laughed, as now, she saw them set to dancing.

Hesitating for a second, she closed the lid of the laptop, putting it back in the bag. 'Too noisy to think straight,' she smiled.

'It sure is one big angry beast. There's only one plane bigger anywhere – Russian – but not by much. We call these fellas FRED.'

On an impulse, she took off her beret, throwing it in the bag, and shaking her hair free.

He watched her, intrigued. Some of her gestures signalled a degree of confidence, yet he couldn't help but notice her hands trembling when she'd pulled out the laptop. She looked so much better without the headgear, too.

Although Alex knew what the fuel-guzzling Galaxy's acronym stood for, she feigned ignorance. 'FRED?'

'Ah, Ma'am, I couldn't say.'

'Go on,' she teased.

She saw him start to blush.

'Okay, let's have a guessing game.' She relaxed in her seat, watching him grow more uncomfortable. He rubbed the end of his nose, embarrassed.

He had a square jaw, softened by a shade of prominence in his cheekbones. Good looking, yes, she thought.

'Right, I'm going to have a go,' she said, pursing her lips, toying with him. She watched his eyebrows rise in anticipation, a crease across his forehead. 'How about... Fucking Ridiculous Environmental Disaster!'

He burst out laughing, doubling up and slapping his knees, his body shaking. Alex couldn't help but join in. Still giggling a minute later, she produced a tissue and dabbed her eyes.

It struck her she hadn't laughed like that for months. Nor had she made anyone else laugh, something she liked to do. Pleased at how she'd managed to bait him, she still had a wicked gleam in her eye when she turned sideways. 'That's one up for me, I think,' she said.

Shaking his head, hardly believing he'd been suckered, he let out a deep breath. 'Yeah, you got me good and proper. I can see I'll have to watch you.'

They talked, interspersed with laughs, for the rest of the journey. She was intrigued by him, so un-military like and with none of the overt macho characteristics of some of those she'd met. He was two years older than her, an army helicopter instructor, currently based at their destination, the Kuwait-US Ali al-Salem airbase, forty miles south of the Iraq border.

'Do you like what you do?'

'I like flying choppers – hope to have my own charter company when I get out. Thankfully, I don't get involved with Iraq and wouldn't want to. I just train the younger guys in Kuwait. Until all this kicked off, I was working for an oil company but, as an army reserve, got called up. So here I am.'

The noise of the Galaxy's engines dropped a beat.

He handed her his card. She saw his rank was a chief warrant officer (class 4).

For some reason, she found herself wondering if he was married. Just out of curiosity, she told herself. Probably had a wife and a couple of kids back in Philadelphia.

The plane came into land, touching down sharply.

'Say, Alex, I'm going into Kuwait – two days left of my R and R. I'd be pleased for the company, that is unless... '

She hesitated for a moment. How else was she going to get into the city? Besides, she was enjoying his easy manner. She'd be safe with him, surely?

'That'd be great,' she said.

The process of taxiing in the Galaxy proved a protracted affair. At a loaded weight approaching 380 tons, the plane had to manoeuvre on to special reinforced ramps to stop its undercarriage sinking into a runway that often melted in the 120-degree heat of this bleak desert outpost.

Finally in position, Steve picked up Alex's luggage and allowed her out of the plane before him. She scanned the vista. No wonder they called this place The Rock, she thought. Perched on a barren hill, surrounded by sand and scrub, it comprised a runway and more tents than she could count.

'What goes on here, then?' Alex said, feeling the heat wash over her like she'd just opened an oven door.

'Aircraft in and out all day,' Steve said. Then, pointing to the far side of the base, 'That's where the geeks hang out – air defence. Patriot missiles at their fingertips. Occasionally they send up a UAV.'

'Ah, the video gamers,' Alex said, smiling to herself. She was sure the military could speak using only the odd full word in a sentence full of abbreviations. 'Unmanned aerial vehicles – drones, right?'

Steve nodded. They walked a short distance to a mini bus, which soon whisked them off to a large tent – the customs and immigration hall. Waiting in a queue, she leaned over his shoulder to peek at his open passport.

'Sorry, can't resist looking at people's photos – hey, who's that good-looking guy?'

Steve laughed. 'Can't be me, that's for sure.'

'But you're not seeing mine,' she said, snapping her passport shut. 'Most unflattering.'

'That's okay. I like what I see in real life.'

Now, it was Alex's turn to flush. She felt the heat rising from her neck to her cheeks. Compliments had been thin on the ground. No one had said they liked her in an age. She gave him a shy smile, admitting to herself that she kind of liked him, too.

They reached what looked like a car park, a vague assembly of vehicles haphazardly placed wherever there was a space.

'Sorry, this is the best I can offer,' he said, putting her luggage in the boot of a rather battered Japanese compact. She had trouble closing the door so that he had to go round to help. 'There's something of a knack to it,' he laughed lifting the door upwards and slamming it shut. 'The result of a slight argument with a Kuwaiti cab not too long back.'

'Well, you sure know how to impress a girl,' she said mischievously.

'Aw shucks, you ain't seen nothin' yet,' he parodied in a southern drawl.

They turned on to a highway, refreshingly clear of the burned out vehicles and wrecks of Baghdad.

'So what do you do on leave?'

'Oh, you know, the usual for us army guys – strip joints, bars, nightclubs.'

'I see,' she said, a hint of disappointment in her voice.

He sensed her demeanour. 'Alex, I'm joking – Kuwait is a dry country and that's not my scene anyway. I... er... well, the rest of the guys think I'm crazy, but I'm rather fond of Islamic art. So I take myself round a few galleries with a notebook and try to escape from what's going on the other side of the border.'

'That's interesting,' she said, happier.

'What time's your flight?'

'Oh, not till just before midnight – the red-eye to New York.'

'Wish I was coming with you,' he said with a hint of melancholy. 'How about we go for a bite in the city – I know a great little Italian. We'd have time to eat and I could still take you to catch your plane.' He glanced at her expectantly.

'Are you sure? I mean... '

'I've never met anyone yet who likes eating on their own – unless you do?'

She laughed then. It was a tempting offer. 'I don't always say yes to strange men... '

* * *

They clung to each other, both of their bodies racked with sobs.

'But what will become of us?' Farrah said taking a deep breath. 'The boys... '

'We will be all right,' Aban finally said, composing himself. 'It is just the shock, the rebuff – it was not what I was expecting. You go up to bed and I shall bring you a drink in a little while.'

Farrah gave him a squeeze and went up the stairs. The sound of gunfire in the distance added to her unease. It was becoming a more regular occurrence.

103

Choosing her favourite china pot, he made her usual bedtime chamomile tea and took it up. 'I'll be along presently, just need to attend to something at my desk.'

He retreated to his study, moving swiftly over to the bookcase. By removing several volumes, he exposed a wooden panel, then a safe. Twisting the dial to the correct combination, he opened the door.

The contents were all too familiar; their wills, birth and marriage certificates, passports. He picked up several pieces of expensive gold jewellery and laid them aside. Farrah hardly ever wore it – especially not these days. In keeping with many Iraqi families, the collection was considered 'final resort' investment.

From the back of the compartment, he withdrew a large brown envelope, sealed with the official stamp of the Iraqi government. He noticed his hands shaking as he took it over to his desk and studied it, hesitant. It had been given to him two days before the invasion by a senior official in the government, a distant relative of Saddam, who feared he might not survive the invasion. The man wanted Aban, his trusted friend and colleague, to keep it safe and confidential.

Until now, he had been fearful of breaking the seal, lest someone else called for it. Aban had learned his friend's depressing prophecy had become self-fulfilling. On reflection, Aban suspected the presage had simply been a sad, coded metaphor. The story had soon reached him that his colleague had steadfastly remained in his office. It was the first to be hit in the bombing.

The seal broken, a sheaf of papers and a computer disc spilled on to his desk. He inserted the disc into his machine and waited for it to play.

When it did, he could scarcely believe what he was seeing.

* * *

'So, what's your take on all this?' she asked, guiding a forkful of shrimp and clam linguini into her mouth, savouring the crushed red peppers in the sauce; it was delicious.

He studied her for a second, wondered whether to be diplomatic, toe the usual army line. But, heck, that was not his style, even if he did keep his own counsel back at base. 'I think we've created one helluva mess, a tragic mistake that's going to take a mighty long time to sort out... you?'

'Check that. What in God's name were they all thinking?'

'Well, maybe they launched this thing in God's name but they sure as hell didn't think that way about the consequences. Some of the stories the guys on active over the border tell me... Jeez.'

'And you train them,' she said passionately, a hint of condemnation within her voice.

'Look, I joined up because I thought I could contribute, you know, do my bit in exchange for them teaching me to fly. I always figured I'd be willing to defend my country against an aggressor but, over there,' he gestured with his fork, 'it's got me wondering just who are the aggressors.'

Then, there was a silence between them as they both ruminated on their pronouncements. He normally did not voice his opinions so vehemently. She was glad he had. It was as if they had both been swimming together under water, hand in hand, lost in the lucid buoyancy of mutual accord. Now, they had breached the surface and needed time to gulp for precious air.

'Sorry to have sounded off, so... ' he eventually said almost apologetically, aware he had been lost in her thoughts as well as his own.

She smiled, looked into his eyes. 'That's exactly how I'd want it.'

At the airport, he insisted on waiting for her while she checked in, then he walked her to the departure gate.

'Listen, this might sound crazy,' he said stroking his chin self-consciously, 'but I just wanted to say that, well, I kinda' feel as though I've known you for ages – if that doesn't sound too screwy. You think we'll see each other again?'

'You married?'

He looked surprised. 'No,' he said with a hint of indignation. 'I wouldn't have asked if I was.'

She kissed him on the cheek. 'Maybe.'

Then she quickly turned and walked towards the gate.

'I'll email you,' he shouted.

Just before she went through a set of double doors, the urge to look back proved too strong. He was still there, waving. She waved back. A lightness swept over her as she joined the other passengers waiting to board. He seemed a really nice guy and she would love to see him again.

It was just before her plane took off that a terrifying thought struck her, sending shock waves through her body. What if she allowed herself to fall for someone like Steve?

How the hell could she guarantee he wouldn't be a heartbreaker, too?

11

Matt McDermott lay on his bunk, reading the Bible; the Book of Revelation: 'And a star fell from the sky.'

Just lately he had been reading a lot of Revelation in the excerpts from his Scofield Study Bible. Placing great store in the book, it was his escape, an antidote to the increasing horrors on the outside of that wall and the seeds of doubt Alex had planted.

Two evenings past, he had suddenly felt a heavy, pervading dread envelop him as he walked across a moonlit parade ground; a physical feeling so strong inside him that, at one point, he was forced to stop and look around. He was convinced that he was surrounded by evil forces. And they were closing in.

Feeling drowsy, he lay the Bible open on his chest and closed his eyes, breathing deeply. A pair of smiling baby brown eyes loomed out of the darkness. Suddenly, his body began to tingle, as if an electrical charge coursed through his very being, his heart soon hammering away, so fast. Floating, a benign sense of wellbeing enveloped him where he was able to look down at himself, an eerie feeling he had never known. He could feel his eyelids fluttering but could not stop them.

Next, soaring, high up somewhere, the background a blur. A roaring sound blasted his ears. Along the line, he saw his Aunt Dorothy who had been dead at least ten years. She floated by, wistfully, without saying a word.

More frightening, he felt his body in a state of dull paralysis. He wanted to move his arms but seemed incapable of any action. Someone was pressing down on his legs. He could feel the weight of them on the bed but he was incapable of opening his eyes. It was then that the Devil himself appeared. For a short terrifying moment in his mind's eye, he could see Satan's horns only inches from his face. From afar, he heard the sound of his own groaning as he tried to brush the Beast away. He wanted to kick out, but his body had given way to a hopeless inertia. Then, rigid, fists clenched, he was in a tunnel, flying towards a brilliant white light. He passed through it to a stunned, irrational consciousness.

Shaken and confused, several minutes passed before he was able to ease himself to a sitting position. With great effort, he slid his legs over the side of the bed, unable to stop himself trembling.

He struggled to comprehend what was happening. It was as if everything was beyond his control, his mind incapable of any rational thought. Within seconds, he was totally overwhelmed with a deep despair; so dark it consumed him, mercilessly.

He cried out to stop himself reaching for his Beretta 9 mm service revolver, but was powerless. His right hand seemed a separate entity as he watched it slide the pistol out of its holster.

Grunting involuntarily, he took out the Check-Mate 15-round magazine from his drawer, slowly snapping it into place, hearing the light click. *Was he still dreaming?*

Sobbing now, shoulders shaking with grief and pity and self-loathing, images of the baby and its mother, the other women killed, flashed before him. Did they have children who were orphans? Parentless because of him?

Raising the Beretta, the barrel felt cold in his mouth. He flinched. One round was all it took. One round to salve his sins. One round for heavenly release.

He screwed his eyes. Tighter, tighter, tighter. Shutting everything out. The effort hurt him. Orange flashes streaked across his skull. He undid the safety catch, fingered the trigger. Now. Now. Now, a voice told him. *For God's sake do it now.*

Rocking to and fro on the bed, strange whimpers oozed from

his lips. The sweat poured off him. His finger squeezed slowly on the trigger.

From the blackness, his mother's face appeared, serene, loving. She smiled. Her lips moved: 'My darling baby boy.'

Startled, he opened his eyes fully, expecting her to be there. 'Mommy,' he cried out.

He put the gun down. The tears ran down his face and soaked his neck. He buried his head in the pillow and let it all go, wailing like the day he was born.

* * *

For days afterwards, his nerves danced wantonly with his emotions. Teasing him and turning him in every direction, he tried his utmost to hold himself together. Once, he very nearly lost his composure in front of his men, just about rescuing himself from the brink at the last moment.

Then, on an almost-perfect spring morning, the torment ended. He came up with a measured reasoning; God had surely been testing him. It was Satan who had urged him to pull the trigger, ending his life in disgrace, devastating his loved ones. Now, McDermott knew he had won. The victory gave him strength. If he had seen 'the fallen star' and been repulsed, surely this was a sign of his indefatigable belief in God? It left him convinced this tour of duty, indeed his very reason for joining the army, was pre-ordained. He could feel it, deep down, a gradual re-awakening of his soul, an affirmation of his faith. The visitation, the temptation to shoot himself, had held that very message: God was checking him out.

Walking proud, shoulders back, and with a determined stride, he left his billet on his way to the mess. Lifting his head to the only pink cloud in an orange sky, he suddenly cried out, 'Dear Lord, you may be testing my obedience. But my faith will earn your grace.'

His face creased into a wide smile as he saw P.J. approaching.

'Lieutenant, sir, the major wants to see you straight away.'

'Right, my son,' McDermott said calmly, altering direction.

P.J. stood and watched him go, perplexed. The lieutenant had addressed him like a priest. Not only that but he had seen him talking to the heavens. There was no doubt about it; something was getting to the lieutenant.

The rest of the guys had noticed it, too.

* * *

Major Walter Douglas stood to attention and greeted McDermott with his smartest salute. 'Come in, Lieutenant, at ease, rest your feet,' he said, gesturing to a new leather chair that McDermott had not seen before.

'Sir?'

'It's good news, Lieutenant – a Silver Star.'

McDermott gulped. It was the third-highest American military honour. 'I just don't know what to say, sir.'

'Congratulations, Lieutenant, well done,' the major said shaking his hand profusely. 'And that's not all. Your boys get the Valorous Unit Award, the unit Silver Star. We're all very proud of you.'

The major pulled out a large cigar and lit up, his face disappearing behind a cloud of smoke as he clenched it between his teeth. He smashed a fist into his palm. 'Goddam, son, this is one helluva boost to all of us. When this gets out we'll be the toast of Baghdad. You'll want to gather your boys up and break it to them. It means we'll probably be losing you for a little while sooner than I thought – Washington beckons. They want to give you the full works up there.'

The major studied him, a scrutinising stare. 'You're up for that aren't you, soldier? For the sake of your comrades?'

'Well, I guess... '

'Good man.' The major slapped him on the back. 'That Pentagon guy, Kowolski, he wants to brief you on events, says it'll be a grandstand show.'

The major's telephone rang and he turned away to answer it

so he did not see McDermott's hands on the arms of his chair. His grip was so tight the blood drained from his knuckles.

Only one vision sprung to the lieutenant's mind – that of a smiling brown-eyed baby boy with pudgy legs.

* * *

'Jesus, I don't believe what I'm hearing.' Kowolski turned to one of his assistants. 'What did you say?'

The assistant, a young law graduate who, in Kowolski's opinion, was too straight to be trusted for this job, began to stammer. Kowolski cut him off, rushing to check the memo on his own computer screen, leaning forward, pressing keys as if possessed. 'Bremer's disbanded the whole fuckin' Iraqi army with a month's pay-off? You sure?'

The assistant nodded, although the implications looked lost on him.

Kowolski's screen checked in. He quickly scanned the page. 'Holy shit. This means, my friend... ' he said, exhaling loudly, '... this means there'll be half a million of the mothers out there roaming the streets, all armed, looking for a job they'll never find. Talk about guns for hire, jeez. D'you think they'll give a fuck who they're shooting at as long as someone pays them to feed their families? How the hell did this get past Washington?'

'Maybe it's all part of a plan,' the assistant chimed, returning to his own screen, anxious to calm Kowolski's rising temper. 'Yeah, chief, it says here the plan is to rid the army of its previous Ba'athist influence, like in all the other institutions – and start from scratch.'

'Start from fuckin' scratch? How long d'you think that will take? Listen, pal, most of them couldn't organise a game of pool in a well-lit bar room. They're about as useful as tits on a boar hog.' He shook his head in exasperation. 'There's going to be a bunch of flak flying in the next few days. Call Bremer's office and find out what the hell's going down there.'

111

As the assistant picked up the phone, Kowolski fixed him with a stare. 'You see the kinda' shit I have to deal with?'

He read the memo more slowly. Paul Bremer, US head of the Coalition Provisional Authority, had not only declared the army illegal, but had also just disbanded several government ministries. Thousands more civil servants out of work.

'The purge of the fuckin' Ba'athists – now this!' Kowolski stormed.

In the last few days alone, the Ba'athist clear-out had become the talk of the town.

'Hey, kid,' he shouted to the assistant, just leaving. 'Make damn sure you never have an accident outside the Green Zone – because there'll be no fucker left out there to patch you up.'

How the hell was he supposed to come up with a line to mitigate this disaster? The media would have a field day proclaiming that no one knew what they were doing.

He decided he had to go to the bathroom. Sometimes he could think more clearly while taking a leak. The questions from the media would come tumbling in now, a veritable avalanche.

He thought quickly, splashing noisily into the pan. He would have to go over to Bremer's office this afternoon, brief the Press Office on how to play it. 'Okay,' he said to himself, tossing ideas around. He'd tell them that any mention of the Iraqi army and the Ba'athists must always include the name of Saddam in the same breath. Tar them all with the same brush. Killers, torturers, despots.

Disbanding the Iraqi army was a no-brainer, he would tell them to say. They would have to get a quote from someone, too. No problem. 'How could anyone trust them not to rise up?'

His mind working overtime, the vision of mass graves flashed into his head. He'd been planning to push out an update piece for some time. This struck him as the perfect opportunity to remind people who they were dealing with.

112

'Got it,' he whistled. Weren't search teams still digging all over the place? They must have found more corpses by now. Well, they could dig for his salvation from this Bremer shit.

He washed his hands, studying himself in the mirror. Pictures of bullet-ridden skulls, decaying bodies, skeletons with their hands bound. That would deflect the people back home from the real issue. The public were susceptible to that – especially if something was said often enough.

He smiled back at the face before him. 'Any smart-arsed journos who ask what a Ba'athist administrator has got to do with mass graves, we'll remind them they asked the same about the Nazis,' he said.

He only hoped to God it would work.

* * *

Aban al-Tikriti loaded the CD into his computer drive and brought up the file he had begun to read the previous night only to give up in the early hours, exhausted.

As part of Saddam's response to the UN Security Council resolution 1441 – the resolution eventually used by the US and Britain to wage war – Iraq had made two copies of a top-secret report on their disarmament process. It was more than 12,000 pages long.

One copy was delivered to the International Atomic Energy Authority in Geneva, the body responsible for all previous weapons inspections in Iraq. The other was destined for the United Nations in New York, to be delivered by secure means to the then-current chair of the UN, Colombia.

The report was, in fact, intercepted by US officials, virtually at the doors of UN headquarters, who took it to Washington for 'photocopying' so it could be distributed to the remaining four permanent UN members, Britain, China, France, and Russia, and then to the other fifteen non-permanent member countries.

The four permanent members duly received the full dossier,

113

but the other member states were made to wait several days. And, when they got their version, it was a heavily-edited manuscript which had been cut by more than 8,000 pages.

Intelligence agencies were aware that Saddam had warned the dossier would list everyone who had supplied Iraq in its thirty-year weapons programme – each government, every public and private company, and each individual. But these references had all been removed by the US in the redacted copies.

And, now, Aban was staring at that full unedited list on screen, a mind-numbing flow of information he found difficult to fully comprehend. Exports from America, sanctioned by the Reagan administration, then continued by the government of Bush senior, included regular shipments of anthrax, strains of botulism toxin, *Brucella melitensis*, gangrene bacteria, West Nile fever virus, and other agents used in germ warfare.

So too, were detailed plans for chemical weapons-production facilities, chemical warfare agent precursors, missile production and missile guidance equipment, chemical and biological warhead filling apparatus. The list of WMD seemed endless.

The file showed seventeen shipments and some eighty batches of bio-material had been sent to Iraq during the Reagan years alone.

There were almost 800 approved US export licenses for dual-use technology. Some of those deliveries continued after Saddam had carried out the gassing of more than 5,000 men, women, and children in the Kurdish town of Halabja, near the border with Iran, in 1988.

Aban recounted the Kurds always claimed they were subjected to many more gassings. Estimates reckoned more than 100,000 people perished. Survivors and their offspring were left with virulent cancers, congenital abnormalities, blindness, and many other serious health problems.

He read further. There was a multitude of international companies involved; American, British, Russian, Chinese,

French, German – Singapore featuring prominently, too. But, what use was all this? The names of the companies, the individuals, meant nothing to him. What would be to gain in dragging up old history?

He stretched his arms out wide to relieve the tension in his shoulders and paced the room. Suddenly, the incongruity finally hit home. It struck him so hard he was forced into a loud raucous laugh, so surprised with the absurd paradox of it all.

So, it was the father, George Bush, first as Vice-President, then President, who had helped Saddam build his array of WMD. And now, it was the son, George W. Bush, who was destroying Iraq because of that.

* * *

It was raining when Alex got out of the yellow cab from JFK. The cool drizzle on her face felt good; such a refreshing contrast to the merciless heat of the Middle East.

Her apartment was in a former warehouse block on the borders of SoHo and Greenwich Village, third floor, one-bedroom, in a six-storey building that dated to the 1880s. Part of it she used as a studio where the light flooded in through large cast-iron windows and where she sometimes had clients sit for portrait work. It was, as her friends said, 'pretty hip' and she knew she had done very well to have landed it. Now, with Kowolski's money, she could pay the mortgage.

'Hey, Alex.' She was just paying the fare when the Badgeman came ambling up the street. He gave her a high-five. 'Say, girl, where you been the last few weeks?'

She scanned his garments, not a piece of cloth that was not covered by a badge of some description. 'This here's new – and this,' he said pointing to a couple of pin-ons. 'Got this at the gas station. It says BP, guess you don't know what that stands for, heh?'

'Well, Badge, I guess it could be British Petroleum. They're mighty big in the States right now.'

115

'Gee, British Petroleum,' he mumbled, wiping the badge with his thumb while his eyes darted up and down the street, his usual custom. Badge was a familiar site in these parts, seemingly covering an area that stretched from Sixth Avenue to east of Lafayette Street into Little Italy, sometimes handing out leaflets of one sort or another, occasionally washing a car. She had once seen him up on Houston Street wearing a sandwich board advertising a new restaurant.

They talked often, like this, on the street, and she had once suggested that she take some photographs for a magazine feature, but he appeared reticent so she never pursued the idea. It was Richard Northwood who'd let slip the reason for the Badgeman's hesitancy one night when he got drunk at her apartment.

Gazing out of her window, Northwood had spotted him shuffling along in the street below. 'You see that guy down there,' he'd slurred.

'Yeah, Badgeman – he's not too bright but he's harmless,' Alex had replied.

'He's a Fed, Alex. Known in the FBI as one of their street-walkers, cute eh?'

In a more sober frame, Northwood had sworn Alex to secrecy about the revelation – not that she would have told a soul anyway. But not before he told her the Badgeman's intelligence-gathering on drugs, prostitution, money racketeering and such like had led to several invaluable arrests.

Now, she sometimes wondered, when she looked into the Badgeman's blue eyes with something of a hint of amusement, whether he knew she knew. She also thought he was in the wrong job. He should have been on the stage.

It was one of the many things she liked about New York. An ants' nest of activity where, among all that aping of myrmecological dash, there was just no guessing who was the soldier, the worker, the male or the queen.

She punched a series of numbers into the security device on

116

the front door, hoping the monthly code had not been changed while she was away. She was in luck as the large heavy door buzzed open.

'Hey, you didn't tell me where y'ouse been,' Badge shouted after her.

'Baghdad, man.'

'Jeez, that's hot – and dangerous.'

'Yeah, treacherous in more ways than one,' she said, closing the door behind her.

Dropping her bags in the hallway, she gathered up her mail. Then she switched on her computer to see she had a stack of emails since her last pick-up in Baghdad.

Among them, as she hoped, was one from Steve Lewis. The note was bright and cheerful, trusting the flight had been okay. Would she mind if he continued to correspond? He had enjoyed her company so much, could he be her 'cyber friend' over the Internet? Her heart suddenly felt lighter.

She replied straight away, saying that if he was ever in New York, she, too, knew a great Italian restaurant and would be delighted to return the favour.

Throwing her jacket over a chair, she sauntered into the kitchen, smiling to herself. 'Cyber friend', she thought. But would she ever see him again? She hoped so. Romance? She let out a sigh and opened the fridge.

A half-full bottle of white wine greeted her. Removing the cork and lifting the bottle to her nose, it seemed drinkable. From a cupboard, she took a wine glass, something she could have done with her eyes closed. Then she suddenly stopped. Memories flooded back. After several seconds, she put the glass back and emptied the bottle down the sink. Alcohol hadn't been the crutch she'd envisaged needing in Baghdad – she'd hardly drunk any. The thought bucked her up no end.

Making a lemon tea, she returned to her computer. An email from Aban caught her eye. She thought about leaving it until later, guessing the message contained a brief pleasantry. She clicked it open, her face immediately taking on a puzzled frown. Just a pleasant few words of introduction but with a lengthy attachment included.

Scanning several sheets of the contents, her eyes widened. She let out a gasp. A shock of overwhelming disbelief rattled through her.

For every page was stamped with the words 'Top Secret'.

12

Alex spent the next day in high tempo mode, feverishly checking out Aban's amazing file. Having worked solidly on the Internet from early morning, her right hand ached.

Forgoing lunch, it was late afternoon before she paused, sinking back in her chair and trying to take stock of the notes she'd made. Her mind swam with detail. Wondering whether to call it a day, she pressed on. A new page caught her eye. Quickly scanning the contents, a feeling of despair suddenly hit her as if she'd just rushed headlong into a brick wall.

She groaned, throwing the mouse down on the desk and watching, disinterested, as the back cover fell off and the batteries fell out. 'Shit,' she cried. The story wasn't new.

Many of the companies and individuals responsible for arming Saddam over the years had already been exposed by a German newspaper, *Die Tageszeitung*, several months earlier – something she'd missed.

The revelations, from the paper's Geneva UN correspondent, Andreas Zumach, had been picked up in the US but not reported with much enthusiasm by the mainstream press. The thought flittered through her mind that they'd slapped a gag on anything that might undermine the war effort in Iraq. Kowolski probably had a hand in it.

Alex stared in disbelief at her screen. The Los Angeles alternative paper, the *LA Weekly News,* had gone further, publishing a list of ninety US or affiliate companies who had supplied Iraq with its many chemical poisons and military aid. The stories, run over several days, had been printed while she was in Baghdad.

Kowolski must have known about them, she thought. Maybe

that was one of the reasons he'd been so on edge. But why hadn't she seen them? Her mind wandered. She knew why. The stories had originally broken slap-bang in the middle of her depressive phase when she'd hardly spoken to anyone. Keeping up with any news had been of no interest.

Damn, if only she'd seen the reports. She'd have loved to hear Kowolski try to explain them away.

While it was prima facie evidence of America's involvement in the arming of Saddam, Alex quickly decided it was pointless trying to take the story further. Now the facts were in the public domain, no doubt politicians would want to examine the material and act on it – a committee of inquiry or such like, she figured.

She'd initially been flushed with the excitement at what she thought would be a tremendous scoop. But it had all been a waste of time. Now, frustration consumed her because she had a full schedule of work for Kowolski and she'd been side-tracked. The downtown photo lab which was producing her Baghdad photographs, expected her this morning and she'd put them off.

Kowolski hadn't given her a deadline, but he was just as likely to stun her with a surprise date for McDermott's big day in New York. She needed to be ready.

She was just about to pick up the phone to call the lab when it rang. Unmistakable; the voice of Greg Spencer.

'I'll have to be quick,' he said, a nervous edge to his voice. 'You get the message from our friend?'

'I've been working on it all day – there's nothing new. It's all out in the open here. We'd been secretly supplying Iraq for years with chemicals.'

'No, not that stuff, the other info. It's dynamite.'

A shiver ran through her. 'What other stuff?'

But the line suddenly went dead. Frantic, she tried to call him back – no response. Hurrying over to her computer she scrolled down the pages of Aban's email, convinced she hadn't missed anything. Page after page flashed by. No, she'd covered every-thing. So what the hell was Greg talking about?

Slumping back in her chair, her mind began racing. There'd been over a hundred emails waiting for her when she got back – and she still hadn't read half of them. Opening her inbox, she ran down the list. Nothing else from Aban. Many of the others were simply junk. She often cursed why they weren't always filtered to the spam file on her Hotmail account, the one she used to pick up her emails when abroad. It always confused her how some got through to her main account and some didn't.

Then the thought struck her. Her spam file! Logging into her Hotmail server, she waited for the tab to appear, impatiently tapping her fingers on the edge of her desk. She clicked on the spam box. Her eyes flicked over the lines of blue type – and there it was. Another email from Aban, with the heading: 'Greetings'.

Opening it, Alex began devouring the contents. She gave out a low whistle as she took in the implications of Aban's overview of the material. It was just as Greg had described, dynamite. Hundreds of firms from around the world, including America, had paid kickbacks to Saddam during the seven terrible years of sanctions against Iraq in the UN's oil for food programme starting in 1996. This definitely had not been published.

She nodded to herself as she read further, understanding Aban's take on how the scam worked. Companies exporting a controlled range of goods to Iraq had their invoices paid from a UN bank account. In turn, Iraq was allowed to sell oil, the proceeds going back to that UN account to balance the books.

But Aban's documents showed firms had been secretly sending ten per cent of the invoice value as an upfront payment directly to Saddam's coffers. These payments were classed by Iraq as 'trucking and service fees'.

The company then inflated the price of its invoice by that ten per cent – which the UN, unknowingly, paid in full.

Aban explained he had heard rumours of such a slush fund.

Now he was convinced Saddam and his inner circle had obviously raked in millions of dollars, probably billions, while the country grew steadily weaker. Children had died in their thousands because of the sanctions. The tales of suffering were endless. Infant mortality alone had sent Iraq scurrying back to the Dark Ages.

Aban was hoping Alex and his other 'good friend', Mr Greg, could bring the matter to the public's attention.

Alex read further, discovering there was an extra edge to the situation. It appeared some powerful foreign individuals, friendly to Saddam, had received millions of dollars of oil credits. Through a myriad of shell companies, the Iraq government had given them the rights to buy several million barrels of its oil at a reduced price. This was then sold on at market rates to earn a healthy commission for the individual.

She sat back in her chair, astounded. It was fraud and corruption on a mammoth scale.

But what could she do about it? Who could she tell?

* * *

It was a little after two in the morning – eight hours ahead in Iraq – by the time she switched off her computer, shattered. Summoning a final reserve of energy, she called Greg's cell phone from her quick-dial menu. He would have ideas what to do about Aban's material – his contacts were first class. The number did not ring out. She dialled it again, this time deliberately pressing each button, so she could hear the tune of each key. The number sounded unobtainable.

Maybe he'd left Baghdad and was on his way back to Oz although, when they'd spoken earlier, he'd made no mention of it. Perhaps he'd meant to before he was cut off.

Tiredness quickly taking over again, she felt somewhat relieved she hadn't made contact. A dull ache pounded her brow and her head swam with questions she hadn't the strength to answer. She made her way to bed, vowing to speak to him in the morning.

Pulling the duvet tight around her, she lay there thinking what a strike for democracy it would be if they could make everything public.

Kowolski wouldn't like it; Richard Northwood would hate it. And the White House would go berserk.

* * *

They came for Aban at 6.10 a.m. Iraq time.

A hammering on his door woke everyone in the house. Deep thuds like someone was trying to break in. Throwing on his dressing gown, he rushed to the window, could see five soldiers outside, one thumping the solid wooden door with his rifle. A Humvee lay parked at an angle in the street. He ran down the stairs, his heart in pieces, drew the bolts, and turned the key.

No sooner had he released the catch when the soldiers burst in. Two grabbed him before he could utter more than a cursory protest. Forcing his hands behind his back, he was quickly subdued with plastic handcuffs. Farrah appeared on the landing. She screamed.

'Shut the fuck up,' a soldier shouted, running up the stairs towards her.

Their sons appeared. Aban could see they were as scared and confused as he was.

'On the floor, NOW,' the soldier shouted at them, pushing Farrah roughly.

Aban tried to struggle free. A soldier hit him with his rifle butt, catching him to the right side of his forehead, blood immediately spilling down his face. Fighting hard not to faint, he felt his legs starting to wobble. Two soldiers entered his study. Panic gripped him. Then, a black cloth hood was roughly forced over his head and he was dragged outside. His head swam and his eyes stung from the blood dripping down his face.

'What are you doing? What do you want of me?' The words

123

came out in a disconcerted mumble. No one answered. They bundled him into the vehicle, pushing him down. Suddenly, he felt the bulk of two powerful bodies, one either side.

He wasn't sure if he had passed out or not on the journey. Still dazed, he lurched against both captors each time the Humvee made a turn, could feel them pressed close. Their sweat smell taunted his intestines. Was the nausea that gripped him the result of his own fear? Where were they taking him? What for?

He sensed the vehicle finally stopping, stiffened when the door opened. A blast of warm, fresh air hit him. Trying to gulp a lungful of the sweet solace, he groaned as he was marched double time, a soldier either side grasping him firmly under each shoulder. He stumbled and was roughly pulled upright.

The jangle of keys, booming voices, a door clanging shut behind him. Then another door. Finally, he was pushed down into a sitting position, the cold of smooth metal chilling the backs of his knees through his thin pyjamas.

Foosteps, fading. Another heavy door closing. Now, alone. His wrists were numb where the plastic handcuffs seared his flesh. He tried to wiggle his fingers to ease the feeling back into them. Screwing each eye, he could tell the blood had dried, but still felt as if he was wearing a mask beneath the hood. And his head ached violently.

They left him in this state for more than twelve hours.

* * *

She was sound asleep when the shrill of her mobile on the bedside cabinet stirred her.

'It's me again.' Greg's voice carried the same edge as the previous night.

'What the... you okay?' Squinting at the clock, she cursed. It was just after 10 a.m. and she'd overslept.

'Listen, no names, this thing – I got my room broken into. They stole my laptop and my phone.'

She sat up, startled, reached for her dressing gown. 'How would anyone know – maybe just coincidence?'

'It's dangerous. Know what I'm saying?'

'No one would know we...'

'Don't want to think about it. I can't afford to get kicked out – I've been contracted for another three months in Baghdad. Just watch your back and get rid.'

The line went dead again. Alex wasn't sure if it was Greg simply hanging up. She sat on the edge of the bed staring at her mobile. No wonder she couldn't get through to him last night. Stolen? And his laptop? It was unlike Greg to scare like this. The man she thought she knew would have grabbed the Aban material with both hands and worked it until the cows came home. What did he mean by dangerous? And his opening words – 'no names' – did he think the lines were tapped or something? *Shit.*

Fastening her robe, she hurriedly made coffee, taking quick short sips from the steaming mug as she carried it to her desk. A blinding headache accompanied her – the price of oversleeping. She rubbed her temples with both hands. When she sat back, the sight of the blinking red button of the answer machine almost made her jump. She didn't have a main line into the bedroom, relying on her mobile for emergencies. So, someone had called her main line during the night – and she had slept through it.

Greg's call had frightened her. She stared at the machine, hesitant. Her finger trembled, hovering over the play button. Summoning her nerve, she pressed it. The voice was strained, pleading.

'Alexandra. This is Farrah al-Tikriti, Aban's wife. They have taken him, the soldiers. I don't know where he is. Please help us.'

She replayed the message several times. The anguish in the voice was unmistakable.

'No!' Alex cried. Why would they take him? But she

125

answered herself just as quickly. He'd been a member of the Ba'athist Party – like everyone working for the government. There was a purge going on against former members. They'd rounded him up, probably a routine sweep.

Jesus, the email. If they hadn't known about it then, they would now. Soldiers didn't march off with anyone without turning the house over. She could imagine the scene; garbage bags emptied, toilet cisterns lifted, files and papers removed. And computers taken.

Greg's laptop stolen? Surely too much of a coincidence. If she was right, it would mean only one thing.

She was next on the list.

* * *

Quickly, she dressed. Pair of jeans, old sweater. Then tried to think. She switched on her laptop. Aban's email jumped at her. *Just too good to dump*. But what the hell should she do? Who could she send it to? Who to trust? Who had the balls to investigate such stuff, never mind print it? Besides, might it be classified, therefore illegal? She couldn't afford to be caught in possession of it, not now.

Opening the email again sent her into a spin. A receipt box appeared on the screen asking the recipient to acknowledge they had read the message.

Shit. Did she see this last night and click the 'yes' button? If they'd taken Aban's computer, the acknowledgement would show up and they would definitely know she'd read it. Alex couldn't answer herself. She'd ended up so tired last night that, right now, she simply couldn't remember.

Her mind flew in all directions. Surely she hadn't given herself away with a weary click of the mouse? She stared at the screen, trying to concentrate, going over the sequence of last night's events.

Then it dawned on her. For some reason, known only to computers, there mustn't have been a box to click last night – or

126

she hadn't noticed it – that's why one was appearing now. Logic told her the message wouldn't appear a second time had she already acknowledged receipt. She checked her 'sent items' file just to make sure. Nothing.

Relieved, she leant back in her chair and stared at the ceiling, puffing her cheeks and blowing out the tension, a slow, measured rasp from deep within. She wasn't that computer literate but, she asked herself, if she deleted the email from all her files, could anyone tell whether or not she had actually read it?

It took only another thirty seconds before a detached logic hammered at her heart; this was the CIA she was dealing with. They could find out practically anything about anyone. The organisation hired the best brains in the business and, for all she knew, they'd already tapped into her email accounts. Maybe they knew at what time she'd opened Aban's message.

Even if they hadn't secretly investigated her, the last thing she needed was for a team of goons to call with a search warrant and whisk her computer away. Some of the research she'd done on Aban's earlier email would be on her hard drive and the CIA would have no problem accessing that and pointing an accusatory finger her way. Being thrown into a cell didn't figure on her list of things to do right now.

Working feverishly for the next couple of hours, half expecting a knock on her door at any minute, she transferred Aban's material to a memory stick then deleted all his emails. She double-checked she'd wiped all trace of any correspondence from him on either of her servers. Next, she began work on her McDermott photos, transferring them to a different memory stick.

Her final job was to return to her email inbox. When she scrolled down to the bottom of the remaining list, she came to the oldest message on file, one she had opened and read countless times. It was from Richard Northwood, a passionate note sent only hours after they had first made love. She thought of deleting it, but checked herself. Then she called a cab.

While waiting for it to arrive, she unplugged everything from the back of the computer, lifting the modem on to the table. Fetching a screwdriver from the kitchen, she undid the back of the casing and peered inside.

'This looks like it,' she murmured, locating the hard drive among the confusion of wires and circuit boards. She reached in and scratched the lump of metal with the screwdriver – two marks that looked like a cross.

* * *

The electrical store was surprisingly busy which meant Alex had to stand in line for several minutes. At her turn, the shop phone rang prompting the sole assistant to throw up his arms in a gesture of helplessness. Resigned to further delay, Alex gestured for him to answer the call.

When she finally had the young man's attention, she explained she needed a new hard-drive.

'I could normally do that while you wait, Ma'am,' he said, flashing a grin and taking the modem out of Alex's large hold-all bag. 'But just now... '

'That's okay – I have to do something else. I'll be back in twenty, though,' she said by way of warning.

Turning left out of the store, she began the walk three blocks north to a post office she often used. On edge, she stopped at a shop window, pretending to be interested in the display, glancing back nervously. She felt foolish, but if Northwood was on to her she'd have to play his silly games.

Crossing a junction at the last minute a block further on, she turned round halfway, darting back on a red light and almost knocking a man over waiting at the kerb. He seemed to have stood in her way on purpose.

'Well, pardon me,' she blurted, indignant. Glancing at him, her embarrassment came king-sized when she saw the guy was carrying a white stick and wearing shades that were impenetrable. 'Oh, sorry,' she murmured.

'Ain't no bother, lady,' the man said, nodding his head as if listening to music on his headphones – even though Alex couldn't hear anything.

'Okay, green for go now,' she said as the lights changed, feeling obliged to lightly guide him by the arm.

'Well, thank you kindly, Ma'am,' the man said, sweeping the stick before him as if searching for mines. 'Say, you goin' far?'

'Post office,' Alex said.

'Hey, me too,' he drawled.

* * *

'We have contact, sir.'

In a secret CIA office on East Forty-Eighth Street, near to the United Nations headquarters, Richard Northwood leant over the shoulder of a technician watching two red dots on a screen map of central Manhattan moving side by side.

'Heading?'

'She said the post office, sir,' the technician added.

Northwood smiled to himself. He had to hand it to Kowolski, it was a sheer piece of inspiration that he'd called the bureau in Baghdad after searching Alex's hotel room at the Palestine. Finding nothing of note among her things, Kowolski suggested they might want to bug her cell phone. So they'd sent round one of their surveillance experts to carry out the simple task.

'Sometimes small insurance policies pay big,' Kowolski had remarked as he'd watched the CIA man take off the back cover, remove the lithium battery from inside and replace it with an identical-looking one.

'Two thirds battery, one third GPS tracker,' the guy had told him. 'She won't know any difference.'

Northwood returned his gaze to the twin red dots. He knew he was playing a hunch. But long shots came in every day.

* * *

ROY DAVID

Inside the post office, she guided the blind man to a counter and stood in front of him in the line, eventually buying two envelopes, one smaller than the other.

'I'm done – it's your turn now my friend. Good luck,' Alex said, ushering the man forward.

Moving over to an empty counter, she wrote a hurried note on the front of the smaller envelope: 'Dear Mom, Please put this packet in a REALLY SAFE place for me – it's a back-up file of important pictures. xxx.'

Quickly retrieving the memory stick of Aban's material from her pocket, Alex slipped it inside the package, secured it, and placed it in the larger envelope, which she addressed. She suddenly became aware of someone standing close by and turned round sharply. The blind man was at her side.

'Oh, it's you,' she said. 'If you want the way out, it's directly behind you.'

'I didn't say thanks back there – so thank you, Ma'am,' he said, slowly moving off towards the exit, nodding his head to his music and sweeping the floor with his cane.

Alex found a counter clerk who was free and said she wanted it sending by registered delivery, watching as he tossed it nonchalantly into a nearby red mailbag.

If only he knew what the contents were, she thought, he might just have treated it with a little more reverence.

She headed back to the electrical store in a more positive frame of mind, even managing to hum one of her favourite songs to herself. At least Aban's material was now safe – no matter what Northwood and his crew got up to. She'd decide how to broadcast it to the world as soon as the McDermott show was over when she would have the time to sit and think. Steve might be able to help, too, she thought. Sometimes an outsider could see the wood from the trees.

* * *

130

When Alex had gone from his sight, the man took off his shades, folded them, and put them in the inside pocket of his jacket next to the stub of his collapsible white cane. Then he strode purposefully into the post office and asked to see the most senior person in charge.

* * *

The electrical store assistant was serving someone else as Alex entered the shop, but he raised his hand to signal he'd seen her. Presently, he joined her.

'All done, Ma'am – a new hard drive installed and here's your old one.'

Alex turned the lump of metal in her hands, checking it had the two fine scratches she'd made on its outer casing. She ran her finger over the marks. Was she becoming paranoid about all this? She quickly dismissed the notion. If the Badgeman could be FBI, then anything was possible.

'Say, do you have a hammer back there?'

'Think so,' the assistant said, disappearing behind the counter. He returned with a heavy lump hammer. 'This okay?'

'A backyard?'

'Follow me.'

He unlocked the rear door. Alex found herself in a high-walled enclosure, the tops decked with rolls of razor wire – just like Baghdad, she thought. Placing the hard drive on the concrete floor, a jumble of images and fears flooded her mind.

Pent-up frustration taking over, she raised the hammer and began smashing the metal for all she was worth. If the CIA were going to put her life under the microscope, they'd get no help from her.

The last two blows were particularly satisfying – one for Gene Kowolski, the final one for Richard Northwood. Her arm aching, Alex stared at the twisted piece of scrap, allowed herself a contented smile. She just knew Northwood would soon make contact.

And she reckoned she was now ready for him.

13

'You okay, Lieutenant? I mean, if it's all going too fast, you just holler.'

Kowolski paced the floor, clicking his fingers in frustration, and hearing with increasing boredom McDermott's version of the raid. It was so matter-of-fact, so one-dimensional, he knew the media would find themselves scraping the barrel to colour it up.

'Well, it was sorta' like I said, sir, routine sort of stuff,' McDermott blustered.

'No, no, no,' Kowolski interjected, irritably. 'Wasn't routine at all. No, SIR.'

If McDermott noticed the sarcasm in Kowolski's voice, a withering impatience brought on by the feeling he was not giving it his best shot, he did not show it.

'Surely, it's more like this.' He ran a hand through his hair as if the dark mop was a fountain of inspiration. 'Okay, you were not sure what to expect – intel is never that precise – then you came under heavy fire. You and your men were in grave danger. It was a tricky situation with it being dark and all, but you had the best equipment the US Army could provide, illumination flares, night sights, powerful spotlights from the Bradley... and, of course, the firepower and the best of trained soldiers in the unit. That's right, isn't it?'

McDermott blinked. It was a nervous twitch, both eyes at once, that Kowolski had noticed earlier. 'Well, sort of, sir.'

'Okay, remember what I've just said. Learn it off by heart. Then what happened?'

'Well, we kinda just let rip an' all – there was no taking any chances.'

'Exactly, Lieutenant, nice pitch. There was no way you were going to risk the lives of any of your men in such a combat situation because they're all like brothers to you – that's what you say, right?'

He nodded, blinking some more.

'So you followed your training, your instinct as a soldier, the way they taught you rigorously at West Point where you learned... let's see now... yeah, courage, discipline, exemplary behaviour – remember that, Lieutenant, CDE, easy enough.'

'Yes sir.' It was beginning to dawn on McDermott that this was all going to entail a lot more than he had ever envisaged.

'And your haul – what was it?' Kowolski read from a copy of the commendation. 'Fifteen enemy combatants, all killed. A large cache of armaments, let's see... bomb-making equipment, guns, ammunition, RPGs, a very substantial amount all told. It doesn't say here how many you personally knocked off? Be great if you could say, you know, one of my guys was about to be hit when I opened up... something like that.'

'Sir, it wasn't really like that.'

Kowolski began to feel his temper rising. 'Well, tell me soldier, what was it like for Chrissake?'

McDermott stared at him for a moment, indignant at Kowolski's tone. Okay, he was no prude and, in the heat of the moment out there on the street, he was now forgiving his men the odd cuss or two. But there was no pressure on here. The major had said this was going to be just a friendly little chat.

Kowolski, sensing the atmosphere he had created, picked up a chair, moved it closer to McDermott, his voice more conciliatory. 'Look, Lieutenant, I know it's difficult. Battle-hardened soldiers like yourself – well I guess you don't like talking about certain aspects of war. Hey, my old man was in 'Nam and could I ever get him to open up?' He snapped his fingers loudly. 'Schtum – like a clam.'

He watched McDermott's face break into one of those half-smiles, a look of understanding. Too distant for Kowolski's liking; almost melancholy.

There was a knock on the door. 'Not now,' he shouted angrily. Then, turning back to McDermott, 'Look, son, it's just that I know what it's like dealing with the media – they're hungry for information and we need to give them all they need. They want to know every twist and turn, every single burp and fart. That's why we're having this little talk. Best if we can operate on the same wavelength, okay?'

McDermott let out a long sigh. 'Affirmative, sir. I'll do my best. I... I'll try not to let you down.'

Kowolski slapped him on the back, got up and paced the room once more. 'Thataboy, soldier – think of the men in your unit, all the boys here away from home, all the tens of thousands of them. You're their talisman, Lieutenant, you'll be speaking on their behalf – they'll all be looking to you to tell it like it is. You're in a privileged situation; you mustn't forget that. You're going to be the public face of the war in Iraq.'

'Right, sir,' he said, gulping.

'There's something else to take onboard here. We can go over everything again several times when we get to New York but I just wanted to tell you this. When you get to meet the media, the TV people, the newspapers and magazines, I can guarantee there's always one smart-ass among them trying to make a name for themselves who'll ask you a shit question, you know, something awkward.'

McDermott gave him a furtive sideways glance. 'What sort of question, sir?'

'I don't know precisely – just be ready for it coming. What you gotta do is turn it round. You ask THEM if they've ever been in Iraq. It'll be a dime to a dollar they haven't – that puts them in an inferior position straight away and you can just leave it like that, watch them shrink into their seat. Nothing more needs saying. You understand?'

McDermott looked as if he was about to say something, but merely nodded.

'If, by any remote chance, they say they have been here, well you play the buddy buddy card, and get them onside like you're sharing something the rest of the bunch don't know about: "Well, as you know from your own experience out there, it's a real tough situation, an ever-changing event – things move at an alarming rate"... something vague along those lines. And if you can't answer a question without embarrassing yourself, simply say that you have no knowledge of whatever they're asking.'

When McDermott finally got up to leave, Kowolski shook him by the hand, grabbing his shoulder at the same time. 'Don't you worry about a thing, Lieutenant, I'll see you through all this in good style. Believe me, we'll have them eating out of our hands in no time. Everything's going to be just rinky-dink.'

Alone in the room, Kowolski's final words echoed in his own ears as a feeling of dread enveloped him.

Finally meeting McDermott had convinced him it was going to be anything but rinky-dink.

* * *

Out on patrol later, Bobby-Jo stamped hard on the Bradley's accelerator, inducing an immediate clanking deep growl from the 600-horsepower diesel engine as the vehicle lurched forward.

The sudden movement caught some of the men off guard, throwing them out of their leather-padded metal seats.

One of them shouted, cursing him. 'Hey, Bobby, you leave your fuckin' pantyhose off today and take a bite on the ass by a sand flea?'

This brought a rumble of laughter from the men, painfully aware of the nasty bites from the tiny mosquito-like creatures. Like the heat, they were another torment, here. To combat this particular pest, the men had taken to wearing women's nylon tights.

McDermott's face appeared from the commander's turret to see what the shouting was about. The soldier caught the lieutenant's glance, raised his hand in apology at the outburst.

Bobby-Jo was in an uptight mood. He'd been carrying the gloom since the men were told there would be no special leave for them. Only the lieutenant. So he was continually moaning to the rest of the boys that 'the whole deal sucks'.

It was an opinion shared by several others, but who said nothing – and had no intention of doing so. Sergeant Rath had threatened to 'get personal' with anyone who bitched, anyone who mouthed off, about the night in question.

McDermott sensed something was troubling his driver. He shot a downward glance his way, made a mental note to have a word with him back at base. Beyond the raised driving hatch, the lieutenant could see Bobby-Jo's head, shaking side to side, as he gunned the Bradley abruptly on to a deserted highway. Burned out car wrecks, trash of every description, littered the side of the road, the central reservation scarred with stumps of shattered palm trees.

He was just about to tell him to cool down when, without warning, the Bradley swerved violently from the inside lane to the outside, Bobby-Jo accelerating hard.

Flung forward, McDermott grabbed the rim of his turret with both hands, the metal digging into his skin. Below, a chorus of shouts rang out as the men were sent sprawling inside the cramped rear quarters.

A split second later, the roadside bomb exploded.

McDermott had often discussed the effects of an IED attack with his unit; the drill, the repercussions, wondered how the Bradley with its flat belly might cope with a central underside assault.

Now, his senses shook with the brutality of the explosion; a blinding orange flash and a deafening roar that stunned him, lifting the front of the 30-ton vehicle several feet into the air and skewing it sideways.

'What the... ' McDermott screamed as a powerful rush of hot air hit him, its intensity forcing his feet off the floor and shaking his body uncontrollably. The Bradley came to a grating halt with a final jolting thud, spilling him down into the turret. Powerless as he slid, he smacked his head on the bare metal side. It left him dazed for a moment, his ears ringing. Someone helped him up.

'Everybody out – NOW,' he shrieked, his mind suddenly screaming alert. 'Watch for snipers.'

A fog of grey smoke enveloped the Bradley and the acrid smell of bleach hung in the air. Sand, dust and dirt rained down in a dense drizzle forcing McDermott into a violent coughing spasm. Turning to Joe Herman in his turret, he could just make out his gunner was sporting an ugly bruise on the side of his face. Herman's thumbs up reassured him it was his only injury.

His heart racing, McDermott made to jump to the ground, but, just as he transferred his weight to his right leg, his foot slipped off the side of the vehicle.

Double damn. As he landed, his knee twisted under him. Steadying himself on the side of the Bradley, the sudden pain, burning, shooting down his leg, made him grimace. Fighting hard to suppress the agony, he tried to clear his mind of nerve-endings that were yelling knee-injury trauma. His breathing came in short gasps. The sweat began pouring off him. *Shit.* He desperately needed to assess the situation outside.

The unit's procedure was well rehearsed; each of the six infantrymen from the rear of the vehicle took up crouched cover positions in a 360-degree arc. Herman's finger hovered over the machine gun, his eyes sweeping over the low-lying scrub beyond.

McDermott dragged himself slowly along the side of the Bradley. He tried half-hopping for a couple of strides, a tight grip on his rifle, but gave up as the pain jarred his thigh. Still blindside of the driver's port, he kept low against the vehicle, now dragging his injured leg behind him as he inched forward.

Reaching for a spot near the front end of the Bradley, his hand touched hot metal and he cried out. Glancing forward, he could see what was left of the Bradley's offside track, a smouldering, twisted, tangle. Smoke rose from the damage in thick, indolent, coils. High above, a black plume of smoke drifted. A feeling of relief swept over him that fire had not taken hold.

His eyes, narrowed with pain, scoured the surrounding flat landscape. Not a place for harbouring snipers, he decided. 'See anything?'

'Negative, Lieutenant,' Herman shouted first.

Reaching the far side of the Bradley, he resorted to half-crawling, using his rifle to prop himself. It was only when he raised his head that he caught sight of Bobby-Jo's dark outline against the midday sun. 'Bobby, man. You okay?' No reply. McDermott put a hand to his forehead to shield his eyes, at the same time moving a couple of steps nearer.

Now he could plainly see Bobby-Jo, slumped forward in the driver's well.

'Oh, Lord, no,' he moaned as he got within touching distance, suddenly letting out a pitiful wail. Bobby-Jo was obviously dead. McDermott fell back against the vehicle, burying his head in the crook of his arm.

Although the sides of the Bradley were covered in explosion-reactive armour tiles, it was evident Bobby-Jo had taken a shrapnel hit. His helmet was lying upside down in the middle of the road.

McDermott struggled against a faintness rising up inside him, his gut churning. He called HQ on his radio for assistance. As he blurted details of the hit, Bobby-Jo's gaping wound was all he could see, his eyes drawn to it, refusing to look away. Suddenly conscious again of his knee, it throbbed, pounding in unison with his rapid heartbeat.

'Help, we need help here,' he shouted.

Two of his men backed up to reach him.

'You been hit, Lieutenant?'

He shook his head, pointing to the driver's well.

'Fuck,' one of them shouted. 'Jesus, he was only a kid.'

'If he hadn't swerved like that, we all would've bought it,' McDermott faltered. 'He... he died saving us, man.'

Tears appeared in his eyes. His body heaved, shivered, his face ashen. He exhaled slowly, shaking his head. He murmured a prayer for Bobby-Jo's life – all twenty-one years of it. *Thank you dear Lord for the life of our beloved brother.*

Then, the sound of sirens. He looked up, thankful to see two medics' trucks racing towards them. An Abrams tank, travelling in the opposite direction, had stopped and was pulling across the median, its gunner sweeping the vicinity.

'Set up road blocks, both carriageways,' he ordered.

A helicopter appeared, hovering above the scene. He radioed HQ again, an assessment of the damage. They told him a recovery truck was also on its way.

He turned to see Joe Herman being attended to by one of the medics on the rear steps of one of the ambulances. McDermott struggled towards them. One of the medics quickly moved forward, took the lieutenant's weight on his broad shoulder, helped him to sit next to Herman.

'Bobby-Jo's dead, Joe. Man... ' he let out a shuddering sigh, 'he died saving us – just like Our Lord.'

* * *

'But is McDermott okay?' Kowolski growled down the telephone, his voice tense.

He eventually replaced the receiver, exhaling deeply. Thank God the boy was all right, only ligament damage, he thought to himself as he poured a double shot of bourbon, downing most of it in one. When he first heard the news just now, his first reaction was to suspect the worst – and that Northwood's grand plan had bitten the dust.

It was too bad for that kid, the driver, who had apparently

been driving with his hatch up. They said he must have seen evidence of the roadside bomb or something suspicious and that was why he swerved at the last moment.

He walked to his desk, topped up his drink and, after a few minutes contemplation suddenly felt brighter. The incident would do the cause more good than harm. After all, it wasn't every day the media would meet a young lieutenant who had not only proved a hero in one operation – but had cheated death by inches in another.

Okay, he reasoned, the lieutenant would probably be hobbling for a while. But that was even better. Perhaps he could bring the whole show forward now the lieutenant would be laid up. What better than McDermott to appear on crutches, injured. A war casualty. The embodiment of a hero.

He almost rubbed his hands in glee at the very thought of the emotive pictures, now guaranteed to accompany the large banner headlines of McDermott, his Silver Star – and the President.

14

The mid-summer humidity of New York added to Alex's discomfort as she lugged the heavy computer bag up two flights of
stairs to her apartment. Once inside, she contented herself that
no one had been in and touched anything. The red light was
flashing again on her answerphone. It would have to wait.

Quickly, she assembled the computer stack and switched on
the power, patiently waiting while the monitor started up. She
began loading the programmes that would bring it to life.
Sophisticated photographic software needed for her work, she
put to one side for now. If the CIA came for her computer,
they'd find there wasn't much treasure in the chest.

Relieved, she went to the bathroom, splashing cold water on
her face. The phone rang. It was Kowolski.

'You get my message?'

'No, I just got in.'

'McDermott's been injured, the Bradley took an IED hit.'

Alex took a sharp intake of breath. 'Oh, God.'

'He's okay – just ligament damage, twisted his knee. He'll be
laid up for a few weeks here – they won't let him travel. But I
reckon he'll still be okay for the dates I arranged. Oh, and that
kid, the driver...'

'Bobby-Jo?'

'Yeah, that's him. He was killed,' he added blithely before
hanging up.

Shocked, her heart suddenly heavy, she went to the window
and opened it. Gulping at the cloying air gave little relief for the
tightness in her chest. Outside, only the sound of yellow cabs'
honking horns, their drivers and their fares impatient to move
their lives on apace.

Poor Bobby-Jo. Other than an exchange of smiles, she hadn't really got to know him on the embed because he was always in his driver's seat – never seemed to leave it, in fact. All the same, another mother without a son. More lives blighted. Opening her diary, she made a note to dig out some pictures of him, vowing to send them to his folks. She'd enclose a card saying what an 'angel' he was. It might give them some small degree of comfort.

She pressed the button on the answerphone, heard Kowolski's message. He hadn't even mentioned Bobby-Jo. *The pig.*

The next message held another unmistakable voice, that of Richard Northwood. Fingers twitching, she plucked at the silver bracelet on her wrist as it played. He simply asked her to call him on his cell phone as soon as possible. It was an official matter, he added icily.

So, minutes later after summoning up the courage, she dialled his number, taking a deep breath as she heard him answer.

'Hi Richard, it's Alex,' she said, trying to sound as light and bouncy as she could.

'You received an email from Iraq recently?'

'Lots – Kowolski's almost been jamming up my computer.'

'Let's say from one...' she heard a rustle of papers, 'Aban al-Tikriti, an Iraqi national? And, like, yesterday?'

'I wouldn't know because I've just got back from Mom and Dad's and haven't had time to take my coat off,' she lied. 'It's weird you should mention his name, because I was going to call you about him. He's a good guy, Richard – his wife just left me a message saying he's been arrested or something. She and their boys are worried sick.'

'And how would you know him?'

'We met through a mutual friend when I was over there.' She thought about adding that Aban had been the main source of her intelligence brief that Northwood requested, but decided against it. No use muddying the waters at this stage. 'What's going on here, Richard? His wife tells me the soldiers have taken him.'

142

'It's classified business – but what I can tell you is that he's being held on suspicion of spying. And it could prove very serious for anyone who has, shall we say, collaborated with him to any degree. Do you hear what I'm saying, Alex?'

'Just how official is this conversation – and where do I fit in?'

'Look, for the moment let's call it semi-official because… well, you know why… but things could quickly ratchet up a notch. Alex, you must report to me if you have received such an email or if you might be tempted to do anything with the information it contains. I don't want to see you incriminate yourself. Is that understood?'

'I won't – sure thing,' she said with as much seriousness as she could muster.

'Good girl,' he said. Then with a final, chilling, warning, added, 'Your friend's fate could lie in your hands if you do anything foolish.'

* * *

'Damn,' Richard Northwood said out loud to nobody but himself as he snapped his cell phone shut. There were so many things he'd wanted to say to her – that he knew exactly what she was up to and that she was lying through her teeth on all counts. But he'd been forced to play it softly, softly. His agent had produced a great result at the post office, switching Alex's memory stick for a blank one then jumping in a cab to the secret CIA office in Midtown Manhattan with the treasure in his pocket. But was that the end of the story or the beginning?

Northwood returned to his desk and unlocked a drawer. Removing Alex's memory stick, he sat down with it in his hands, turning it between his fingers. Could he be sure this was the only one? Was the damn file still on her computer?

He knew from the Baghdad bureau's work on al-Tikriti's computer that the information had been sent to only two people. The threat from the other recipient, the Australian journalist, Greg Spencer, had been nullified. He only possessed

143

a laptop and they'd soon lifted that. An examination of it established he had not forwarded the email to anyone.

But if Alex had made more copies, he was in serious trouble. If so and, as was more than likely, she went public, the consequences would be too frightening to contemplate. Exposure in the media would be disastrous for the Administration. The Democrats would have a field day. They'd accuse the government of being involved in breaking their own sanctions against Iraq – either through complicity or carelessness – and lining Saddam's pockets to boot.

The White House would be livid; fraud on a grand scale, all going on under its very nose. Such revelations would reflect gravely on the President. Who could tell the enormity of the damage?

He suddenly went chill with the thought that all and sundry would come looking for a scapegoat. Northwood had done well under the present government; he was well connected, had gratefully accepted several promotions with the intimation of higher things to come. The fingers of blame would point squarely at him. The buck stopped right at his desk. He could hear the comments now: *Yeah, he had it all in his grasp and then let it slip.*

His career in ruins, how would he keep the house, his wife and young children? Their home was now worth a million and a half, but Coralie had seen a bigger one up on the hill. She reckoned they could afford it if he made assistant director. He gulped, fetching himself a drink of water from the cooler. Swigging it back, the cold water should have refreshed him, but instead, he suddenly flushed as another thought hit him.

In a panic, he grabbed the phone on his desk that would scramble his call to Langley. Cursing himself, he'd earlier asked the tech boys in Langley's basement to see if they would retrieve and monitor the emails from Alex's main server – the one she logged into when she was away from home.

It only just occurred to him that Alex might have kept the one

144

email he'd sent her just after their affair started. He'd written it in the thrill of the moment, but regretted doing so ever since. Even so, he never thought it would come to this. Women were like that, he thought. So fucking sentimental.

Fuck, if she had saved it and the boys downstairs read it, he was a definite gonner. Even though he hadn't sent it in his own name, it was the sort of material the tech boys would follow up and, one way or another, soon trace it back to him. His link with Alex, then and now, would be fatal.

The phone answered, he tried to quell the agitation rising within him.

'Richard Northwood here – say, you had a look at that computer server I asked about?'

'Just a moment, sir.'

Northwood heard muffled voices in the background. He could hardly stand the tension, his heart pounding, hands so moist he nearly dropped the receiver.

'We were just about to get on to it, sir,' the voice said.

'Okay, well cancel that. The situation's been resolved.'

He put the phone back on its cradle with a feeling of utter relief. He was off the hook for now. But he knew he couldn't sit on this al-Tikriti information forever. Sooner or later he'd have to pass it higher up the line. Maybe they'd order the retrieval of all Alex's emails. They'd certainly want to know how he was going to contain the problem. Maybe a covert operation on her apartment, one where they'd make it look like a robbery, trash the place – take the computer and hi-fi, the television. The work of a junky.

Maybe he could get the Badgeman involved? Plant drugs, tip off the Feds? Then again, the CIA and FBI weren't sharing beds at the moment. He'd have to think of a way to get Alex's computer. It could provide a mine of information.

And it was the only safe way of saving himself.

* * *

Now, Northwood faced one more question: who else had this guy, al-Tikriti, given the information to? There was no knowing if he'd passed on a hard copy to anyone else. Even though they'd recovered one from his safe, was it the only one? Currently in Abu Ghraib prison under CIA jurisdiction, they would soon find out.

Northwood called the Baghdad bureau and spoke to his senior field officer. 'We're going to have to hold our man. We need to know who else has seen this stuff. It's up to you to find out. Just give me the answers. I don't want to hear how you got them – go to the maximum if necessary.'

Inserting Alex's memory stick into his modem, he turned his attention to the file. He shook his head, almost in disbelief, as he read the documents. It was a truly damning catalogue of fraud on a grand scale. A shiver ran through him at the thought it might enter the public domain. All these companies had their snouts in the trough.

For a fleeting moment, he broke off, wondering which of the enhanced interrogation techniques his colleagues might use on al-Tikriti. The CIA and US Military Intelligence had a list of measures they could adopt – all approved at the highest level of the Administration where the subject was delicately referred to as an 'alternative set of procedures'. The word 'torture', of course, was never used. Recalling a conversation with Kowolski just before the invasion, Northwood had been struck by Kowolski's determination to ensure that nuance, particularly of a negative nature, was never to be allowed in media reporting of the war. How funny, he thought, that in Washington the meaning of the word was adopted policy.

Shuddering, he loosened his tie, undid the top button of his shirt, and got back to work.

* * *

The sound of footsteps echoing nearer in the corridor roused Aban al-Tikriti from a semi-sleep. His body stiffened as the steel door clanged open. Still hooded, he could only sense the number of men entering the cell, but guessed there were three. He waited nervously, desperate for a voice to tell him there had been a mistake and he was free to go home to his beloved family. But no one spoke.

They yanked him to his feet, hands tearing off his dressing gown. Fingers dug into his midriff as his pyjama bottoms were tugged down.

'No, no, help me, please!' he pleaded, now terrified.

Strong arms either side lifted him upwards until the pyjama bottoms came free. Gasping for breath, he tried to speak again but only a shocked, pitiful, croak came out as his top was ripped off his back.

Totally naked, save for the black, bloodstained hood, they began turning him round and round repeatedly until his head swam. He felt like vomiting, just able to catch the foul taste of the bile that rose from his stomach. His arms were forced backwards until he feared they would snap. The cold of metal dug into his wrists and he heard the click of the manacles closing tight, pinching his skin. Next, his ankles were shackled so he was completely powerless.

A sharp blow to the back of his head forced him down to a kneeling position and he felt the unforgiving courseness of rope being pulled over his head, then tight around his neck. He screamed as he was dragged across the floor, the friction of the rope biting deep into him, the flesh shredding from his knees on the rough, pitted, cement. They pushed his face up hard against the bars of his cell so he could barely move his head and he feared he would suffocate.

Still kneeling and unable to alter position, he heard the cell door begin to close. Summoning one last piece of strength, he managed only one word: 'Toilet,' he moaned.

'Go fuckin' shit yourself,' a voice laughed as the door slammed shut.

And, at that moment, with cramp already setting in, all Aban al-Tikriti wanted to do was die.

15

Alex looked in the mirror. The strained half-smile that greeted her did little to ease the anxiety that had been gnawing at her over the last twenty-four hours.

She was concerned about Aban, worried about his email and its ramifications. Northwood's threat had been implicit. Okay, he had a job to do – but not at her expense. She didn't want to be looking over her shoulder everywhere she went, waiting for a knock on the door. The CIA could turn over her flat, hack into her emails for all she suspected. There was no time in her life right now for such nonsense.

To make matters worse, she'd just finished an elaborate telephone conversation with Kowolski regarding McDermott's presentation day. He'd kept the news that most distressed her to the last.

'Oh by the way, did I tell you we've got a big name to pin the medal on McDermott's chest?'

'No, who?'

'The President.'

She put the phone down in a daze. Kowolski had her by the balls. Whichever way she turned, his grip was relentless. Only now after digesting the implications did she realise the whole show was a stunt to boost the President.

If only she'd thought everything through when he first offered her the McDermott job. The outcome never occurred to her. Political chicanery. Shouldn't she have known it lay lurking in every corner to trap the unsuspecting? Now, she was an integral part of Kowolski's sophistry. She'd been a fool again. Such a fool.

McDermott deserved his medal as far as she knew. Bravery

was bravery. For whatever cause, it had to be admired. Her distress lay solely with Kowolski and Northwood and their ilk and the greasy machinations of politics.

The venue had been booked for what he called 'the launching of our star'. A formal lunch in the grand ballroom of a glitzy Midtown hotel. Two hundred guests would be invited, selected members of the armed forces, politicians, a couple of former presidents, city leaders and civic dignitaries, international embassy staff. And, of course, the whole media pack.

Topping the list would be the President himself. He would pin the medal on Matt McDermott.

And the whole world would see it. *Shit.*

* * *

Alex tried to call the only number she had for the al-Tikriti family. Just the sound of an unobtainable line. She'd tried it several times with the same result. What could she do to help?

Hurrying over to her desk, she switched on the computer and went to her emails. Only the one from Richard Northwood, now some six months old, remained. She opened it, reading her former lover's words with a remoteness which, not that long ago, she would never have considered possible. There was only one course of action she felt she could take. Setting the file to 'print', she watched as the paper edged out of the printer bit by bit.

Then she called his number.

'It's me again.'

'And?' His response was cold.

'I'm afraid I had to switch on my computer – there was indeed an email from my friend Aban. I haven't had time to read it yet,' she lied.

Northwood sucked in a breath. He had to play the game her way at the moment. 'You must not open it – do you understand?'

She could hear the desperation in his voice. It pleased her.

'Delete it – permanently – without reading it. You'll find yourself in serious trouble if you don't and I won't be able to protect you.'

'Well you're going to have to protect me – and Aban. I've just printed off another email from around six months ago. It's one you'd recognise and it's in an envelope sitting on my desk. Anyone comes into my apartment uninvited or hacks into my emails is likely to find it staring straight at them – do you know what I'm saying?'

There was a chilly silence for half a minute. She wanted him to be the one to break the void but she finally gave in.

'You're not the only one capable of dirty tricks so the ball's in your court, Mr Northwood.'

'What do you want?'

'Safe passage for me and Aban. Call the dogs off.'

'I'll see what I can do. And the emails?'

'I'll delete the Aban email,' she lied. 'The other will have to stay put – let's say for insurance purposes.'

'Alex, you're a fucking bitch,' he said slamming down the phone.

* * *

He paced the office like a tiger in a small cage, turning this way, stopping, peering out of the window at a grey New York afternoon, turning back, scowling.

Richard Northwood had crucial decisions to make, yet he felt incapable of making any. Twice he'd picked up the phone to the Baghdad bureau, hesitated, and replaced the receiver. In the mood Alex had just portrayed, he felt she might well have made several copies of the file. Its incriminating contents could be winging their way to every news outlet in the country for all he knew. And he was powerless to stop it.

The doubts and frustration gnawed at him, spreading like a rash. He'd half dismissed the idea she might shop him to his wife although he couldn't be certain. Under attack, who knew

151

what lengths she'd go to? He took a deep breath and forced himself to think rationally. Okay, her moves so far appeared to be purely defensive. He consoled himself there was no reason to suspect she would switch play for the time being. No point yet – she didn't know they possessed her memory stick. And if she had made further copies, wouldn't she have tried to post them at the same time as their pick-up?

For the moment, he had to believe just as she'd told him; she didn't have the time or the inclination for anything other than to see the McDermott job through to the end. If there was only the one memory stick then he was home and dry.

Could he rely on that assumption? No, of course not. The more he turned things over in his mind, the more irrational his thoughts. Maybe he would have to retrieve the goods from her apartment himself.

But the thought of it immediately filled him with panic. Would he be up to it? What if someone saw him and raised the alarm? How the hell would he explain his actions if he was caught? He was good at directing other people to do the dirty work. Doing it himself scared him half to death.

He slumped forward in his chair, head in his hands, and let out a loud groan.

* * *

They half-dragged Aban, naked, along the bleak prison corridor.

He could only moan, a pitiful wailing noise that echoed off the grim bare walls. Splayed against the bars of his cell all night, excruciating pain had tormented his body, relieved only when he'd blacked out. Twice they doused him in cold water, once after he lost control of his bowels. The shock of it set him shivering uncontrollably, each tremor intensifying the agony of the tight manacles that dug into the flesh of his wrists and his ankles, the noose around his neck chafing ugly red blotches on his skin.

It was known in CIA circles as the softening-up process.

Delirium now numbed his mind. Still hooded, he felt himself being shuffled into a room. Was he back home? Weird visions of Farrah and their boys taunted him, playing tricks. Farrah stretched a hand out to him, then she was gone. He could no longer tell whether his eyes were open or closed.

A sickening smell of cheap disinfectant assailed his senses. *Fried onions.*

Rough hands gripped his arms and legs, lifting him horizontally. His body tensed as he was manoeuvred onto a hard wooden bed, tilted so his head was lower than his feet. Leather straps pulled tight, pinning his legs and his chest.

His head swam, disorientated, faint and dizzy. Suddenly, a blinding light as the hood was removed, dark figures around him. A towel was draped loosely over his face. A voice, very close to his right ear. American; low and earnest.

'Who else did you send it to?'

Was someone talking to him? Or was he hearing things? Send it to? What did they mean?

'Fried onions,' he slurred, incoherently.

A hand touched his temple, resting firm and sure. He tried to move his head to see precious light but the towel was suddenly twisted tight from either side of him, blinding him once more, and covering his nose and mouth so he could hardly breathe.

He felt a trickle of water over the towel. It seeped into his mouth. Instinct taking over, he tried to cough, move his head aside, but he was totally powerless. A one-second pause, then another trickle, this time heavier. He could feel the water slowly filling his nose, starting to dribble down his throat.

Soon with sinuses full, he put all the energy he could summon to gasp for precious air. But his tormentors had been well trained. As he gulped, they poured so he sucked in only water. A brutal realisation immediately screamed from his brain: he was drowning.

More liquid splashed over his face and into an open mouth

153

that was trying to plead for mercy, pushing down further, overriding his epiglottis, entering his lungs.

Then the voice in his ear again: 'Who else? Just tell us and we'll stop.'

But he couldn't think straight. Someone talking to him? How could they? He was in a river, under water, battling the current, fighting for his life.

Another splash, straight down. The water now weighed heavily on his upper chest, his lungs bursting. From somewhere deep within him, a final alarm from nerve endings in utter panic.

He began kicking out, both feet thrashing wildly, crashing into each other. His body arched into a violent spasm, shaking uncontrollably and straining helplessly against the straps.

In the room, the senior of the three men present held up his hand to pause proceedings. The man with the half-empty two-litre plastic carton stood poised to pour more water on command.

They watched as Aban gave a last pitiful, shuddering, con-vulsion, and collapsed.

'Holy fuck,' the senior man shouted. 'Call the fuckin' medic.'

The third man opened the door, dashing out. 'Medic... MEDIC,' he could be heard shouting frantically as he ran along the corridor.

* * *

Alex took a taxi downtown to the specialist photo lab to check on the progress of her work. She had now been there so often, she knew all the staff by their first names.

Kowolski had given precise instructions on what he wanted. He ordered life-size cut-outs of some shots. These to be printed on a fibre-based paper, backed on card, air-dried and matte with no sheen to reflect the spotlights on stage.

There was to be a vinyl backcloth in colour, some thirty-feet wide, that would reflect the lieutenant's 'dedication'. They had argued over this one, Alex winning the battle by suggesting a montage of various shots, telling Kowolski the exact pictures it would comprise.

'Okay, okay,' she remembered him saying impatiently. 'But get an outdoor one, twice as big – that shot of him with the Iraqi kid on the street, a great shot. Just imagine that strung across the hotel facia on Times Square.'

Her work, on display like this, was at least a positive. An exhibition of her photographs in the hotel foyer would only credit her reputation. She had to agree with Kowolski when he said her pictures would 'knock them dead'. She knew just which shots she needed in colour, and which in monochrome, all on fine art silver gelatin paper of gallery standard.

Though resigned to Kowolski's trap, it still didn't lessen her anger – mostly aimed at herself for falling into it.

* * *

Richard Northwood pored over the briefing paper he'd just finished writing. It included the information Alex had provided together with a fresh intelligence report from the CIA's own heavily-manned station within the Green Zone. The next day, his work would be eagerly digested by the dozen pairs of eyes of the Senate Defense Committee.

Some of Northwood's agents were currently engaged within the Iraq Survey Group, the massive multi-national force of scientists, military experts, security and support staff, scouring the country for traces of WMD. Many of those agents had been attached to the same weapons inspectorate that had failed to turn up anything of note pre-war.

He raised his head and stared into the distance. The public had bought the White House line that the weapons inspectors were thrown out by Saddam because he probably had something to hide – not because his agents' cover had been blown.

It mattered in the past, but no longer, he answered himself. All the intelligence agencies had their people out there now, sniffing and digging for WMD. But they were proving to be bloodhounds leading the posse on a trail to nowhere.

And no one had yet come up with a whiff of a link between Saddam and al-Qaeda.

He scanned the document. He'd purposefully toned down the warning in Alex's brief of a probable threat to stability from the cleric, Muqtada al-Sadr, calling it only a 'possibility'. The Shi'ite religious leader's band of followers within his Mahdi Army presently numbered in its hundreds.

Signs were, Northwood wrote, that al-Sadr would find no difficulty recruiting many more from among the Shia population of the several million Iraqis who were not only without jobs, but, seemingly, devoid of hope. There were a couple of million Shia in Baghdad itself, festering in the slum-ridden area now known as Sadr City. The report said groups of his followers, armed with weaponry looted from Iraqi army arsenals, had taken to setting up their own patrols in their Baghdad neighbourhoods.

How ironic, he considered, that they were the group now controlling law and order, preventing further outbreaks of looting and general lawlessness.

While writing the report, he'd posed himself the question if the Shia Mahdi Army was growing as the report suggested, what about the other parts of Baghdad that were Sunni?

In such a power vacuum, he feared it could lead to a mass outpouring of ruthless self-interest on both sides. He'd considered mentioning this, but, not wishing to over-egg the threat, left it out.

Placing the report on his desk, he checked the time, and called Baghdad.

The bureau chief answered, a man Northwood had worked with in the field in Kosovo. He didn't particularly like Don Brady, considered him a hard bastard, unpossessed of the political finesse that would have seen him rise to any higher rank within the agency.

'Say, Don, this guy al-Tikriti, I want you to... '

But Brady cut him short. 'The guy's dead – the doc thinks he probably had a heart attack under questioning.'

It was all Northwood could do to stop himself from collapsing in a heap.

16

Kowolski sat hunched over his desk, putting the finishing touches to his schedule for McDermott's New York itinerary. The latest medical bulletin said the lieutenant would be fit to travel in a couple of weeks and, providing he wasn't 'strenuously tested' should be fit to resume duties in Iraq 'sometime before Christmas'. That gave Kowolski plenty of leeway to exploit the situation.

Deciding it was time to pay the lieutenant another visit, he marched out of the villa, nodding to the Marine guard at its entrance – receiving a crisp salute in return. He would never have cut it in the military, not like his father. Too much brass and bull, 'an excess of rigidity', he always called it. No, he savoured the freedom of this job even if his stratagem did involve a degree of military-like scheming. There was nothing wrong with that – he just didn't need to battle his way through the haze of a command structure that, by its very nature, he always considered a stultifying process.

'Howdy, Lieutenant.' Kowolski bounded into the hospital room, a wide smile on his face that beamed camaraderie. 'How's it going?'

McDermott lay on a bed, his heavily-bandaged knee elevated and supporting an icepack. 'Okay, sir,' he said, shifting slightly as Kowolski pulled up a chair.

'I guess it's a case of PRICE, eh, Lieutenant?' Kowolski noted the puzzled look he evoked. 'Thought you'd have known that one – if I remember my college football days correctly, it was protection, rest, ice, compression and elevation. Talking of which, you remember your CDE?'

'Courage, discipline, exemplary behaviour of my men, sir.'

'Good man.' Kowolski's eyes wandered around the sparse room. He noted the Bible lying open on the bedside cabinet. 'Is there anything you need... books, magazines, a video game or two? Looks like Hell in here – you could die of boredom,' he blurted, immediately regretting his choice of words.

McDermott shot him a glance. 'Hell is out there, sir. I got everything I need.'

'Yeah, right,' Kowolski said, suddenly ill at ease. There was something odd the way the lieutenant had fixed on the words, *Hell is out there.* What the fuck did that mean? 'Well if there is anything... ' his voice tailed off. He felt like telling the lieutenant he could send along a pretty blonde who gave great head, but was certain the quip would have been wasted. Strange dude.

'Actually, sir, there is something I just remembered,' McDermott said, sitting up. 'A book about Iraq.'

'Iraq? Gee, I don't know.' Kowolski looked stumped. 'I mean, the Grand Canyon, the Statue of Liberty, the Yosemite National Park – I can get you books on all those. A book on Iraq? I'll have to see what I can do.'

'Thank you, sir.'

'Oh, and I'll let you have an outline of the planned itinerary. We'll soon have you up and wowing them – don't you worry.'

But worry was all McDermott had been doing these past weeks. The thought of Kowolski's intentions made him sick with it.

* * *

In the hospital corridor, Kowolski sought out a doctor he'd spoken to before. 'Hey, doc. How's our boy doing? He gonna be okay on those crutches?'

'Ah, yes. Lieutenant McDermott. Well, he's doing okay, physically.'

Kowolski felt a surge of panic resonate through him. 'Physically, he's doing good – but?'

159

The doctor rubbed his nose. 'He's been put on sleeping tablets.'

'So? Everybody takes goddam sleeping pills – it's the only way you can get a decent bit of shut-eye round here. I mean, that knee looks pretty swollen, must still be painful.'

'And tranquilisers. We had to up the dose because he was still hallucinating.'

'Jesus, I... '

'Precisely – he told me yesterday he thought he WAS Jesus Christ.'

Kowolski shook his head, turned to face the wall, grasping for words. He fixed the doctor with a ruthless stare. 'You know he's due to meet the President to have that Silver Star pinned on his goddam chest – are you saying he's gonna freak out?'

'Look. I'm no shrink – and I don't know how he'll react to anything. You'd have to take it easy with him, that's all I'm saying.'

'Can we get him further help – you know, a psychiatrist or something?'

The doctor made a clucking sound, an exaggerated sucking in of his breath as if to say 'don't go there'.

'It's an option,' he eventually said. 'Most of them are mad as hatters themselves and you might not see your man again if he falls into their clutches.'

Kowolski nodded in acquiescence. He opened his wallet and gave the doctor his card. 'Call me, day or night, if his condition gets worse. You've no idea how important this is.'

'Important? The lieutenant's condition – or your date with the President?'

Kowolski didn't answer. He merely flashed the doctor a strained half-smile, turned on his heel, and left.

He returned to his office in the fiercest of moods. A young secretary, who'd rebuffed his advances on her first day in the job, took a direct hit and left the room in tears. His young assistant jumped out of his seat abruptly, a rolled up newspaper in his hand.

'What the hell are you up to, son?' Kowolski growled.

'There's a bug, right there by the window,' the assistant said, arm raised, ready to swipe it.

'Let it out,' Kowolski said.

'No. It's going to get it.'

'I said. Open the fucking window and let it out – NOW.' Kowolski turned red with rage. 'There's been enough goddam killing round here,' he stormed.

The assistant stopped in mid flow, his face wan at his boss's sudden outburst. Kowolski leapt up and opened the window, ushering the bug to safety. 'See how easy it is to let something live? Get out my sight – go get me a coffee, black.'

Slumping into his chair, he rubbed his eyes, pondered the immediate future with McDermott. It was impossible to cancel now. Everything depended on the lieutenant performing well – all their futures – including that of the President of the United States of America. *Jesus Christ, indeed.* The boy would just have to pull himself together. Goddam it, wasn't he a soldier of the highest calibre? A guy everyone on camp looked up to? Hadn't he led by example on that night of bravery? Well, Kowolski decided, he could fucking-well lead by example again – under the Star-Spangled Banner and with a soft bed in a five-star Manhattan hotel.

* * *

Kowolski picked up his glasses, and with a sigh, put them on. He had to admit he was beginning to feel more comfortable wearing them. On a few occasions, he'd glanced at himself in the mirror, thought they gave him an air of erudition. With all the reading he was doing, they were a boon.

Switching on his computer, he concentrated on the screen. The daily headlines had just come in from the major newspapers; New York, Washington, LA, London, all closely monitored and sent to him daily by his staff at the Pentagon. Some of the banners contained a two or three-line resume of the article's main points. It was such an important part of his modus operandi to follow up events, anticipate embarrassing situations, quash them before they materialised.

Avoiding the flak was his forte. A word of praise in the ear of a few editors and publishers was par for the course. Several times recently he had called to express his delight on a particular story. It was simply to let them know he was over here, finger on the pulse, watching.

On the occasions when he'd had to take issue with a newspaper's particular slant on a story, he'd come across the usual recalcitrants, the awkward ones who argued back. Then, he played his patriot ace. It was amazing what compliance he got when he launched an attack.

'Let me ask you this, would you fight for your country? Are you as patriotic as those losing their lives out here every goddam day? Dying in their hundreds so you can sit on your fat ass and take your wife out shopping Saturdays.'

He usually got a positive response to the tactic.

Many long hours had gone into developing his blueprint for coverage of the war. The contract that had to be signed by all embedded journalists was one of his favourites. Its conditions were watertight, weighted totally in the military's favour. No expelled journalist would have a leg to stand on if considering litigation on some breach of human rights or other such fancy.

Now, they knew his rules and, by God, he would do his utmost to see they stuck to them.

In his pre-war paper to the White House, he had called for 'sophisticated and subtle manipulation' to control the flow of information and images emanating from Iraq. There was simply no room, he said, for the alternative view.

For Kowolski now, however, it was a case of so far, so good. The gung-ho coverage of the TV networks at home was as gratifying as he had envisaged, while the majority of newspapers had taken their lead and acquiesced. There would be no more mistakes with the media as in Vietnam, nor as for the Brits in the Falklands.

And on no account would there ever be pictures of our slain men and women coming home in body bags, draped with the flag. Those press 'freedoms' were well and truly over.

His only negative of any consequence so far; no one had uncovered the slightest whiff of WMD. He had seen the weapons inspectors' classified reports and, like them, seriously doubted there were any. The spectre of their absence had not yet hit the news pages, so that was a bonus. Only one or two of the more shrewd political columnists had broached the subject; their ramblings confined to columns on the inside pages. Hardly anyone had time to read such smart-ass political comment.

Kowolski's ongoing worry was that some writer scratching his fanny on a slow news day might just broach the subject with his home editor after reading such a column. It was a potential front-page landmine. He knew they all copied off each other, sneakily window dressed a theme to make a piece sound new. The 'exclusive' tag was old rope these days. In Kowolski's view, very few of the whole rotten barrel had an original thought in their heads.

Although WMD was a potential booby-trap, he was quite at ease to push the subject to the back of his mind. For now. But he knew, sooner or later, he'd have a battle on his hands trying to deal with the public fallout when the reality dawned.

* * *

Alex gunned the motor to a few miles per hour over the speed limit. The highway north was quiet so she flicked on the cruise control of the hire car. Ahead of schedule on her work for Kowolski, the idea of a short visit to her parents had become a priority; she needed relief from the pressures building up around her. There, in the quiet little town of Stamford, she hoped she might be able to switch off from the turmoil within.

She thought of Steve Lewis. He'd been a rock these last few weeks, their phone conversations and emails becoming more intimate. He was a great listener, reassuring her, cajoling, teasing. Smiling to herself, she wondered at his patience as she'd poured her heart out to him; his calm, measured advice acting to quell the panic that often threatened to overwhelm her.

Now, he knew everything: about her affair with Northwood, what she'd done to counteract his threat over Aban and his top-secret file, how stupid she felt about letting Kowolski use her to his own ends. Was it possible she was falling in love with a guy she hardly knew? But, surely, she did know him? Wasn't he the man who'd already spoken of his fondness for her, how he wished he could be near her – not some 5,000 miles away, 'spitting sand' in his desert outpost and counting the days until his release from service?

This man, so unlike the standard military cut she'd worked with, was a different animal. Those kindly eyes that seemed to crinkle when he laughed, his laidback manner, yet his ambition and determination to set up his own business endorsed her view that he was a good man. She wished Steve could be with her now, driving him to meet her folks, secretly hoping for their approval. Something inside her desperately needed him at her side to see everything through. Thinking about him, the journey seemed to pass in no time, adding to her guilt that she didn't make the trip more often.

Turning into the driveway, she was pleased to see the flagpole on the front lawn bare. Devoid of the Stars and Stripes, it was an action of protest her father had taken when the first bombs dropped on Iraq. She didn't see eye to eye with her parents' views on a variety of issues, but, she guessed, that was a generation thing. Taking down the flag must have been difficult for both of them. But she was proud of their stance. 'To hell with what the neighbours think,' he'd told her on the phone. 'I'm not gonna fly that flag until we're outa there.'

Turning off the ignition and grabbing her bag, a shudder ran through her as she asked herself how she would explain her work for Kowolski. The President's name was now spoken with disparagement in this house.

So, how would she tell them that, within a couple of weeks, she'd be party to bolstering this man's reputation?

A feeling of dread enveloped her as she got out of the car.

* * *

'What is it, honey? A man?' Alex, curled up on a sofa, managed a half-smile. Her mom was so damn intuitive. Apart from the usual jibes about wanting grandchildren before they reached the ga-ga stage, her parents had given up asking about her private life. The subject had become a running joke because Alex always steered such hinted conversation away from the topic. And her mom and dad now knew to keep their counsel.

'Why d'you say that?' Alex said, irked, as if an unwritten rule had been breached. She stole a sideways glance at her mother, returning her gaze out of the large picture window to the backyard lawn where her father was riding a mower.

'Hun,' her mom said, sitting on the edge of the sofa, 'this is your mother speaking – perhaps I know you better than you think... so?'

Alex sighed. 'Yeah, I've met a guy... do you believe in, well, sorta love at first sight?'

'Sure. It happens. Look at Grandpa – he always said he fell for Nana first time he clapped eyes on her.'

'Hmmm... '

Her mom stroked the back of Alex's hand. 'C'mon, baby, out with it.'

For the next half hour Alex recounted her meeting with Steve. How they had corresponded, talked for hours on the phone. Even when she became exuberant, and her dad walked in, she continued, regaling them both with her innermost feelings. So lost in words, she failed to see her dad exchange a look with his wife. One that seemed to say, 'Wow, this girl's got it bad.'

Later, after talking some more, Alex had her best night's sleep for ages.

* * *

It was over breakfast the next day that she told them of the Kowolski business.

Reluctant at first, she gave her parents a blow-by-blow account of the events, at one stage unable to hold back the tears.

'What a bastard,' her father said.

'Frank!' Her mother gasped.

'Well, what a snake, then,' he said, admonished.

He got up and put his arms gently on Alex's shoulders. 'Never mind, baby. What do I always tell you?'

'Something'll turn up,' Alex said, sniffing.

'It will, hun,' her mother said. 'We're sure it will – right, Frank?'

'You bet,' he said, reaching for the coffee pot and topping up Alex's mug.

A little later, sitting in her father's den catching up on her emails, her mother popped her head round the door.

'Thought you might need that thing you sent me, honey.'

'Thanks, Mom,' Alex said, taking the memory stick and putting it on the desk. When her mother left, she sat looking at it, lost in thought. She didn't have the time or the inclination to do anything with Aban's material at the present. It would have to remain her ace up the sleeve. At one stage, she'd thought about telling her parents about the whole business, but decided against the idea. It would be unfair to burden them with something she alone must handle. But it wouldn't do any harm to glance at the file again, remind herself of its bombshell contents.

She got up, gently closing the door, and returned to the computer inserting the stick. Tapping a few keys on the keyboard, she waited. *Nothing.* She swallowed hard. The stuff was

166

on here – she'd checked, made doubly sure before posting it. Maybe she'd hit a wrong key. She withdrew the stick then reinserted it. Biting her bottom lip, she could feel the panic rising in her chest. *Still a blank screen.*

Frantic, Alex repeated the procedure with the same empty results. She asked her dad to help. He tried several times to load the stick, each effort unsuccessful.

'Hope it wasn't that important, Alex,' he said, resigned.

Alex just shook her head, unable to comprehend what might have gone wrong. An empty feeling verging on nausea gripped her, spinning her inside out.

Then the sudden realisation of her own powerless insignificance; that she was but a mere speck in the momentous forces ranged against her. Something had happened beyond her control. She had no idea what. But her body still trembled with an overwhelming sinking acceptance of defeat. She stared helplessly at the worthless stick – the only copy she had made.

* * *

Alex headed for Manhattan late afternoon, her heart heavy, mood sour. Being around her folks had initially calmed her. Now, her thoughts in turmoil, she needed someone to confide in, someone with a sense of sangfroid, like Steve. Staring ahead at the rippling shimmer of brake lights stretching into the distance, all she could think was that she needed him.

Traffic going into the city crawled like cattle herded into a narrow corral. A late summer storm had dumped torrents of water on the road, which collected in deep pools on the underpasses causing motorists to meander from lane to lane. Her phone rang. She ignored it. Seconds later, its familiar alert tone told her someone had left a message.

It was unnaturally dark when she finally parked up. Great gloomy clouds threatened overhead and a smell of newly-drenched dust filled the air. Her phone beeped again, impatient to be silenced. Making sure the car doors were still locked, she reached for this nagging piece of technology, saw a voicemail beckoned, and called the service.

'Hi Alex, it's me, Greg. Listen babe, I don't know how to tell you this... it's about Aban... I'm sorry, but he's dead. They say he had a heart attack while being questioned... I just don't know any more than that – don't know what to think. I've only spoken briefly to Farrah – she's devastated. She thinks they killed him.'

The shock hit Alex like a tornado, the force lifting her aimlessly high into the air, battering and shaking her whole being, flinging her feelings in a crazy, haphazard maelstrom then hurling her down with cruel abandon.

Numbed to the bone, all she could do was to drop the phone – and scream.

17

The grief, the tears, and the desolation had begun to wane. She'd been tempted by the thought of alcohol over the last few days, but her resolve stood fast. Now, Alex felt consumed by an all-powering rage. Her whole being bristled with an intense loathing of Richard Northwood and his ilk. How could she make them pay for their contemptible blind loyalty to an administration such as this and for the consequences of such loyalty? Especially Northwood. He'd promised her Aban's protection yet, obscenely, hadn't lifted a finger. The poor man was dead because of him.

Fearful that her phone might be tapped, she'd spoken with Steve from a public pay phone that had cost her a small fortune. Urged to recall the minutiae of her movements, he'd asked her to accept that the CIA most likely knew about Aban's email from the off and had placed her under surveillance.

'The post office counter clerk, the blind guy – hey, do blind people walk round listening to music? Someone switched that memory stick, Alex and one way or another, they got you. Accept it, you can't win them all.'

While relieved to have shared her worries, Alex was in no mood to let the matter lie. In fact she now found herself doubly determined to hit back. When and where, she couldn't answer. She simply knew she must.

Alex was also wrestling with herself to call off the whole McDermott show. But her pictures were ready and, try as she might to ignore them, professional pride wouldn't allow it. At least, she determined, she should go and view them.

Kowolski called her just as she was leaving for the lab in a supine fit of reluctance.

His voice was different, softer, much more subdued. 'I heard about your friend – I'm so sorry. This thing's getting harder for everyone out here. There isn't a day goes by now without...'

'You know they killed him,' she said, her eyes welling up.

'Alex, I don't know that and neither do you. They say he had a weak heart – it could've happened any minute.'

'God knows where they kept him, what they did to him. It's what his wife is saying,' she stormed.

'You spoken to her?'

'No, I can't get through. It's what I hear. I've arranged for flowers but I don't know if...' she began to cry, soon sobbing full flow.

Kowolski sighed, a long labouring breath. 'Listen, I'll see what I can do – I'll recommend compensation for the family, see they're cared for. I've already spoken with Richard Northwood – he's as shocked as anyone.'

Alex glanced at the letter sitting beside her computer. 'No he's not. He's just a cold calculating bastard. You all are.'

'That's not fair, Alex.'

'And I suppose your plan to bolster the President is just an afterthought? I'm sick of it all, everything.'

'Hey, hold on a minute.' He hesitated a few seconds, his voice dropped a notch. 'You remember when you got that picture published, the one of that poor mother with her dead son?'

'Well?'

'It had an effect on me, Alex, got me thinking – not that I expect you to believe me. Maybe I'm not as tough as you think. And, boy, could I do with a break from all this. But, remember how you responded when I bawled you out? You said, "It's what I do." Well, this is what I do, Alex. It's a lot tougher than I imagined and I might not like the job as much as I thought I did, but I set out with a goal in mind and I have to see it through. I need you to understand that.'

She was stunned by his admission, not knowing how to respond. 'I gotta go to work,' she finally said, hanging up.

In the cab to the laboratory, Alex stared at the thick metal security grill separating the cab from the rear-seat passenger, a fact of big-city life. You could see the driver, talk to him, but make no closer contact. Kowolski's revelation sounded almost like a confession. So the war was getting to him. Shame others weren't out there to taste the vile concoction they'd created. Perhaps she'd been wrong to sully him in the same breath as Northwood.

She'd always considered the space between them as opaque and impenetrable. To a large degree, she was sure this was still the case. He was still the enemy. But, were holes beginning to appear in the barrier between them like the mesh in front of her? Recalling his ranting at the time, she was amazed her picture had touched him. She only remembered his flashing, steely eyes and set jaw. There'd been no semblance of any feeling other than anger.

Kowolski was a loner, no family, no real friends. Why had he reached out to her? Had he just given her a glimpse of the real person? Did he feel some sort of bond between them? Perhaps there was a hint of humanity about the guy after all, she thought, as the taxi pulled up outside the photo lab. She pushed a twenty bill through the mesh and told the driver to keep the change.

* * *

The lab's production people had assured her countless times they were in sympathy with her aims and would translate them to her satisfaction. Until she viewed the final product, however, she couldn't be sure. So it was with a certain amount of trepidation that she entered the building. Met by the company's art director, a Slovak called Milo, she was ushered with great ceremony down a narrow hallway towards the main studio.

'This is where we ask clients to close their eyes,' Milo said with a fanfare as he opened the door.

171

'Right, you can look now,' he shrieked excitedly, clapping his hands in delight.

In front of her, suspended wall to wall, her montage. Measuring some 30 feet long, almost 6 feet deep, it thrilled her more than she'd ever imagined. From the planning stage to reality was sometimes a leap too far in her business. She'd known colleagues whose pictures had been annihilated in the lab. Shaking her head in disbelief, she scanned the work. Her face creased into her first smile for a long time.

'Milo, it's fantastic,' she said, hugging him in delight.

'Will look good on the stage, high up and behind your hero,' he beamed.

'Sure will,' she said, moving closer to examine each shot in more detail. One of the photographs was of the Bradley squad, Bobby-Jo at the end of the group giving a thumbs-up.

'This poor boy's dead now,' she said, gently running a finger to caress Bobby-Jo's cheek. She gazed at the impish face staring out of the canvas and a shiver of remorse snaked through her.

'You want to keep him in? I mean, we can take him out if... '

'No, no, of course I want him in – he's very important. They're heroes, all of them,' she said, the melancholy all too apparent in her voice.

'I guess it's tough out there, huh?'

'It's hell,' she said firmly, 'for everyone.'

Eventually, Milo gestured to another room. Here, her large monochrome photographs adorned the walls, laid out in smart recessed mounts with black borders, hung on portable screen boards ready for wheeling into the hotel foyer for her exhibition.

The art director stood back admiring the work. 'You like?'

Alex put both hands up to her face, felt a tear trickle down. 'They're amazing.'

'But we are merely the conduit. You are the artiste,' he said, a note of deference in his words. After a few minutes, he took her by the hand. 'Come, Madame, you can study them in greater detail later – we are not yet finished.' He led her back towards the main studio. 'I present to you the *pièce de résistance*.' He rapped on the door. It was opened quickly.

Milo stepped to one side. 'We cannot do it full justice here, Alex. But, on the side of the hotel and over several stories deep, I'm sure it will knock them dead.'

Alex's jaw dropped. Hoisted up to the high ceiling, a giant canvas in full colour of McDermott and the toddler he'd picked up in the Baghdad street. Several assistants unfurled the canvas as best they could so it spread towards them on the floor. Now, Alex let the tears flow freely.

It was a remarkable picture; McDermott's uniform and the glimpse of a gun barrel a stark reminder of the brutality of the conflict, the little boy in a red sweater with a worn pair of shorts displaying his little chubby legs. Alex had captured the child's brown eyes looking up into the soldier's face. And McDermott's expression was one of almost sublime beatitude, one hand looming large in the foreground, protectively around the boy's waist.

'We put some colour in the hero's face – it was a little too white on every shot,' Milo exclaimed.

Suddenly, Alex was back on that dusty, debris-strewn street, the stench of raw sewage assailing her nostrils, the stultifying heat that elevated water over oil as Iraq's most precious commodity. And, there, with trembling fingers and a deathly pale, McDermott and his mystifying reaction to an innocent child.

'Yeah, it's the intensity of the sun out there,' Alex bluffed, immediately shutting the memory from her mind to concentrate on this surreal vision before her.

Later, she left the lab with her spirits raised, her immediate anger blunted. Her work had been polished so it shone like a beacon. Did she have the nerve to call everything off? She would speak again to Steve and tell him her dilemma. He was such a good listener.

* * *

173

'Babe, you've just gotta do it.' Steve was as enthused over her pictures as she'd been when describing them. 'Forget about everything else for a while and just think about yourself, your career and all.'

'Maybe,' she said, only half convinced. 'Be pragmatic you mean?'

'You've had a rough time. I only wish I could have been with you, put my arms around you and given you a real Philadelphia squeeze.'

Alex laughed, a girlish giggle that tinkled in her throat.

'So do I,' she murmured.

There was a moment's silence between them. She heard Steve's voice waver a little.

'Alex... I think I'm falling in love with you,' he said, clearing his throat.

She pressed the receiver as close as she could to her ear.

'What?'

Detecting a split-second hesitation, she heard him swallow hard.

'I said I think I'm falling in love with you.'

Feeling her face flush, her words came out in a whisper. 'So am I with you. There, we've both said it now.'

'Alex, sweetheart, you've made my day.' Then he roared. 'No, not my day, my month, my year – my life!'

They both burst out laughing in a fit of relief and delight. She eventually hung up, her heart soaring. This was madness, exhilaratingly so. But wasn't everything just plain senseless at the moment? Turning to the photograph of Steve at her bedside, she blew it a kiss.

'Lovely, crazy guy,' she said, turning off the light.

* * *

McDermott walked slowly along the hospital corridor, limping. Dressed in uniform, he held a walking stick in one hand and a small bag in the other.

Kowolski watched him approaching. 'You're doing good Lieutenant,' he said, relieving McDermott of his bag. He'd hoped the soldier would have remained on crutches – so much better for the media. The doctors, however, were pleased with McDermott's recovery and agreed with the physiotherapy people that a stick would be sufficient. Still, Kowolski mused, a walking stick was nearly as good. The sympathy when he met the press and TV would be nearly as emotive.

'We got one of your buddies to pack your gear and send it on to the airport,' Kowolski said, ushering the lieutenant into the back of a waiting SUV, sandwiched between a Bradley and a Humvee.

'Sir, what time's the flight?'

'Whenever we're ready, Lieutenant. This is a first-class trip.'

An army photographer met them at the airport, spending longer than Kowolski had planned taking his shots.

'I don't suppose we could get you up on the Bradley, Lieutenant?' the photographer gestured.

Kowolski cut him short. 'Son, we got a prized cargo here and you wanna risk him doing his other knee? Go take a jump. Anyway, you've got enough – we're outta here.'

The pictures would soon be on-screen on the army's official website, married to a press release from Kowolski's own hand. He thought it only fair to give the army first bite of the ripened cherry. He'd primed the prominent home media, of course, telling them to watch for the piece and take from it whatever they wanted as a teaser story for their own websites. By Kowolski's reckoning, the President's Silver Star hero would be on his way to full launch by the time they touched down on American soil, ready to face the waiting media pack.

* * *

Kowolski fastened his seat belt and braced himself for take-off. Fiddling with his hands, he rubbed one against the back of the other as if washing them, finally screwing his eyes shut as the plane reached critical speed. When he opened them, still flustered, he glanced at McDermott. The lieutenant was staring out of the window, seemingly unaware of Kowolski's discomfort.

'You like flying, Lieutenant?' Kowolski said, shifting in his seat. 'Makes me kinda nervous.'

McDermott fixed him with a strange smile. 'Perfect love casts out all fear, sir.'

Kowolski raised his eyebrows.

'John, chapter four, verse eighteen sir.'

'Er, right,' Kowolski said, bending down and opening his briefcase.

'No one has ever seen God, but if we love one another, God lives in us and his love is made complete in us,' McDermott added.

Kowolski smiled thinly. This guy was weird, just like the lot of *them*.

He gestured with his head towards the window. 'Not much love down there, Lieutenant... I see only hate, yes sirree, just hate and fear.'

Taking a sheaf of papers from the case, he handed a set to McDermott. 'This is the itinerary – better study it. You know we've got a small reception tomorrow night, a sort of eve of the big ceremony. You're booked in a real swish place, the Carlyle on Madison Avenue. White-gloved waiters everywhere. You heard of it?'

'No, sir, I've never been to New York before.'

'You're gonna like it. Hey, I've even booked Alex in there next door so you'll have a friendly face.'

McDermott nodded his agreement. It would be good to see her again. He'd been troubled for some time about something she'd said when they'd last met – the reason the US was in Iraq. He'd like to talk to her further about the subject. It was extremely important to him right now.

Taking his Bible out of his hand case, he began reading from a bookmarked page. After a few minutes, he turned to Kowolski.

'Can I ask you something, sir?'

'Fire away, Lieutenant.' Kowolski immediately regretted his turn of phrase, not sure if McDermott would have recognised the irony. Besides, he thought, from what he'd seen of this soldier, he wasn't totally convinced McDermott was capable of firing at anything at the moment, despite his undoubted act of past bravery.

McDermott's demeanour, his whole appearance in fact, had caused Kowolski some debate with himself in the past few days as he made final preparations for their trip. In one sense, presenting the media with the hackneyed vision of a US soldier, a beefy, uncomplicated young man with a ready smile and a slap on the back for all and sundry, would have been the simple solution.

But a guy who looked as if he'd just come out of college? Fresh-faced and a trifle gangly, there was no way McDermott fitted the stereotype. Some might even wonder if he had the strength or the stamina to march around Baghdad with a 33 lb supply pack on his back, never mind tackling a bagful of bad guys. Still, Kowolski concluded, a studious-looking McDermott might fit the bill in another way; it would show that the US Army had room for the thinking soldier. And if someone like McDermott was willing to put his life on the line, it might even reinforce the public's acceptance of the invasion.

'Have we found any evidence of WMD yet?' McDermott stared at him, blinking several times.

Kowolski eyed him, uncertainty playing in his mind. Several months ago he would have told the lieutenant it was only a matter of time before a whole raft of mass destruction weapons were found in some secret desert hideaway. Now, he not only doubted it himself, he wondered if it was worth keeping up the pretence to a hero like McDermott. He glanced at the open Bible in the lieutenant's lap, the thought suddenly reminding him that he'd never found McDermott a book on Iraq.

'You're a good kid, Lieutenant. You gonna stay in the army forever?'

'I don't know, sir. I guess I never thought about it until recently.'

'Recently?'

'Being out here, seeing what it's really like. And lying in bed in hospital, thinking.'

'What if we didn't find any WMD – that bother you?'

McDermott slowly raised a hand to his face, rubbed the side of his chin. 'I don't really know, I mean, why are we here?'

Kowolski pursed his lips, put both hands to his mouth, fingers together. To an outsider, it would have been misconstrued as a conscious act of praying. 'You're glad we toppled Saddam, right?'

'Sure, everyone is.'

'Well, that might be the sum total of it – isn't that enough?'

'And al-Qaeda?'

Kowolski shrugged without answering.

McDermott stared at him expectantly for several moments. When there was no further response, he turned his head to the window. 'Thank you, sir,' he said resignedly, gazing at the clouds.

'But you stick to the official line, soldier. That's your duty,' Kowolski cautioned.

Moments later, Kowolski closed his eyes to try for a nap so he was unable to see McDermott staring straight ahead, lost in thought, the corners of his mouth turned up in a deeply contented smile.

It was if he had just made a monumental decision – and was pleased with himself for doing so.

* * *

Kowolski couldn't sleep. His was a deeply troubled mind. Restlessness prevailed, bombarding him with a barrage of reflections. He'd put his heart and soul into this whole Iraq war media project, McDermott merely the sugar paste on a perfectly-formed slab of preconception. His masters were pleased, passing on their congratulations, delighted at the amount of 'media control' his vision was delivering.

But did anyone back in Washington count the true cost of their actions? Were they ever touched by the actuality? The architects drew their plans with glee, but never saw the ramifications of the shapes they were trying to create. Did Rumsfeld and Cheney and Wolfowitz and the President never see the blood? More frightening, if they saw it and didn't care – while Kowolski struggled daily to rid his nostrils of its deadly stench.

He considered his latest remark to McDermott that, below them, he could only see hate and fear. He was sure the Washington cabal viewed such notions in the abstract. Not for them the heartbreaking surety of death and destruction. Think *the big picture.*

But hate and fear abounded in Washington, too. Among the seething myopic mass of opinion layers and policy-makers, people were afraid. From newspaper editors to the politicians themselves, hate and fear was endemic. Everyone in fear of losing their job, their status. Hating their rivals with a ferocious intensity. Kowolski had seen it all. Wasn't his own function to allay the President's fear he might not be re-elected? Sanitising a war to palatable sound-bites and agreeable verbiage.

And if there was a God, how did they square their belief with their actions? And how would God judge such people? Even Prime Minister Blair in Britain expounded his religious views ad nauseum. Kowolski now wondered if their fervour increased in relation to the bloodiness of the outcome of their actions.

His own role? How would he be judged? Disturbingly, such questions had begun to permeate his consciousness in recent weeks. He'd had to keep telling himself not to waver, gritting his teeth and reminding himself he had a job to do.

But it was all looking so different from just a few months ago.

* * *

179

The media turnout at the airport exceeded all Kowolski's expectations as he looked about him, stepping from the plane on a windy, overcast day. He took a deep breath of the air, found it immediately refreshing. Standing back, he let McDermott venture out on to the aircraft's top step to a barrage of flashing cameras.

'Smile, Lieutenant and wave your goddamn walking stick in the air,' Kowolski hissed from inside the open door. He counted at least a dozen TV cameras filming the scene, perhaps twice as many reporters and photographers.

Kowolski waited for several minutes before escorting McDermott slowly down the steps, over-exaggerating his show of help before two medical orderlies rushed forward to take over. Several army personnel lined up to greet them, a lieutenant-general, a home-service colonel from McDermott's cavalry regiment, and, to Kowolski's great pleasure, an array of civic dignitaries.

The welcome handshakes concluded, McDermott and Kowolski found themselves being ushered to a waiting golf buggy at the head of a convoy, and whisked off to the terminal's VIP gate where a room had been set aside for a press conference.

The general, a large man with a vice-like grip, beamed before the assembled media. It had been a good while since he'd been anywhere near the limelight. Just weeks away from his retirement as a three-star general, he hoped his wife had remembered to set the TV to record. The grandchildren would get a kick out of seeing old Grandpa in all his splendour. So would he.

Waiting until the assembled throng had settled down, the general raised his frame to its full 6 feet 3 inch height and addressed the ensemble with a resume of McDermott's 'daring night-time' raid on a 'deadly bunch of killer insurgents'.

McDermott cast his eyes around the packed room. Everyone was looking at him, paying scant attention to the general. Kowolski, sitting alongside, gave him a reassuring grin.

Cameras flashed every few seconds and, near the front, television crews recorded his every move. He felt the tension building inside him, his stomach swirling, a tightness across his chest. If the air conditioning was on, it wasn't working very well. His mouth dry, he reached for a glass of water, almost spilling it.

He gulped. The TV lights seemed to grow in intensity, almost blinding him, causing him to blink. Each time he did so, the vision of a lifeless little body flooded his mind, a pair of big brown eyes staring at him. Only now those eyes were no longer smiling. McDermott was sure their gaze held only a touching innocent puzzlement.

The questions came, thick and fast, staccato like the burst of Herman's 25 mm cannon that rang in his ears. 'How did you feel, Lieutenant?' 'Were you frightened?' 'How long did the fire-fight last?'

He began to answer his interrogators as if in a dream, barely conscious of his mundane words and unaware he had slumped back in his seat and away from the microphone like he was sheltering from the barrage. Some journalists at the back of the room obviously couldn't catch every word and became restless, turning to one another with pained expressions.

Kowolski, constantly sweeping the room like a radar dish, was soon alert to the problem. Scribbling furiously for a second or two, he slid the piece of paper along the desk top. Glancing at it, McDermott saw the large capital letters: 'SIT UP. SPEAK INTO MIC – CDE!!!'

As if shaken to life, McDermott pulled himself upright, leaning forward to the microphone. 'I'm sorry, ladies and gentlemen, I was kind of reliving the moment just now. I can honestly say it was an alarming experience, in many ways a humbling one that has had a profound effect on my life. But, throughout, I knew that God was with me. I would also add that had it not been for the courage, discipline and exemplary behaviour of my highly-trained men, the mission would not have been successful.'

'Hear, hear,' the general said, banging the desk with a clenched sledge-hammer fist. A ripple of applause broke out. It grew louder as several in the audience stood up, encouraging others to do likewise. Kowolski jumped to his feet, followed by the rest of the top table. McDermott, smiling coyly, was hoisted from his seat and embraced in a bear hug by the general.

'Soldier, we're all so damn proud of you. You're a great credit to the armed service,' he bellowed.

As photographers jostled forward to capture the scene, McDermott tried desperately to hide the pain from his knee, which had stiffened up and was beginning to throb.

Kowolski viewed the proceedings with a measure of ambivalence; it had started disastrously. Anyone leaving halfway through to file copy for an early deadline would have missed the rousing finale. Still, he thought, it was doubtful such reporters would write anything downbeat on a hero's story. Journalists were all pretty good at embroidery.

But would McDermott be able to handle everything else that would come his way? Kowolski hadn't told him the half of what he planned. The offers would come rolling in and would have to be chosen with care.

One false step and he feared the kid just might crack up.

18

McDermott almost bumped into Alex as he limped out of one of the two lifts near the Carlyle's reception desk, his walking stick slipping on the highly polished marble floor tiles. His eyes down, he didn't see her at first, issuing a polite 'sorry Ma'am' for getting in her way.

'Well, is that all you're going to say?' Alex didn't move. Her head tilted to one side, a teasing, quizzical expression filling her face. He looked so different in a t-shirt and jeans.

McDermott looked up. 'Alex!'

Pecking him on the cheek, she noticed him flush. 'Well, look at you. Back home in one piece – almost. How's the knee?'

'Getting there.' He hesitated. 'You heard about it, Bobby-Jo an' all?'

She nodded sadly, felt like mentioning Aban, but caught her breath.

He waved his walking stick in the direction of the hotel's front door. 'Thought I'd check out a couple of places.'

'Right,' Alex said, aware that whatever he was doing, his body language suggested he didn't want company. 'Well, I'll see you later – I'm your escort at the reception this evening, don't forget.'

He pulled a face, turned to leave. 'People, people and even more people,' he grumbled.

'Hey, make sure you check out the side of the big hotel on Times Square – can't miss it,' Alex shouted after him.

Outside, it was one of those crazy New York autumn days; the temperature already in the high eighties, the humidity at steam-bath level. McDermott put on a pair of sunshades, felt the first trickle of sweat roll down his body. A doorman, sizing him up in an instant, blew a sharp shrill blast on a whistle, which beckoned a yellow cab kerbside before McDermott could blink. Holding the car door open, the doorman wished him to 'have a good day, sir,' as McDermott slid in, careful to keep the strain off his outstretched leg.

'Got no a/c,' the cab driver said bluntly.

McDermott sighed, feeling the hot plastic of the car seat through his jeans. The Bradley was bad enough in the Baghdad heat although, with senses tuned to more important issues like life and death, discomfort always came second.

Now, he might as well have been sitting in an oven. 'The public library on Fifth Avenue, and go via Times Square,' McDermott gasped.

Despite all the cab's windows being open, only a trickle of warm air filtered through. Traffic crawled in a stultifying mass, blaring car horns reflecting everyone's inflamed frustration.

When they got to Times Square, McDermott was awash, his t-shirt clinging damply to his skin. He ogled the scene; crowds of shoppers packing the sidewalks, street artists entertaining gaggles of tourists, flashing signs everywhere competing with the sun. He glanced up at the towering Reuters building, dwarfing its neighbours like a concrete sequoia.

The cab stopped at a red light. He looked up again and, almost at once, turned cold. From the façade of a large hotel, a giant photograph stared down at him; a soldier with a child in his arms. It stretched several stories high. Unmissable. Beneath it, a wrap-around banner proclaimed 'A HERO COMES HOME'.

He gulped hard at the sight of himself. Shivering, he felt the agitation rising. He fought for air, gasping mouth open and hunching his shoulders up in a desperate effort to fill his lungs. But there was no respite from the crushing sensation and, closing his eyes, he was back in Baghdad, cradling a dead baby. Its eyes fixed him, now sneering and spiteful. Their gaze burrowed deep within him, accusing, mocking. And, for the first time in all his flashbacks, the eyes were bloodshot.

Shocked, he raised a hand to his lips. 'No,' he murmured.

The driver peered in his rear-view mirror, saw McDermott transfixed.

'Some guy, eh? Watched them putting it up yesterday,' he drawled. 'Passed it a dozen times already and I still get a lump in my throat.'

McDermott wanted to take off his sunglasses, wipe the cool sticky perspiration from his face. But, fearing recognition, all he could do was to sit back stiffly in his seat, saying nothing, his hands trembling. Relief only came when the cab finally dropped him at the library.

Taking his time and walking unsteadily up the steps of the columned building, he was forced to pause outside one of the three solid oak-panelled entrance doors. His mind swam. What had he let himself in for? This was all utter madness, a sham. He looked back down into the street. On the corner, a newspaper seller was plying his wares, too far away for McDermott to hear his staccato bark. But the billboard on the newspaper stand was plain to see. It said simply 'Silver Star Hero'.

Steeling himself, his face set firm, McDermott entered the building, convinced that what he was about to set in motion was his only escape. He'd decided there was no other choice.

No one had left him any alternative – not even God.

* * *

Alex's mobile phone buzzed impatiently. The tone annoyed her intensely. She told herself she *must* get round to changing it to something more melodic.

Kowolski's voice sounded urgent. 'You got the lieutenant with you there in the hotel?'

'No. And why do you think I'm in the hotel?' Alex resented the assumption.

'Is he with you for Chrissake?'

'No, he went out somewhere. I just reminded him to be back in good time for tonight's reception.'

185

'Shit. I told him to hang around. I could have had him on the lunchtime news – everybody's clamouring for a piece of the action,' Kowolski said, cutting the call.

Richard Northwood eyed Kowolski across the desk. 'Do you want us to send out a search party?'

Kowolski sighed. 'No, we'll have to make up for lost time. I just don't like missing any opportunity, no matter what.'

He rubbed his chin, hoping Northwood hadn't picked up on his near-fatal blunder with Alex. He'd known she was still in the hotel because of the flashing red dot on the screen map in front of them.

One thing intrigued Kowolski about the bug in Alex's phone. When he'd first mentioned it during a conversation with Northwood some time back, the guy hadn't responded with much interest. But from what the technician at the screen seemed to indicate, the CIA had been tracking her movements quite regularly over the past few days.

* * *

Alex cast a contented look around the spacious foyer of the hotel where McDermott's medal ceremony was to be staged. Her photographs featured prominently on smart display boards just to the right of the entrance. She'd agreed with the hotel manager that they should cordon off the exhibition until tomorrow's official opening and the area now lay in semi-darkness.

She checked her watch. Almost time to get back to the Carlyle and prepare for tonight's reception. Seeing Kowolski again would give her the opportunity of telling him face to face what she thought of his tricks. If nothing else, she'd feel better for giving him a blast.

'Very impressive show.' The voice from behind her, instantly recognisable, stopped her short. She turned, could feel the adrenalin starting to pump.

'Richard.'

Northwood leant forward as if to kiss her cheek. Alex moved back a step. Feeling the rebuff, he glanced about him, forcibly taking her arm and guiding her to a quieter corner.

'Let go of my arm or I'll scream,' she blazed.

'The game's over, Alex,' he said, slackening his grip.

'Is it now?'

'You'd only get your fingers burned meddling in stuff against the national interest.'

Defiance in her eyes, she spat out the words, 'And was it in the national interest to kill that poor man?'

'The autopsy showed he had a heart problem – he could've gone any time. It's the truth, believe me,' Northwood said, his face set cold. 'We've got your memory stick, Alex, and we know it's the only one.'

She stared at him, her mind in turmoil. How did they know it was the only one? Was he bluffing – or could they really tell?

Northwood kept up his gaze, steadfast and intimidating. Alex swallowed, suddenly with no fight left. She didn't want this turning into a prolonged set-to. Her eyes moistened as she thought of Steve and his advice to 'let it go'. How she wished he could be here at her side right now.

'You bastard,' she hissed, defeat evident in her slumped shoulders. Turning on her heel, she darted for the exit. She could feel Northwood's eyes tracking her, burning. She did not look back so she didn't see the thin cruel smile of triumph on his lips.

Her body was still shaking as she hailed a cab back to the Carlyle. This bruising round with Northwood might be over – for the moment, she thought. But she vowed with a ferocious passion that if the opportunity ever arose, she would resurrect the whole contest anew.

* * *

Showered, changed and feeling more glamorous than she had in ages, Alex gave McDermott a shy smile when he complimented her on her turnout.

'You're looking pretty smart yourself, Lieutenant,' she said, admiring his regimental dress uniform.

For the rest of the short journey to the reception, they rode the chauffeur-driven Cadillac in silence. She sensed McDermott's nervousness so quit the small talk.

'You ready for this?' Alex touched his arm lightly as they pulled up at the venue.

McDermott nodded. He gazed up at the monolith, which in the inky-blue murk beyond the glare of the streetlights, seemed to stretch ever-upwards. 'As ready as I'll ever be,' he groaned.

They walked through the ground-level mall, McDermott's boots click-clacking on the hard walkway, taking an elevator to the sixty-sixth floor. Two security men stood outside the doors to a private entertainment suite. Alex flashed their invitations and she and McDermott went in. A buzz from the guests already assembled dropped a couple of notches as they entered. Cameras started flashing, immediately making McDermott shift, uncomfortable with the attention. He felt like retracing his footsteps right back to the quiet of his hotel room. A waiter came by with a silver tray of champagne.

'Go on, enjoy yourself,' Alex said, thrusting a glass in McDermott's hand while choosing an orange juice for herself. He took a tentative sip. Not realising how dry his mouth had become, he knocked the rest of the glass back in two gulps.

From the middle of a pack of people, Kowolski came bounding over.

'Just great to see you guys,' he bubbled. 'Lieutenant, let me introduce you to a few people,' he said, dragging McDermott away. After a few strides, Kowolski turned round. 'By the way, Alex, you look good.'

Alex watched McDermott standing bashfully by Kowolski's side among a group of guests, a couple of the men in uniform.

Several of the women seemed to be sizing up the lieutenant. The cut of their clothes, the glitter of the jewellery brazenly stated they were from the right side of town. Alex wondered if their obvious interest in the lieutenant might be for their daughters – or themselves. A frown crossed her brow when she also observed McDermott accepting another glass of champagne. What had she started?

'One helluva story,' the deep voice beside her exclaimed. Alex turned to see the man towering above her, immediately noticed the three stars of his general's uniform and that he was slightly drunk.

'Are you with anyone?' The general seemed to rock on his heels as he spoke.

Alex wasn't sure how to take the question. The man looked older than her father. Surely he wasn't trying to pick her up?

'I'm with Lieutenant McDermott – I was embedded with his unit in Baghdad,' Alex said, mimicking the clicking of a camera.

The general's hopeful bushy eyebrows dropped half an inch, his mouth turning down at the corners. He gestured towards McDermott. 'A good soldier – I was part of the lieutenant's homecoming committee at the airport. He's done us proud.'

'Ah, yes, you made the front pages hugging him,' Alex remembered.

The general puffed his chest out. 'So, a photographer? Interesting life. Never been to Iraq myself. What did you make of the place?'

Alex looked him in the eye. 'Well, if you must know, General, it was a total crock of shit.'

He let out a belly laugh that shook his vast frame, almost spilling his drink. He leaned towards her, so close she could see a couple of stubby hairs at the base of his nose that he'd missed while shaving.

'Sweetheart, Afghanistan and Iraq are only numbers one and two on our list. There's another five to go.' He drew away, taking a swig of his drink, with a defiant 'well what do you

189

think of that' look in his eyes. 'But thank God I'll be out of it by then – retiring soon.'

Alex stared at him, shocked. 'Five... what, countries?'

The general nodded matter-of-factly. 'You go and ask a certain Mister Clark about it.'

Racking her brain, the only Clark of any prominence Alex could come up with was Wesley Clark, the retired former NATO Supreme Allied Commander in the Kosovo war. Did she mean him? The US declaring war on five more countries? Surely the general was talking nonsense.

Someone called him from nearby. 'Sorry, young lady, I gotta split. I take it you won't be going to Iraq again,' he said as a parting shot.

'Not on your life, never mind mine,' she shouted after him.

* * *

Kowolski beamed. He'd left McDermott talking to a couple of prominent columnists, one from *The Times*, the other from the *Washington Post*. Everything seemed to be going well. The lieutenant had loosened up, cracking a couple of jokes – even if they were terrible. People still laughed – out of politeness or respect. Kowolski couldn't figure which but at this moment didn't care.

He felt a tap on the shoulder. Alex faced him, confrontation written all over her face.

'Look,' he said, knowing what was coming, lowering his tone. 'I know I didn't mention the President but if I had, would you have still gone ahead with it all? I couldn't take the gamble that you'd cry off. Everything just seemed to come together out there. Anyway your results are fantastic. You're very talented, Alex.'

'Bullshit, Kowolski. You pig-stuck me like a slaughterman. You know exactly what I think of the lot of them yet you took me for the big ride.'

'It's the job – it goes with the territory, Alex. Someday I'll explain, not now. When all this Iraq shit's over and I get back here permanently, I was hoping we might work. . . I've got a few plans.'

'Count me out, buddy boy,' Alex said, her face earnest.

He stood closer, glanced about him. 'But you don't even know what I'm suggesting. Nothing's ever what it seems. I've had my fill, Alex.' He spread his arms out, palms upwards, as if in appeal. 'Being out there, seeing things first hand – it makes you think. War can change people, you know.'

'Jeez,' Alex said, brushing a hair from her face. 'You telling me you're actually human?'

Kowolski allowed himself a weak smile. 'Can a leopard change its spots? You might be surprised, Alex.'

They conversed for several more minutes, skirting Iraq and its implications and concentrating on her exhibition – which, she admitted, was looking good. Spotting McDermott momentarily on his own, Kowolski excused himself and left Alex to join him.

He put an arm around the lieutenant's shoulders, like a father to a son. 'I want to show you something,' Kowolski said, ushering McDermott over to stand at a quiet corner of the room. They stood facing a massive picture window, almost floor to ceiling, the impressive brightly-lit Manhattan skyline stretching out before them. Nearby, the art deco Chrysler building, its terraced crown illuminated in all its glory.

McDermott stood transfixed, his eyes following the radiance of this impressive building's spire pointing to the heavens.

Kowolski stared straight ahead. 'How's the knee?'

'Getting stronger every day, sir. I could probably get along without the stick.'

'Keep the stick,' Kowolski said. 'Definitely keep the stick.'

For a moment there was silence between them. Kowolski eventually pulled several folded pieces of paper from his pocket. They were stapled together and Kowolski carefully unfolded the file, handing it to McDermott.

'This is the rough itinerary for the following few weeks,' Kowolski said.

McDermott looked at the list. His head spun as he tried hard to focus on the contents. Eventually skipping over the detail, he registered only the names of the places – Boston, Philadelphia, Washington, Charleston, Miami. Then Houston, Okalahoma City, Los Angeles.

'We'll probably skip New Mexico and Arizona,' Kowolski said. 'Television and newspapers mainly, the odd radio show.'

McDermott's hands dropped to his side, shoulders sagging. 'I can't do it, sir. I just couldn't do it.' Eyes screwed tight shut, he began to sway.

Kowolski quickly retrieved the list, put an arm out to steady him. 'Take a good look out there, son,' Kowolski said, sweeping his free hand at the window as if he'd just conjured the glittering vista from thin air like a magician. 'See it, take it in. This could all be yours – it's all at your fingertips. You won't be in the army for the rest of your life. Think about that. Everyone in the whole goddamn country will know Lieutenant Matt McDermott and what he stands for. The top companies, banks, finance houses – they'd all be falling over themselves to have you on board. You could snap your fingers and name your own salary.'

McDermott shook his head slowly. 'Get thee behind me,' he hissed from the corner of his mouth.

Surprised, Kowolski glanced around nervously, hoping no one had heard the remark. 'Hey, take it easy fella, I just mean you could... '

'GET THEE BEHIND ME, SATAN,' McDermott thundered, turning away abruptly. He stormed unsteadily across the room and out of the door before Kowolski or anyone else could stop him.

* * *

Alex returned to the Carlyle in a cab feeling rather deflated, the evening having fizzled out with McDermott's sudden departure. Worried where he'd got to, and blaming herself for not keeping a check on his drinking, she stepped out of the elevator and approached his room with trepidation. She tapped lightly on his door – no answer.

Kowolski brushed off the incident, claiming it was one of McDermott's awful jokes that had backfired. Alex got no further than that. But she knew the lieutenant was the sensitive type. Who knew what he could get up to with alcohol on board?

In her own room before getting ready for sleep, she tried to call Steve but couldn't get through. She poured herself a glass of water and lay on the bed in a bathrobe flicking through the catalogue of her exhibition. The people at the photo lab had done a brilliant job of that, too.

A loud thump in the corridor startled her. She looked at the clock, realised nearly an hour had passed and that she must have dozed off.

Still groggy, another thump quickly followed by a groan, set her heart racing. Shouldn't she just call down to reception and report it? Looking through the door's spyglass didn't help – she couldn't see a thing. Another groan sent a shiver through her. In two minds whether to open the door or not, she let curiosity get the better of her. Making sure the security chain was in still place, she inched the door open a crack.

'Oh, for God's sake,' she said. McDermott lay slumped in a sitting position, his back against the door. When she opened it fully, he fell into the room. Glancing both ways along the corridor, she was relieved no one else had ventured out to investigate the noise. She spotted his walking stick, further up the corridor and quickly retrieved it.

By now, McDermott had managed to crawl through the doorway and lay on his back, moaning.

'Someone downstairs in the bar bought me a drink. I had a

large bourbon,' he mumbled, barely intelligible. 'The ceiling's moving up and down – up and down, round and round.' He started giggling.

Shit, this is all I need, she thought. 'Let's see if we can get you on the bed, okay?'

With much huffing and puffing, she managed to get him to a standing position, leaning on her heavily for support. Suddenly, he pushed her away, stumbling towards the bathroom and knocking over a chair in the process. Seconds later, she heard him throwing up.

Several minutes passed before he reappeared just as quickly, lurching past her and flopping on to her bed. Alex watched, horrified, as he went out cold before she could protest.

She couldn't leave him like this; sleeping in the uniform he'd wear to meet the President. Starting with his feet, she undid the laces of his boots and eased them free. She managed to get his tunic half off before he groaned, turning sideways. That helped her – a tug of the sleeve and, thankfully, it came loose. For a second, she considered his trousers but then thought better of it – to save McDermott's embarrassment in the morning rather than her own.

Resigned to sleeping in the armchair in the corner of the room, she suddenly hit on the idea: she'd use his room next door. If she could find his key, she'd be assured of a reasonable night's sleep.

Feeling a little guilty, she began searching his tunic, which she'd draped over a chair. Her fingers felt what she thought was the room card key. It was the same size, a folded piece of card, with the Carlyle's gold-embossed shield and crown on the front. But, below that, the words 'Central Park Runner's Guide'.

Alex opened it up. What the hell was McDermott doing with a runner's guide in his current state? There was a map of the park showing the different routes and their distances from the hotel. She was intrigued to read an estimated 20,000 people a day used the 'reservoir route'. As she went to return it, she noticed a series of numbers written in pen on the otherwise blank back page: 31–1–4 and 47–26–3. She stared at them. For a moment, she thought they might be someone's telephone number – an admirer from the reception. She repeated the numbers to herself, but they were meaningless and she put the card back.

Eventually finding his key card, Alex threw her clothes into a bag and made sure McDermott was comfortable. She was just about to leave the room when he started mumbling in his sleep. She turned, heard him call for his 'mom', then say something about a baby.

'Another crazy guy,' she whispered, switching off the light and closing the door behind her.

* * *

Across town, Richard Northwood sat at his desk reading a fresh intelligence report from Baghdad. He leaned back in his chair, rubbed his tired eyes. A feeling of relief swept over him. As far as Alex and her threat were concerned, he was off the hook. Her reaction when he bluffed her confirmed she had indeed only made the one copy of the al-Tikriti file.

That was why he asked the tech boys back at Langley to wipe all her emails from her main server and her computer. She might be upset when she found out – but it would enforce his warning that the CIA was not to be messed with. Despatching a trusted assistant to oversee the operation, they'd confirmed that every one of Alex's emails had been wiped at a stroke – without anyone reading as much as a line from any of them.

Northwood's only remaining worry; if Alex would shop him to his wife. But he felt fairly sanguine on that score. She wasn't the type.

Even in a war, there were some things you didn't stoop so low to do.

19

Lieutenant Matt McDermott woke with a start. For a few seconds he thought himself back in his Baghdad quarters. Jumping out of bed, dizziness overcame him. He reached out to steady himself on a chair. His tunic hung neatly over the back of it. Running his fingers lightly over the fabric, recollections of the previous night flooded back.

His head thumped. Finding a glass of water on the bedside table, he gulped it down. He let out a long, labouring sigh. A sense of foreboding clung to him like a shroud. This was his big day and it scared him rigid. Worse, Kowolski was going to put him through the mangle with a whistle-stop tour of heaven-knows how many towns and cities.

'Alex,' he called out, his mind in a whirl. The bathroom door was open – no sound from within. Had she slept alongside him, or in the armchair, got up early? He felt guilty he'd acted so badly. Flexing his bad knee, it felt stronger. His walking stick lay in the corner. It had been useful but he could manage without it. Kowolski's insistence that he still use it annoyed him. It was a sham. But no more than his whole life had become a depressing, never-ending charade.

There was a way out, however. He'd prayed harder than he ever had in his life, begged forgiveness, sought guidance. And he now felt the Lord had concurred with the only solution left open to him. McDermott knew that God would tell him when to act.

He glanced down at his creased trousers. His shirt, too, needed pressing. Studying the bedside phone, he pressed the button marked 'laundry'.

'Yes, Miss Steadman,' the voice answered, throwing him.

196

'I'm not who you think... I mean, I... Can you have someone press a shirt and trousers in a hurry?'

'Sure thing, sir,' the maid said with a hint of amusement that was lost on him. 'Just leave them in the bag from the closet and put it in the corridor. Have a nice day.'

'Have a nice day,' he mimicked. *You swap places with me – that'd be a very good day.*

Stripping to his underclothes, he found the bag, filled it, and put it in the corridor. He thought about ordering breakfast, but couldn't face the idea. Rather, he badly needed a shower. On his way to the bathroom, he reflected on his brief conversation with the laundry maid. He'd told her he wasn't who she'd thought. That was a remark he would dearly love to tell everyone who would get to know him over the next little while.

* * *

McDermott took great care to shave without nicking himself. Accepting a medal from the President with a face 'like a patchwork quilt' – as Kowolski had put it – would upset everyone. Not quite finished, he heard the doorbell chime. He grabbed the bath-towel, wrapping it around his waist, and went to answer it. Flecks of shaving foam fell on the carpet.

Opening the door revealed a man he didn't know. The guy carried a large bunch of red roses and, tucked under one arm, what McDermott guessed was a box of chocolates.

The man looked surprised. 'Oh, pardon me, sir,' he said, giving McDermott the once-over. 'I thought this was the room of Alex Stead.'

'That's right – it is,' McDermott said.

Steve Lewis took a half step backwards. His jaw dropped. Anger flashed in his eyes so that, when he took a step forward, McDermott thought he was going to be attacked.

Steve thrust the flowers and chocolates so hard into McDermott's bare chest that everything fell on the floor.

197

'Buddy, you tell her from me she's a first-class bitch,' he stormed, turning on his heel.

Shocked, McDermott scrabbled to pick up the pile at his feet. By the time he looked up, the corridor was empty and all he could hear were hurried footsteps echoing down the staircase. Panic set in. What on earth had he done?

* * *

He surveyed himself in the mirror, decided he'd pass muster. His fingers reached into the top pocket of his tunic. McDermott withdrew the hotel's running guide. Silently reciting the numbers to himself, he turned to the back page to check. They were locked in his memory.

The room phone rang.

'Alex. Where are you?'

'Right next door.'

Ten seconds later, he opened the door to let her in. She flopped into the armchair.

'You look smart, Lieutenant. Feeling okay?'

She could see he was not. Something was troubling him, big time. He looked a bag of nerves.

'I've screwed up, Alex. You had a visitor.' He gestured to the battered bouquet and the chocolates on a coffee table.

Detailing the early-morning incident, he gulped, his eyes blinking furiously. The quavering of his voice intensified as he watched her slowly sinking in despair, the look on her face crushing him. 'I'd dashed from the bathroom – just in a towel. I guess he thought...'

'Just tell me what he looked like,' Alex snapped, fearing the answer.

McDermott's description of the man meant only one person.

'Steve,' she said, jumping up, immediately bursting into tears.

'He was so angry... just disappeared. I'm sorry, Ma'am.'

'Why didn't you try to stop him? You could have shouted...'

'Everything happened so fast,' he said meekly, his body drooping. 'I wasn't thinking straight.'

Alex made for the door. He stopped her, his hands gently on her shoulders.

'You won't have time to find him now. Your show opens soon.'

She realised he was right. Her exhibition opened in an hour. McDermott was cutting the ribbon. Kowolski had invited the media. She knew she'd never find Steve in time, which made her more distraught. Where would she begin to look?

'Maybe he'll come back,' McDermott said, hope in his voice.

Alex's eyes blazed. 'He won't come back, you fool,' she spat. 'I thought you were trained to think on your feet. Do you realise what you've done? "Everything happened so fast",' she mimicked. 'You're supposed to be top gun, Lieutenant. Remember the raid? The goddamn Silver Star?'

Right then she felt the urge to slap his face, punch him, kick him, rouse him from this lumbering, unedifying torpor that had brought them to this. He was not the man she'd known in Baghdad.

'You might be a "hero", McDermott,' she said, emphasising the word with as much sarcasm as she could find, 'but, right now, you're nothing but a pain in the goddam fuckin' butt.'

Sinking back into the chair, she buried her head in her hands, sobbing, eyes closed. When she eventually opened them, McDermott was crouching beside her. He touched her hand. She saw he was crying, too.

'Everything's gone wrong, Alex,' he said, his voice low, breaking. 'I'm really sorry. It's all one big awful mess.'

'What has?' She knew she sounded petulant, but reckoned she had every right.

Now he took her hand in his. She stared at him, puzzled at his deadly serious expression.

'I'm no hero, Alex. It's a fraud,' he said softly. 'I killed a baby, a beautiful baby boy, his folks, too.'

Alex gasped, raised her free hand to her mouth. What was he saying? Was he out of his mind?

'His big brown eyes have lived with me ever since, every minute of every day – even in my sleep. I see him all the time. And I never knew his name...'

He broke down totally now, his body heaving in great sobs that shook Alex to her core. He lay his head on her lap.

'I did wrong, Alex, terrible, terrible wrong. Our dear Lord wants me to atone for my sins.'

She began to lightly stroke his neck, unable yet to take it all in.

What had they done to this poor man? Just what in the name of God had they made him do?

* * *

McDermott walked grim-faced with Alex into the reception foyer hosting her show. She linked arms with him at the last minute, gave him a squeeze. Now that he'd told her the full story, she understood his anguish. It was a dreadful secret to bear. Although it had left her with mixed emotions – anger, pity, confusion – part of her was glad he'd shared his deeply disturbing burden. She could feel the torment he'd been under when he explained everything.

'Who else knows?' Alex had said, aware she had to tread softly. 'Kowolski?'

McDermott shook his head.

God, she thought, if Kowolski ever did find out – how would he take it? *Like an atomic bomb*, she considered. She had to admit it was to his credit that he wasn't part of the pantomime – at least not to this extent. So Kowolski had been duped, too. For a fleeting moment she almost felt sorry for him.

'You'll have to live the lie,' Alex told him, not sure she was entirely right. 'It happens to everyone at some time in their life. You can't change the past. Be strong, think of the greater good.'

She didn't really believe her own words. This government,

the President, his despicable war-mongering cohorts, the Richard Northwoods of the world – they'd be the beneficiaries of McDermott's intolerable dilemma. But, what was it to them of the broken spirit of just another soldier fighting for the flag? Thousands had made the ultimate sacrifice; ten times more injured, physically maimed for life. As many again had to carry the miserable burden of their mental scars within a grotesque mask that no one but themselves could see.

* * *

Steve Lewis watched the pair of them from behind a pillar at the rear of the fifty or so people gathered around the exhibition ribbon. Sickened that Alex had obviously been two-timing him, spinning him a pack of lies, he still wanted to catch sight of her one last time before he left town.

His stomach churned at the thought he'd lost her. Their months of long-distance courtship had meant absolutely everything to him. She'd said the same. Now he felt such a jerk.

Alex was preoccupied with the media. Smiling and laughing, she posed effortlessly for their pictures. A television reporter ushered her aside for an interview.

Then, McDermott was asked to step forward to cut the tape. Cameras flashed as he flourished the scissors and snapped them shut to signal the exhibition was open. The foyer resounded to the applause.

Steve stole one last glance at Alex and quickly turned away from the scene. He didn't see a waiter bearing down on him, carrying a tray of drinks. The waiter tried to avoid him but failed, colliding full tilt. Glasses flew in all directions, tumbling as if in slow motion and landing on the tiled floor with a tremendous crash.

For a moment, Steve froze. Everyone at the reception looked his way. His and Alex's eyes met. Sidestepping the mess, he hurried towards the hotel exit, dashing through without looking back.

'Steve!' Alex shouted in vain. But he had soon disappeared.

ROY DAVID

Giving chase, she ran after him into the street. People hogged
the sidewalk in both directions. She couldn't see him anywhere.
Frantic, her heart thumping, she hesitated, didn't know which
way to go. Eventually turning right, she threaded her way
through the crowds, bumping into people and not stopping to
apologise. After travelling a block, she gave up.

She stood outside a shop, body bent in devastation. Among
all these people – coming and going in their daily lives – she had
never felt so alone, so bereft. Her tears flowed freely.

He saw her from a doorway where he'd taken refuge, just in
case she'd decided to follow him. Satisfied no one else was with
her, he reached out.

Alex felt the gentle touch on her shoulder. She spun round.
'Oh, Steve, thank God,' she spluttered.

He stood back, taut, eyes flashing with indignation. 'Why,
Alex? After everything we said to each other, just tell me why,'
he said, arms tightly folded.

A smile lit up her face. Then she started laughing, shaking her
head in disbelief. 'You crazy, crazy guy,' she said, sniffing,
reaching in her pocket for a tissue. 'McDermott slept in my
room – I slept in his.'

'What?' Steve frowned, trying to take it in. 'I thought… '

'Of course you did. He crashed out in my room, drunk. I
stayed the night next door.'

'Oh, jeez,' he said, starting to laugh. He held out his arms.
She fell into his embrace, smothering him with kisses. They
clung to each other for so long that a group of Japanese tourists
stopped to stare and giggle. One took a photograph.

Strolling back to the hotel, arms around each other, Kowolski
strode forward to greet them. 'Well, who's the lucky guy?' he
said, eyeing Steve.

Introductions made, Kowolski guided them to a far corner of
the foyer, away from the guests arriving for the presentation.
'There's someone here I want you to meet, Alex,' he said,
checking his watch.

She saw the old couple sitting on a sofa. The man perched on the edge of the seat, his body language stiff and uncomfortable, the woman fidgeting with a large handbag. McDermott sat between them. He stood up as they approached.

'My folks,' he said, gesturing. McDermott's father, older than Alex imagined and with a shock of white hair, got up.

'Our boy's been telling us about your time out in Baghdad an' all,' he said, shaking hands all round. 'Your photos sure look good, Ma'am.'

Alex sat down next to McDermott's mother, immediately striking up a conversation in an attempt to put her at ease. Kowolski's phone rang so he excused himself, sauntering away.

'How long?' Kowolski spluttered. 'Ten goddam minutes. You kidding me?' He snapped his cell phone shut, striding back to the company. 'I think we should be making our way in,' he said. Looking for someone to confide in, he chose Steve, hanging back as Alex led the way into the hotel ballroom.

'Problem?' Steve said. 'If there's no room for me, I can always. . . '

'No, you're fine Steve, just fine,' Kowolski said, slapping him on the back. 'My trouble's with the President. His guys tell me he can only spare ten minutes for the presentation.'

Steve pulled a face. 'Alex would like it if he didn't show at all.'

'Yeah, well I got a job to do. Not everyone appreciates how important it is – even the man himself.'

They joined the others at a large round table near the stage. Minutes later, a small army of waiters appeared, carrying trays of food and fanning out to serve what Kowolski estimated was a gathering of around 200 people.

He glanced to the three tables on his left; the assembled media people seemed to be enjoying themselves – half the battle. Kowolski stopped a passing waiter and asked him to deposit several more bottles of wine with them. Hopefully, they'd be chilled out by the time of the lieutenant's press conference, arranged for after the presentation.

His main concern was McDermott. Kowolski had to keep him on a short leash. The guy was becoming unpredictable. God forbid a repeat of his storming exit the night before. Excuses wore thin second time around.

McDermott had hardly touched a mouthful of his lunch. Sitting quietly between his folks, a faraway look in his eyes, he pushed the plate aside and stood up. Kowolski watched his every move, a nervousness in the pit of his stomach that meant he'd only toyed with his own food, pushing it around in ever-increasing circles.

'Bathroom,' McDermott said.

'Me, too.' Kowolski slid his chair back. He didn't really expect McDermott to take fright and wander off but, with so much at stake, he was taking no chances. 'Your stick, Lieutenant,' he said, handing it to him, frowning and looking at his watch.

McDermott gave him a querulous look, felt all eyes on him as he left the room. Kowolski ushered him between tables until there was enough space to draw alongside.

'You okay?'

McDermott sighed, blinking. 'Guess so.'

'Be over soon,' Kowolski said, patting the lieutenant's arm.

'Before your wonderful grand tour begins, you mean?'

Kowolski gulped. He'd always found McDermott a supine sort of guy. Just lately, though, splinters of sarcasm had begun to appear, a worrying volte-face that unsettled him. McDermott's mood carried a disdain that wasn't merely the product of their familiarity – Alex had mentioned it, too.

'My wonderful grand tour is going to make you famous, Lieutenant. You just think of the money and remember what I told you last night.'

McDermott stopped in his tracks. He turned to face Kowolski, a thin contemptuous smile on his face. 'I will not be tempted by you, or your den of robbers,' he said, hurrying into a cubicle and slamming the door shut. Kowolski washed his hands, splashed warm water on his face, exhaling deeply. Why couldn't his hero be some simple ordinary Joe? Someone who'd do as he was told without complicating matters – without even thinking.

Back at their table, Kowolski gave the master of ceremonies a nod to indicate he was ready for the formalities to begin. He sat forward on the edge of his seat, playing with the strap on his watch. Glancing around the room, he counted eight presidential security staff in place, easily recognisable by their sober blue suits, dark glasses and earpieces. All would be carrying the Sig Sauer .229 secret service revolver, two or three of them an Uzi sub-machine gun or the Heckler and Koch MP5.

Then the general strode forward, planting himself at the lectern. He began regaling the audience with the 'many fine and courageous deeds of our brave men and women serving their country out in I-raq.'

'But we're here to celebrate and congratulate just one man, a man who represents all those I've just spoken about,' the general said, looking about him as if to dare anyone to differ. 'Lieutenant Matthew McDermott, please step forward.'

McDermott rose from his seat and walked unsteadily on to the stage. Kowolski stood up briskly, leading the applause. The rest of the room took their cue and followed suit. The general clasped McDermott to his giant frame. 'Son, see how proud they are,' he whispered.

'Thank you, sir,' McDermott replied, blinking, turning red.

'And now folks,' the general said, 'please welcome our commander-in-chief, the President of the United States.'

The ballroom's PA system burst into life with the President's traditional musical welcome, 'Hail to the Chief'.

Alex leapt from her seat, gesturing for Steve to stay. Turning to Kowolski, she pulled a face. 'Excuse me, I gotta go and puke,' she scowled, rushing towards the main exit. Pushing one of the double doors outwards, she crashed it into the backs of two more secret service men guarding the entrance. Startled, she saw their hands instinctively reach inside their jackets. Alex gave them her cutest smile. 'I need a smoke,' she lied, pressing on.

Outside, NYPD uniformed officers mixed with other security men, marshalling the passing crowds. A fleet of motorcycle outriders sat astride their machines, two front, four rear of the President's armoured Cadillac DeVille, its twin flags fluttering in a stiff breeze. People stopped to ogle at a vehicle they'd only ever seen on the television news and they were quickly moved on.

Suddenly, a small group of protesters appeared, marching towards the hotel entrance. Alex heard the tinny voice on a megaphone, leading a chant:

'Wadda we want?'

'Out of Iraq.'

'When do we want it?'

'Now.'

A line of policemen surrounded the group, pushing them back towards the fringes of the onlookers.

Alex went to go back inside the hotel, but she was stopped by a row of policemen blocking the way.

'Sorry, Ma'am, the President's on his way out soon – stand back,' a burly cop said.

A flurry of activity started up like a desert wind; secret agents spoke into their lapel mouthpieces, agitated and scurrying. The outriders kicked their Harley-Davidsons into life, red lights flashing. Two Highway Patrol vehicles screeched to a halt. Several others, parked at an angle, had already blocked off the traffic in Times Square, which, for a change, soon went eerily quiet.

Alex found herself behind a line of cops. People strained and jostled to catch a glimpse of the most powerful man in the world. She was pushed up against a policeman, could feel the solid power of the man.

For a few seconds, she was back in a dusty street in Baghdad, fear rising as the shots rang out. She felt the same panic as when wedged into that doorway behind McDermott. Gasping for air, she had to concentrate to quell the breathlessness. A vision of her Kandahar nightmare flashed into her mind, a bloodied arm lay across her throat so that she couldn't breathe. It was slowly choking her.

Frantic, she tapped the policeman hard on his left shoulder. He turned round and she slipped to his right, squeezing past him before he could react. The hotel entrance doors opened. Alex could see the President walking brusquely towards her, surrounded by half a dozen agents. One tried to grab her wrist, but she pushed him aside. The President fixed her, a look of puzzlement on his face. Alex glared at him and he avoided her gaze, walking on and scurrying through the open door of his waiting car.

She just wished she'd had her camera to hand. The sheepish look on the President's face would have been a sight to capture.

* * *

On the way back to Alex's apartment hand in hand, Steve volunteered to collect a takeaway from a well-regarded Thai restaurant on the next block.

'Good,' Alex said. 'I'll go up and make sure the place is presentable.'

Opening her front door, she rushed over to her desk. Picking up the envelope containing the Northwood email, she stared at it for a few seconds. Then she switched on the small machine on the floor and watched as the last remnants of a previous life turned to shreds and was gone.

Later, nestled on the sofa with Steve, they watched McDermott's medal presentation on the early-evening television news bulletins. Most channels made it their lead story and some stations followed on with a piece from the post-ceremony interview.

'This guy's gonna' be big,' Steve said.

'I'm afraid he is,' Alex said, sighing. 'But will he handle it?'

She turned to Steve, her face questioning. He ran the back of a finger gently down her cheek.

'Can we forget about it all for now?' he said. 'I've got two days left of my R and R – how do you think we should spend it?'

Alex smiled, drawing him closer and letting him begin kissing her passionately.

20

Gene Kowolski trod what was becoming a well-worn path of unease on the cheap beige carpet of his room, even though he and McDermott had only been on camp a little over twenty-four hours.

Some people said the cantonment of Fort Hood had that effect on its visitors. The sheer size of the world's largest military base and its 70,000 inhabitants meant it radiated drabness on a large scale; a sprawling mass of Texas flat land, its unrelenting uniformity like a repressive governor on the soul.

He'd felt the depression descending like a fog since passing the small town of Copperas Cove on the 190, heading east to the spread that now consumed him. The base struck him as almost as hot and dusty as Baghdad itself. Kowolski's demeanour had not been helped by the lieutenant's address to several hundred selected troops, a short presentation billed 'My Heroism in Iraq'.

Kowolski watched frowning as McDermott faltered, forgetting many of the points they'd rehearsed. He glanced round the conference hall straining for any sign of a negative reaction. But the audience, while not exactly overwhelmed, seemed surprisingly receptive. For a moment, he wondered if he'd been too hard on McDermott, expected too much from the guy. Was Kowolski's coaching, his urging, that difficult to comprehend? Perhaps so, after all, McDermott was a soldier, not a politician.

Dissecting the performance afterwards, Kowolski still couldn't get away from thinking the lieutenant's frame of mind had deteriorated in the week they'd been on the road. The media response didn't reveal that, of course. True to a man, they cheered and burnished the emerging star until it shone as a

ROY DAVID

beacon to the thousands of men and women serving in Iraq. Those soldiers waiting to embark for their first taste of the action, too, could not have failed to be inspired by the media's embellishment. Newspapers and television pushed McDermott to the fore, the glorification of one soldier's deeds like a salve for the nation's conscience. Even his home town was now festooned with yellow ribbons on every street and municipal building, each bearing the lieutenant's name in blue. Makers of the two-dollar strips of cloth were working hard to keep up with demand from the rest of the country.

Although it was still too early to measure the McDermott effect on the President's popularity, the latest opinion polls were a major source of irritation. Kowolski grimaced as he devoured the statistics, showing a slip in the ratings of three per cent. And this before the President made an appearance in Congress to ask for more funds to sustain the war. Kowolski heard the amount being sought for next year was more than 80 billion dollars. People were beginning to get restless, impatient as to how long the bloody mess of Iraq was going to feature in their lives.

He forced himself to take stock of his situation. Once the McDermott road show finished, he knew he'd have to return to Baghdad. The thought now filled him with dread. Initially, he'd envisaged a three-month stint there – six months max – returning to Washington to a bucketful of praise for a job well done. The chaos of Iraq was already entering its seventh month and, from what he'd picked up, it was going to go on for a good deal longer.

Pouring himself a whisky, he threw it back in one, his mind lurching one way then another. Could he face the chaotic dissonance of Baghdad again? The bombings, the shootings, the destruction? How much longer could he hold out? He'd gone there full of it: full of optimism, full of himself. There'd even been a tinge of excitement that he'd be working in the middle of a war zone – perhaps the same buzz that drove media correspondents from country to strife-ridden country.

210

But he now knew it was a mirage, the reality too stark, too brutal to initially imagine. It wasn't just the McDermott situation that had deflated his enthusiasm. In a way, the lieutenant's strange behaviour only magnified a growing realisation within him. Kowolski's time away from Iraq had given him time to think. For the first time in this present role of his working life, he seriously wondered if he wasn't cut out for the job. First-hand experience led him to second-hand thoughts. The reality of Iraq had torn away the mantle of his misconceptions in a way he'd never imagined.

He let out a sigh, turned his head slowly side to side to ease the stiffness in his shoulders. Replenishing his drink, he checked the time and picked up the phone to the camp's medical centre. Under the pretext of sending McDermott for a check-up on his knee, Kowolski had arranged for a psychiatrist to carry out the examination, see if he could subtly deduce the lieutenant's mental state.

'You had time to form an opinion on our boy?'

'Ah, yes,' the doctor said. 'The good news or the bad?'

Kowolski took a slug of his drink. 'Might as well let me have both barrels.'

'Well, his knee's fine providing he doesn't over-exert himself. Mentally, I'd say he's in something of a mess.'

'I figured that, but how bad?'

Kowolski heard the doctor draw in breath. 'Hard to say without a thorough examination of his mind. Could be paranoia, might even be paraphrenia.'

'Para what?'

'He admitted to having hallucinations. I asked him how he was sleeping, he muttered something about a baby – seemed to be tormented about it. Couldn't press too much, of course. Mentioned God a couple of times.'

'Yeah, our boy's a Bible freak.'

'You want me to see if we can take it further?'

Kowolski sighed. 'No, doc. Our trip's on a tight schedule. Maybe some other time.'

'As long as you're aware the engine might just pack up before your journey's over.'

'Right,' Kowolski said, replacing the receiver. He blew out his cheeks, finished his drink and put his glass down with a thud.

Just what he needed – a kid who might go off the rails at any minute.

* * *

Alex was on a high. The orders for her work just kept rolling in. Sitting at her desk, she allowed herself a smile. Kowolski had promised her the exhibition would be successful and he was right. There was nothing like a burst of good publicity to ramp up the reputation. She flipped through her diary, entering her latest assignment; a week's photo-shoot in Hawaii on a calendar for an international company based in New York. Her only downer, that Northwood had somehow wiped her emails. But she'd resigned herself to losing that particular battle and pushed it to the back of her mind.

It was Steve who had really set her heart alight. Two days and nights together put the seal on their relationship. Their parting was a bitter-sweet affair.

'Wish we could roll the clock forward a few months so I'm out of there,' Steve said at the airport, holding her tight.

'Tell me, Mister Lewis,' Alex said, pulling away lightly, her head to one side, 'was it worth all that time, money and effort flying here when you could have been in Kuwait for a few days touring the galleries?'

He gave her an extra squeeze, kissed her firmly. 'No contest, your honour,' he laughed loudly, his face alight.

She glanced around her apartment, decided a spot of tidying up was needed. A stack of newspapers and magazines littered the sofa. She'd been avidly monitoring the McDermott coverage, his photograph adorning every front page. One picture was particularly pleasing; her photograph of the lieutenant with the little boy that the *New York Times* requested from her exhibition and used big. Alex cut that page out for her portfolio.

Her mobile bleeped, signalling an incoming message. Checking it, she gasped. A short note from Greg telling her he'd had enough and was returning to Australia. He enclosed a number for Farrah al-Tikriti, saying that she and the boys had moved to Jordan.

Alex sat down, cradling the phone and staring blankly at the text. For the last few days, Iraq had been blissfully far from her mind. A sudden stab of remorse flickered through her as she thought of the family without their beloved Aban. His death had saddened her beyond words and she couldn't begin to imagine what it had done to his cherished wife and children. Now they had to find a new life for themselves in a foreign country.

She looked at her watch, let out a deep breath. It was early evening in Iraq, Jordan on a similar time difference. Should she call Farrah? What would she say? Words, any words, she knew would be inadequate. Eventually steeling herself, she dialled the number and waited, her heart pounding.

'Hello, Farrah al-Tikriti.' The voice was weak, quizzical.

'Farrah, it's me, Alex Stead in New York.'

'Oh, Alex,' Farrah said softly, despair all too evident. 'You are so kind to call.'

'Dear Farrah, I was so so sorry to hear... it's the least I can do to speak to you. Greg tells me you are in Jordan.'

'Yes, we came, we had to get out. They are killing each other now, just as Aban warned.' The mention of her husband's name started Farrah sobbing.

Alex gulped, the tears welling. 'Is there anything I can do?'

'No, we are safe here. I have arranged schooling for the boys.' Farrah started crying full flow, her words soon spluttering into a mournful wail. 'There were marks on the body, horrible red marks, deep bruises. He is at rest now but what they did to him...'

Alex wound up the conversation, totally disconcerted, an empty feeling inside that made her feel nauseous. She hoped she hadn't sounded trite. But what could anyone say or do to make the poor woman feel any better? Taking a tissue from a drawer, she dabbed at her eyes. 'The bastards,' she spat, sinking into a chair. Richard Northwood and his group of thugs had contributed to Aban's death without a doubt – just as much as if they had killed him, like Farrah claimed.

Her chin taut, she got up and walked wearily to the bathroom. She splashed cold water on her face. Looking in the mirror, Alex reaffirmed the vow she'd already made to herself: if there ever came an opportunity to strike back, then, by God, she would take it with both hands.

* * *

From his billet window close to the airfield, McDermott watched as the numbers of troops began to swell on the apron. Every couple of minutes, small groups of soldiers exited a process centre, its double doors opening automatically and flooding the tarmac with light from within the building. Further away, a C-5 Galaxy stood motionless, engines thrumming, the big beast stark against the night sky, its nosecone up so that it looked like a giant bird of prey that had come to grief.

With trembling hands, he stashed several more items into a bug-out bag, hastily acquired that afternoon from a store on the base's mid-post mall. He secured the last item, a pack of glow sticks, and fastened the bag, content it resembled a fair attempt at a survival kit. On the airfield, an Abrams tank inched forward up the nosecone ramp and was soon swallowed into the aircraft's belly.

McDermott took a deep breath and stared into nowhere. He just knew this was his moment. He'd been so patient, so trusting, waiting for God's guidance. But, as the end of September had drawn almost to a close, his despair intensified and

214

he'd felt his will wavering. As hard as he'd prayed, doubts still flickered, barbs of confusion tormented.

Then, at once, like a miracle, everything slotted into place; the Lord suddenly offered him the opportunity. In triumph, he could now set out on his journey of atonement.

Chatting to a younger fellow officer who'd witnessed McDermott's presentation, he'd discovered the guy was bound for Iraq with his men that evening on their first tour. The C-5 he was looking at right now would be refuelling at the Rhein-Main airbase in Frankfurt, flying on to Basra and, finally, Baghdad.

'I might just join you,' McDermott said, suddenly flushed with the idea.

'You serious?'

'Why not? I have a piece of paper that gets me on to any flight, any time,' he said, tapping his top pocket. 'I have to get back sooner or later – special assignment,' McDermott smiled. 'But you don't say anything to anyone, now.'

'No, sir,' the officer said, gesturing with a sweep of his hand to zip his mouth. 'It'd be a real privilege to fly with you, though.'

McDermott picked up his bag, stopped at the door and glanced around the room. A surge of excitement rippled through him and he clicked his heels, laughing out loud.

Gently closing the door behind him, he marched purposefully down a sweep of corridors and into the processing centre. The room was empty. Through the glass doors he could see the troops, now in single file, about to board the aircraft. He stepped out on to the tarmac and tagged on to the end of the line.

Up ahead, the younger lieutenant was checking his men aboard from the top of the ramp. His face broke into a grin when he spotted McDermott.

'Welcome aboard, Lieutenant,' he said.

McDermott reached for his pocket. 'You need my credentials?'

'I think we all know who you are, sir. Stow your bag and take a seat.'

Within minutes, the C-5 lumbered out on to the runway. Moments later, it took its short take-off and they were airborne. McDermott felt as if he were floating, a curious sense of well-being pervaded his soul. He closed his eyes and saw a baby smiling at him.

Presently, he was joined by his new-found friend who sat in the next seat. McDermott studied him. Did he once look like this, full of the enthusiasm he now saw shining in the young man's face? The eagerness, the fervour, the innocence?

'Well, we're all ready to go and kick ass out there,' the man said, nodding to himself. 'Yes, sir, we sure as hell are ready.'

McDermott looked the man in the eye, smiling serenely. 'Just make sure you temper your wrath with mercy, my friend. "If the spirit of the ruler rises up against thee, leave not thy place; for yielding pacifieth great offences",' McDermott said, blinking several times. He reached for his Bible. 'Now, I have some reading to do,' he said, brusquely.

The young officer gulped, pulled a face that held signs of disappointment. 'Sure thing, Lieutenant,' he muttered as he got up to return to his own seat. McDermott watched him slope off, arms hanging loosely at his side.

* * *

It was cooler now it was dark. A rare wind blew welcome gusts of air through the gap in the wall of the Basra city morgue. Abu Khamsin finished his cigarette and took one last gasp of the breeze, then lifted the mask to his face once more.

He could never quite get used to the smell of death, even though he was now considered an old hand. Working originally in Baghdad in the place they called 'the slaughterhouse', he had leapt at the chance of a transfer to Basra for more money. Baghdad without dear Aban and his family held nothing for him.

It was also better now it was dark; no pitiful, wailing relatives to confront, no witnessing the pain and terror in their eyes as they sought the remains of their loved ones.

In one room, corpses were now being stacked on top of each other to save space. One section had been casually divided for body bits; the major part of anyone's remains stored in its appropriate place, bottom half or top.

It was a system that seemed to work. Earlier in the day, a family identified the lower body part of a young man from the patterned socks they'd bought him for his recent eighteenth birthday. Abu Khamsin had to guide them to the other pile of 'top bits', then let them rummage among the grisly mound. There, they found the boy's arm, identifying it from the cheap wristwatch still attached. He felt so embarrassed by their gratitude as they left – carrying their haul away in a black trash bag for burial.

No longer did he want to hear from grieving brothers and mothers and fathers details of their loved one's lives. Too personal. Too upsetting to hear of the young man due to get married and shot dead for overtaking an army convoy on his rush to the wedding. Too horrifying to learn that a mother and her three daughters had been crushed to death in their car by an Abrams tank that did not stop at a busy road junction.

No, it was much quieter now it was dark.

He brushed flecks of ash from his red-stained apron and walked back inside, glad he'd managed to buy a new pair of sturdy boots with thick-tread soles to stop him slipping on the blood-puddled floor.

There would be three trucks tonight, big Russian-made open-backed diesels that would be stacked high to trundle the unclaimed spirits on the arduous 200 mile journey north to Najaf, the sacred city. There, the bodies would be dumped, without ceremony, in a mass grave just outside the city.

But Abu Khamsim knew that, in that wondrous place, the

217

eternally-open arms of the beloved saint, Ali Ibn Abi Talib, would take them to his merciful bosom.

And then to paradise.

* * *

McDermott felt safer behind the sunglasses. Unsure as to how far his fame had spread, he wanted to take no chances even if he seemed to be the only US soldier at Basra airport. Wearing them also meant he wouldn't have to make eye contact with anyone, encourage a conversation. But no one gave him more than a casual glance, accustomed as they were to the movement of troops of a dozen nationalities. Surrounded by Brits, he joined a line passing through what he anticipated was some form of immigration. He handed in his common access card, hoping that would be sufficient. It was quickly returned after only a cursory examination.

Outside, a melee of vehicles swarmed like insects around a lamp. Walking away from the main terminal exit, he melted into a quiet area where the shadows of the growing darkness made him almost invisible. Then he watched and waited.

After fifteen minutes, a Chevy SUV headed slowly his way, gliding to a halt on the opposite side of the road. McDermott strained his eyes to count its occupants but was unable to see through its darkened windows. He heard the driver's door slam shut, could just about make out a figure standing near the front of the vehicle. The driver lit a cigarette. From the glimmer of the man's lighter, McDermott deduced he was Iraqi and civilian.

Waiting a little longer, McDermott took a deep breath, exhaling ever so slow, half-convinced the driver might otherwise hear him. He reached for his revolver, his heart starting to hammer, gently unclipped the holster and withdrew the gun.

The driver coughed, a rasping sound that, even at distance, grated on McDermott's ears. Then he flicked his cigarette butt high into the air and got back into the vehicle. Seeing the tell-tale red glow cartwheel to the ground, the lieutenant rushed to the passenger side, dropped his bags in the road and yanked the door open. The man's black moustachioed face, surprised at first, quickly turned to wide-eyed terror as he stared into the barrel of McDermott's gun.

'Ya'allah,' McDermott barked, throwing his bags into the back and sliding into the passenger seat.

Urged 'let's go' by the lieutenant's command, the driver started up and pulled away, his hands shaking at the wheel.

As they approached security at the airport entrance, McDermott lowered his window. He gestured for the driver to do likewise, pushing the pistol hard into the man's ribs. Two British soldiers appeared, one either side. McDermott gave his crispest salute. Each soldier opened a rear passenger door and glanced in. Satisfied, one gave the thumbs up to the control booth to raise the barrier.

At a crossroad, the driver stopped and began gibbering, throwing his hands up excitedly.

'Shamaal, Baghdad,' McDermott said, waving the gun at him.

They drove in silence with little traffic, hitting the main road north. After several miles of open desert, McDermott ordered the driver to stop. Fearing the worst, the man began blabbering, a stream of spittle drooling from his lips. McDermott waved the pistol at him, gesturing for him to get out. When the interior light came on, he could see the man had tears in his eyes.

Quickly sliding over to the driver's seat, McDermott slammed the door shut and sped off. A feeling of euphoria immediately swept over him. He slapped the driver's wheel with his hands, thumping the padded leather and emitting a series of loud joyous whoops.

He would soon be at his goal. And whatever happened to him from then on, it would simply be God's will.

21

Kowolski twisted his fingers in fury and frustration. McDermott was missing – gone more than twenty-four hours – yet he couldn't tell anyone. They should have been on their way to the West Coast by now and he'd had to cancel the media shows there, trotting out the lame excuse that his boy was feeling under the weather and that they'd try to catch up.

He sat, stunned, unable to think straight. McDermott's room was empty when he'd visited, the bed not slept in. An envelope addressed to Kowolski contained a hurried, scrawled note. It said simply, 'I have to atone for my sins – sorry.'

But what the fuck did that mean? After his conversation with the doctor, Kowolski felt McDermott was capable of doing just about anything. Discreet enquiries revealed he had not been seen leaving the encampment and his name wasn't on the passenger log of three outgoing flights. But there was no way Kowolski could raise a hue and cry about the disappearance, organise search parties or the like. As their hosts had reminded him, Fort Hood covered some 350 square miles. Where would you begin to look?

He shook his head in disbelief. Surely the kid hadn't gone off to some quiet corner and topped himself? Maybe he'd just wanted a break from the tour and was chilling out someplace. After all it was pressure-barrel stuff. His instinct told him to give it a little longer.

But the more he tumbled the situation in his mind, the more he worried. If the kid didn't appear, wouldn't they turn round and blame him for pushing the soldier too far? All his carefully-nurtured work would be in vain. As if suddenly cognisant of the repercussions, he let out a gasp, swallowing hard. The whole shebang was turning into his worst nightmare. There was no way he could keep the lieutenant's non-appearance secret, either. The very nature of his scheme involved every facet of the media.

He turned on the television, tuned into to a daytime chat show that was starting shortly and where McDermott should have been appearing. Leaning forward, shoulders hunched, he switched up the volume. The show opened with a still; Alex's picture of McDermott with the little boy. The anchor revealed that the country's number one hero had become unwell so would not be appearing. They wished him a speedy recovery, moving on to the next item.

Kowolski pursed his lips. What should he do? McDermott didn't depend on alcohol so wouldn't have gone on a bender. Women appeared to hold little interest, either. It was most unlikely he'd be found in any of the bars of the locality – word would soon get back. He considered the possibility of a chat with the military police chief on camp, but discarded the idea. The last thing he wanted was the hint of scandal associated with the President's boy.

Then the thought hit him between the eyes. Of course McDermott wasn't your ordinary Joe. Kowolski had used the very words that summed up the lieutenant: a Bible freak.

He picked up the phone and spoke to a receptionist. 'Say, how many churches or chapels do you have on base?'

'Just one moment, sir,' the woman said. A moment later, she came back: 'My colleague and me just counted ten, sir. But it could be eleven if you count the spiritual centre. You should find them all on the chaplain section of our website.'

'Thanks,' Kowolski said, immediately switching on his lap-top. The chapels would be all over camp, taking hours to visit even with a driver at his disposal. He decided the best thing would be to use the phone, casually mention that McDermott had said he was off to pray but hadn't specified which church. 'Is he with you, perhaps?'

221

The task took him longer than he envisaged. He got a couple of cleaners in two of the places who seemed not to understand what he was talking about. Striking them off his list, he reasoned the chapels must be closed if they were being cleaned.

On another call, the man he spoke to seemed anxious to discuss McDermott's Silver Star. He prattled on for several minutes before Kowolski had to cut him short.

At the end of the session, he was no further down the line. Wherever McDermott had gone, it now dawned on Kowolski that it wasn't at Fort Hood. He shook his head. What did the lieutenant have to atone for anyway? The kid had everything going for him if only he'd be smart enough to see.

He put in a call to McDermott's home. They hadn't heard from him for several days. They asked if their son would be able to visit his home town. 'Folks are mighty proud of our boy. We could put on a civic reception with a band an' all,' his father said. Kowolski promised he'd see what he could do.

Stumped as to where to go next, Kowolski finished off the rest of the half-bottle of whisky and turned in for the night, restless for what seemed like hours before finally drifting off.

* * *

Alex stared at her mobile phone, puzzled. Kowolski had sent a message with a number to call – but to make it from a public box. Quickly dressing, she left her apartment and walked the two blocks to the kiosk armed with plenty of coins.

'Alex, thanks for calling back so promptly, how's it going?' Kowolski said, his voice flat.

'Good. Plenty of work coming in thanks.'

'Listen Alex, I need to know that you'll promise me this call is confidential, right?'

She hesitated for a few seconds. Confidential? He sounded quite desperate.

'Okay,' she said. 'Completely off the record.'

'You heard from the lieutenant?'

'No, but I've seen the coverage. You must be pleased – he's everywhere.'

'Yeah,' Kowolski sighed. 'Everywhere but here.'

'And where's "here" if I may ask, and what's with all the secrecy?'

'Fort Hood, Texas. And our man's. . . well, he's gone missing, Alex.'

She gasped. Did she hear correctly? 'Jesus, you mean missing as like he's gone AWOL?'

'Very nearly two days. The reason I'm calling, Alex, is to see if you'd have any idea where he might have gone. I know you don't like what I'm doing but I need your help.'

Alex blew out her cheeks. 'Jeez.'

Kowolski outlined developments since McDermott's disappearance. 'He left a note saying he needed to atone for his sins. God knows what that's about.'

'Oh shit,' Alex said, a chill running through her. Quickly debating with herself whether to tell Kowolski the truth or to keep up the charade, she reckoned it was time he knew what he was playing with. She took a deep breath and ploughed on. 'Listen, Kowolski, I didn't want to be the one that told you this. . . '

'Go on,' he said, an octave or two lower, the despondency clear.

She launched into how McDermott had broken down in her room, his guilt, how screwed up he was. When she finished the full story, she heard Kowolski sigh long and loud. Several seconds of silence passed. She wanted Kowolski to come up with a suggestion, some great piece of analytical thinking that might help solve the problem.

But all he could do was to groan. 'No wonder the kid was cracking up. Sheesh, what a God-awful mess,' he finally said.

'Yeah,' Alex said, sympathising. 'He told me you didn't know anything about it which means you've been suckered, Kowolski – we all have.'

'Well, there's the CIA for you. And people call me devious,' Kowolski said.

'The CIA?'

'Your friend and mine, Richard Northwood. The conniving sonovabitch.'

'Northwood,' Alex spluttered. 'My friend?'

'Well, ex-friend, then. Who d'you think put your name forward for the Rumsfeld job?'

'The bastard,' Alex said, the realisation dawning.

* * *

She hurried back to her apartment, slammed the door in a temper. Sitting at her desk, tears welled. So Northwood was behind everything. And he'd recommended her for the Iraq trip. Christ, she could have been killed out there – lots of journalists had died. A sudden chill enveloped her. My God, was that what he'd wanted? A nice clean and tidy end to their affair? Or was she supposed to be grateful to him for thinking of her?

And there was poor McDermott, a young man broken. Did Northwood know of the lieutenant's soul-destroying secret?

Her mind in turmoil, she tried desperately to think straight. McDermott AWOL. He'd be court-martialled without doubt. She envisaged the disgrace, the unfathomable dishonour he'd bring to himself and his family. What torment the man had had to suffer. Some of her final words to Kowolski echoed in her mind, '*You don't think he'd do anything stupid do you?*'

Was McDermott the type to hurt himself? Alex couldn't answer the question. She was fond of him, a misguided soldier duped into a war on false pretences by those who should have known better. A cohort of political elite had betrayed the trust of the people like an enemy within. But was that foe inside everyone? Was it there, lurking, awaiting the opportunity to rise up, a manifestation of harm and injury to oneself? Alex had come very close to self-destruct after falling for Northwood's charms. Kowolski himself had bulldozed an intense path of

224

conviction only to now veer away with a sudden loathing for his actions. He'd admitted to her that his heart wasn't in the job any more.

'You going back to Baghdad?' Alex had asked.

'I've had a bellyful. Have you heard the word, metastasis?'

'Sounds medical.'

'Yeah it's the spread of a disease. My old man died of cancer, went all over his body. I've felt a metastasis in Iraq, a sort of creeping feeling in my being. It's been telling me I shouldn't be there.'

'Don't blame you,' she said with a shudder. Alex moved to a chair by the window, gazing out across the street almost absent-mindedly. Suddenly she sat upright, a flash of a thought entering her head. She'd been replaying some of her conversation with Kowolski. 'God knows where the kid is,' he'd said several times. Now, the phrase struck a note, slightly discordant at the moment as she concentrated on the strands of her memory aiming to hit full pitch. She thought back to a conversation she'd had with McDermott. Then, a smile spread on her face and she laughed to herself.

'Of course. God knows exactly where you are,' she said aloud, switching on her computer. 'And so do I.'

* * *

The midday news anchor laid it on thick. Over a twenty-five second piece of VT, showing McDermott having the Silver Star pinned on his chest, the effusive voice boomed that the latest polls showed the President's popularity rating had shot up more than six per cent – an unheard-of leap.

Richard Northwood sat on the edge of a desk with several of his staff watching the bulletin. He stroked his nose almost absent-mindedly. Of all the agendas on his plate, success on this one was paramount. His efforts would not be forgotten, it had been heavily hinted.

Northwood reckoned he'd make assistant director by the end

of the year. And if the President were to be re-elected in a little over twelve months, who knew what would happen? New terms of office often meant a new broom. Dare he think of deputy director of the whole CIA by Christmas 2004?

Cutting to a scene outside the gates of the White House, a reporter opined: 'The President's high approval is believed to be down to one man – Second Lieutenant Matthew McDermott, the nation's hero of Iraq. I've just spoken with several White House aides who say pledges of donations to the re-election campaign have intensified in the last four or five days. They forecast that at this rate, they will attract more than half the forecast eight hundred million dollars cost of the campaign before this year is out.'

One of Northwood's staff answered a phone call. 'It's for you, sir, a Gene Kowolski.'

Northwood bounced off the desk. 'I'll take it in my office,' he said, strolling out.

Several minutes later, grim-faced, Northwood replaced the receiver. The news from Kowolski wasn't good. Not good at all. In fact, fucking infuriating, as he told him. McDermott's disappearance spelt trouble. Big time. It meant there was a rogue elephant on the loose, badly injured and liable to do anything.

The lieutenant's charade must never be made public, not now, not ever. Too much depended on it. He cursed his old college buddy, Walter Douglas, too. The major had obviously been eager to please but had suffused fact and fiction. He would be forced to deal with him at an appropriate moment.

He called his tech boys. 'Check the movements of Alexandra Stead over the past three days and report back immediately.'

The surveillance technicians at Langley, when not actively monitoring a subject, relied on a remote movement activator, a system that allowed them to watch a recording of the red-dot figure on a map. At full-speed playback, it took only minutes to indicate Alex had not ventured more than 200 yards from her apartment. Her phone taps over the past week revealed nothing that would tie her in to McDermott.

Northwood slumped back in his chair. 'Fuck,' he said out loud, kicking the waste bin and watching disinterested as its contents scattered all over his office floor.

* * *

Alex excitedly jotted the numbers down from the web page on her screen. She cast her mind back to the Central Park runner's guide at the Carlyle she'd found in McDermott's pocket with the writing on the back, which she'd thought might be a telephone number. The main figures she easily remembered, 31 and 47, her current age and her father's birth year. Those tallied with the approximate co-ordinates on the map of Iraq she was now viewing.

After an hour's work, checking and cross-referencing, she sat back and rubbed her eyes. She had a good idea where McDermott had fled. During the rest of the day, the more she thought about it, the more she was convinced he was back in Iraq.

Should she tell anyone? Not yet, she decided. Kowolski had made the right noises recently but she wasn't sure she could trust him, nor what he might do. McDermott was obviously teetering on the edge. She didn't want to be the person who helped push him over the top.

Sipping her orange juice the next morning, Alex put the glass down and could not help but notice her hand was shaking. While she'd been pondering her next move, her inner self had been gnawing at her. She cupped a hand to her mouth, shocked at the frightening reality of her situation that finally emerged.

'No,' she whispered. 'No.'

But there was no escape. There was only one course of action she could take. She would have to return to Iraq to find McDermott herself. And the thought absolutely terrified her.

* * *

Kowolski finished typing the piece and re-read it. In a dead-end street, this was the only way out. He'd had the action cleared at the Pentagon, informed the relevant people including Northwood. A press release would announce that McDermott had volunteered for top-secret special duties and been despatched immediately. A quote from an army spokesman praised the lieutenant as the embodiment of all that was commendable about the country's armed service.

With a flourish he clicked the send key to the wire agency knowing that, within minutes, it would land on the news desks of every media outlet in the country. He expected to receive a barrage of calls from the more inquisitive of journalists and was prepared for them. The fact that the lieutenant's mission was top secret meant it gave him carte blanche to say nothing at all.

Stretching his arms, he yawned, putting his hands behind his head. He realised he'd just carried out another one of his trademark cover-ups. He'd been doing it most of his career. His face creased into a frown. The bloody chaos of Iraq had forced him to take stock of his life. He'd seen ordinary people there, lives shattered, devoid of all hope. Spirits bent like willow, they lived burdened with grief like a different species of the human race. But hadn't that been precisely the sub-text of his cowardly manipulation? The messages home were designed for the home media to propagate; they were only foreigners, Arabs at that. Therefore inferior. Seeing his fabrications in a new light had made him feel sick, ashamed of the lies and the falsehoods he pedalled.

He thought of Alex. She was a good woman, principled. Was the truth as simple as she believed? He couldn't be sure, but he was now beginning to have sympathy for some of her views. They must give her more fulfilment than the tripe he was dishing out, however subtly it was dressed.

Recalling he'd asked her if she knew the word 'metastasis', he chuckled to himself. He was darned certain she'd have heard of the phrase 'poacher-turned-gamekeeper'. In due time, he planned to seek her thoughts on his latest idea.

* * *

Alex glanced at the phone on her desk. Kowolski obviously thought her calls were being monitored. But did he know, or was he merely being cautious? She'd never had time to ask. Despite his recent murmurings, she couldn't be certain just how far he was tied up with Northwood. Surely they were both still on the same side, scheming and fighting for the same obnoxious ends.

Grabbing her jacket, she strode to the nearest phone booth and tried Farrah's number. She was in luck.

'Farrah, I wanted to see if you could help me.'

'Of course, my dear, whatever I can do.'

'I'm going back to Iraq,' Alex said breathlessly, the words tumbling from her mouth so she had to catch herself.

'I see,' Farrah said, a note of caution in her voice. 'You know things are not good in Baghdad. When are you going?'

'I'm setting off tomorrow, but I'm not going to Baghdad.'

'Then where?'

'That's why I need your help, Farrah. I'm going to the Garden of Eden.'

22

Alex landed in Kuwait after a thirteen-hour flight during which she'd tried to sleep, but found herself too wound up. A rousing cocktail of nervousness and exhilaration meant she'd spent hours in a semi-trance staring at the back of a tall man's bald head in the seat in front thinking about her quest.

Studying beyond the top of the seat in moments of more lucidity, she'd imagined the man's head to be the map of Iraq. A small scar in the middle of the pate was Baghdad while Basra lay at the base, near the top of the man's neck. Her destination, near the village of al-Qurnah, was a little higher than the nape. Studying the lightly-tanned flesh, she couldn't help emit a light giggle. The Garden of Eden was a freckle, just north of Basra.

Carrying only a rucksack, she skipped baggage reclaim in the arrivals hall, heading straight for a bank of telephones. Several calls later, she had organised her onward flight to Basra. Then she called Steve, feeling bad about not contacting him until now. Not knowing how he would take her news, she suspected he might be hostile.

'You're what?' he bellowed. 'Tell me this is a joke, Alex.'

'No joke. I've got to do it, Steve. He saved my life and I owe him. Now he needs help and I don't know where else he'll get it. He's a sick young man, liable to do anything.'

Steve let out a sigh. 'You know where he is?'

'Exactly – here are the co-ordinates.'

'And what happens if you find him and he doesn't want to budge?'

'Well, at least I can say I tried. But if he comes back with me, gets treatment, people will have sympathy with his side of the story. That can be a big part of his rehabilitation. The guy's so riddled with guilt it could kill him.'

'Alex, things have hotted up a mite since you were last here. People don't go out to fancy restaurants any more in case the places are bombed.'

'Yes, I know,' Alex said, biting her lip. 'I'll be careful, promise.' She made Steve repeat the co-ordinates several times.

'You got your cell phone with you?' he said.

'Uh-huh.'

'Should work okay in that area – the Brits have a presence protecting the oilfields. Make sure it's always switched on.'

'Don't worry. I have been in dangerous situations before.'

Steve said he loved her. But Alex had already hung up. It was true; she had been in many inhospitable places, times when she seemed to repel danger like a shower off a raincoat. She knew deep down, however, the fearlessness had deserted her. A wisp of dust from a Baghdad bullet had seen to that. The tour with McDermott proved life-changing in more ways than one. Now she was faced with summoning reserves of courage and fortitude from the bottom of a rapidly-draining tank.

As she made her way to catch the military flight to Basra, a sudden feeling of panic enveloped her. Spurred on by an almost reckless desire to save McDermott, she now wondered exactly what she was letting herself in for.

* * *

'We lost her for a little while but there she is,' the CIA technician said to Richard Northwood, pointing at the map of Iraq on the screen.

'Closer,' Northwood said, leaning over the man's shoulder.

'Basra, sir,' the technician murmured, 'heading east into the city.'

Northwood watched the pulsating red dot. What the hell was she doing back in Iraq? There was no indication she was due to return. Was she on another job for Kowolski? There was only one way to find out.

Hurrying back to his office, he put in a call.

'Kowolski, your girl Alex Stead's back in Iraq.'

'Bullshit – she's scared stiff of the place.'

'I'm telling you, fact, that's where she is – Basra. She know McDermott's gone AWOL?'

'Careful my friend, I've just put out a release to the media informing them he's been recalled to Iraq on a top-secret mission. That's now the official line.'

Northwood smiled to himself. Kowolski was quick to cover the angles. 'So?'

Kowolski hesitated. 'Yeah,' he finally said. 'I told her myself. But she promised she wouldn't use the information, you know, make it public. There's no way she'd do anything to harm the lieutenant in any way.'

'Right,' Northwood said unconvincingly. 'I don't need to remind you that journalists working on their own out there do so at their own risk. It can be extremely dangerous for them working in this sort of arena.'

'But she won't be... '

Northwood cut him off. 'You realise we probably have a very tricky situation on our hands. Keep in close touch.'

Northwood put down the receiver with a frown. He tapped his fingers on the desk, his mind whirring. Unless there was some other reason – one of Rumsfeld's unknown unknowns – Alex had returned to Iraq for one primary purpose and that was to locate McDermott. God knows what she'd do if she found him. She was a loose cannon, liable to cause untold damage. Unlike Kowolski, he didn't trust her. Not at all.

Checking his watch, he made a call to the Ali al-Salem air-base in Kuwait, south of the Iraq border, and spoke to a colonel in charge of the air defence team. Without raising any alarm, Northwood wanted to put the base on stand-by for a possible scenario. He was assured they would be happy to comply.

'We can send up a UAV at pretty short notice, sir,' the colonel said. 'Would that be an RQ or MQ?'

'Well, it's a fluid situation so we'd better go with the latter I think,' Northwood replied, knowing that the MQ-1 Predator drone meant it would carry munitions as well as its array of cameras and sensors.

Sitting back after the call, Northwood put his hands behind his head, hoisted his feet on to the edge of the desk. As he told the colonel, the picture was far from fixed. The fluctuating demands of the case meant he could take no chances. But with a couple of Hellfire missiles on his side, he'd feel a whole stack better.

* * *

Kowolski cursed himself for telling Northwood that Alex knew of McDermott's disappearance. He'd been caught off guard but realised now he should have been ready for it. Perhaps he was getting slow. Either that or his mind was moving to other things.

All the same, he didn't trust Northwood. His tone, while not overly aggressive, had still been menacing. Journalists got killed out there, he'd said. *Jesus*, there was no need to remind him of that. He'd been excusing the fact for months. Well, no longer, he decided.

After the McDermott issue was done and dusted, he planned to resign. They could take the whole goddam mess of Iraq and stick it. He was tired of the charade; the conniving and downright lying. It was time for the truth. He hoped Alex would join him in his future plans.

Now, he was worried for her. Did she know what she was doing? Why hadn't she confided in him instead of just taking off? He would have been able to offer some advice. He reflected that he'd always told her he would look after her. How the hell was he now supposed to do that?

In a sour mood, he snapped the locks shut on his suitcase and prepared to leave Fort Hood for Washington. With McDermott's media tour suspended, he wanted to spend a few days back at the Pentagon monitoring events in Iraq. His superiors would be expecting him to return to Baghdad at some stage, but he had set his mind against it. Closing the door behind him, he reasoned he could spin out a spell in the capital. The time would come in useful for making further plans for the future.

Fending off the media flak over the lieutenant's sudden departure would keep him busy enough in that time. And if McDermott should reappear, it would be even more difficult to keep a lid on the whole affair. In a way, he didn't care one way or the other.

He knew he'd told Alex he had to see the job through to the end. Right now, however, he wasn't sure he still had the nerve or the will to do so. He felt he'd given it his best shot. It wasn't his fault the McDermott show was based on a lie. That blemish threw a whole new light on his *raison d'être*, leaving him in a state of anger and confusion.

Arriving for his flight to DC and bracing himself for the plane ride home, he knew his immediate future lay in the hands of two people.

A sick soldier and a crazy girl.

* * *

Alex had her bag searched before she was allowed into the hospital. She swallowed hard, cast her eyes round the busy reception area. A young man approached, face serious.

'I am Abu Khamsin. Farrah told me what you looked like,' he said without offering his hand. 'Come with me.'

She followed him along a maze of dimly-lit corridors smelling of disinfectant, hurrying in the wake of his measured stride and taking in his athletic physique and mop of unruly hair. Approaching the entrance to the morgue, Abu Khamsin stopped and opened the door of a small anteroom, bare but for a Formica-topped table and two chairs.

'Everything is organised and arranged,' he said abruptly with a sweep of his arm. 'You have the money?' His voice trailed off with a hint of reluctance as he studied her.

Alex nodded. 'You speak very good English, Abu, and the accent?' Alex said, hoping she didn't sound condescending.

'Seven years at university – I'm a structural engineer. Two years in New York for my Master's degree.' He ran a hand through his jet-black hair, his elegant features creasing into a grimace. 'This is all the work I can find ... but maybe tomorrow,' he said, shrugging his broad shoulders.

Alex shook her head. 'You'd think with all the reconstruction going on that... '

'It is, as you call it, a closed shop. But let us not get into that,' he said, a coldness in his voice that made her feel uneasy. He handed her a brown paper bag. 'Here are some things you must wear.'

Suddenly he moved closer, looking into her eyes. Alex stood back, unsure.

'Your eyes,' he said. 'Blue.'

'Oh, no problem,' Alex said. 'I did exactly what Farrah told me,' she said patting the pocket of her jacket in which was a set of coloured contact lenses.

'Good,' Abu Khamsin said, looking at his watch. 'I have to do some more work then I will come back. You must stay here. There is a little food and drink in the bag and there is a toilet next door. We leave in the early hours.'

When he'd gone, Alex opened the paper bag; a pack of sandwiches, a bottle of water, a black abayah and a niqab. She fingered the long cloak and the face-mask nervously. The reality of her situation suddenly intensified. Abu Khamsin hadn't hinted at anything untoward, but she'd noticed an edginess about him and he didn't appear friendly. Putting the clothes back, she unwrapped the sandwiches and began to eat, not realising how hungry she was.

Taking a gulp of the water, she went over the plan in her

mind. Farrah told her Abu Khamsin would take her north out of Basra, on one of his weekly trips to Najaf driving a large truck. At a crossroad near to al-Qurnah, a friend would rendezvous with a vehicle for Alex's use. The man wanted American dollars. Then she was on her own. It was madness, she realised. But she had to stake everything on the co-ordinates.

She just knew McDermott was alone with his Bible in the Garden of Eden, the only place he wanted to be – just as he'd once told her. The feeling was so strong within her that she refused to believe any other notion.

* * *

At five minutes before midnight, Abu Khamsin returned. Alex, dressed in black from head to toe, stood up. She gave him a twirl. He frowned, studying her.

'Yes,' Abu Khamsin said, cocking his head to one side. 'And now you have brown eyes.'

He lowered his voice to explain there was a night-time curfew but that he had special dispensation from the military for his truck-load of unwanted souls on the journey to Najaf. In a mass grave outside the city, they would be taken to paradise.

Privately, this engineer-turned mortuary attendant knew such trips were soon likely to be halted. He had overheard his superiors voicing their concerns that a growing lawlessness in the countryside meant respect for the dead was a diminishing factor of daily life in Iraq. A driver had been stopped and threatened on a recent journey. But Abu Khamsin was still a willing volunteer, the bonus in his meagre monthly pay packet just too tempting to resist.

'Wait. I will return quickly,' he said, slipping out of the room. Entering the toilet, Abu Khamsin locked the door behind him. Rolling up his sleeves, he ran the cold-water tap, washing himself thoroughly three times.

'Allahu akbar,' he murmured just loud enough to hear himself, his hands raised to the side of his head. He continued in prayer placing great faith and trust in the merciful Allah to guide him through the night. When finished, he raised his eyes to the ceiling. He felt an impostor, for he had not prayed in years. He hoped he had remembered the words correctly to see them safely on their journey.

Tonight was a special night and he had a feeling he would need all the help he could muster.

* * *

A heavy green tarpaulin covered the contents of the open-backed truck. Alex glanced at the bulk of the cargo, stark against a moonlit night. She shuddered, wondering about the myriad strands of life each poor soul had left behind, forever burdened with an everlasting grief. Abu Khamsin led her to the passenger side, slamming the door shut behind her.

He turned the ignition key, sparking the rough diesel engine to start almost as if roused from a heavy slumber. Forcing the cumbersome gear lever forward, the gearbox grated loudly in complaint.

'Sounds reluctant,' Alex said.

Abu Khamsin glared at her, his forearms straining to turn the steering wheel.

Five minutes into the journey, he turned to Alex. 'I wanted to tell you that when Farrah asked me to help you I was against the idea. Especially when she said you were American.'

'I guess you don't like us?'

'You have destroyed our country – how could I like you? Let me tell you how they are behaving. They are building a bridge in Baghdad that was destroyed in the invasion. I could rebuild it for ten million. The Americans are charging fifty million. They are raping us still.'

'Just hang on a second and let's get something straight,' Alex countered sharply, eyes flashing. 'Not all Americans are happy with all this – especially me. I'm just as pissed off with it as you are, okay?'

He glanced at her, speaking quietly. 'Farrah said you were kind to her and my dear Aban. More than that I did not ask. I do not know why you are here in this dangerous place.'

'If I told you, would it make any difference?'

'No,' he said, dropping a gear and stamping on the accelerator.

* * *

The lieutenant pulled the blanket tighter around him and over his head. His back resting against the rough wall of an abandoned house, he switched on a pocket flashlight and began reading from his Bible. Outside, the wind began to pick up, sending occasional dust flurries through the open window frames.

Whispering the words, he focussed on Leviticus, chapter 23. At verse 27, his voice grew more urgent as he rocked to and fro repeating the passage: 'On the tenth day of this seventh month there shall be an atonement: it shall be an holy convocation unto you; and ye shall afflict your souls and offer an offering made by fire unto the LORD.'

His body coursed with a tingling sensation, euphoria unlike any other earthly feeling he had experienced. The sensation had been building steadily since he found this place. Earlier, in the fading light, he leaned against the thick wooden frames of a long-since used doorway to gaze out on a landscape that had captivated him for all of the day.

He smiled to himself, a realisation that, at last, he had found his Eden. The garden stretched out into the distance. All around him he saw paradise; a lush landscape of swaying palms and fruit and olive trees, of clear streams gurgling through fields of corn and wheat and brightly-coloured birds of a dozen species. The idyll was just as he had imagined. The peace enveloped him. He felt safe in the protection of its cocoon.

Suddenly he stopped reading, frantically pushing up his sleeve to reveal his watch. He shone the flashlight on it, staring hard and tapping the timepiece for reassurance as he measured the second hand ticking away. He'd told himself a hundred times today that it was October. He definitely knew it; October 2003. And the date on his watch said it was the sixth.

He continued looking to see if the number changed, in case someone was tricking him. But it stayed working exactly the same as it had been a minute ago, and the minute before that. He nodded his head vigorously to himself. Yes, it meant it was still the very early morning of the sixth of October 2003. He'd worked the day out perfectly some months ago – or was it years ago? At the moment he just couldn't remember nor did he want to try.

His biblical calendar told him it was the tenth day of the seventh month.

The Day of Atonement.

23

They were no more than a mile from the hospital when a barrage of floodlights lit up the whole of the quiet road ahead. Abu Khamsin fished in his top pocket, producing a crumpled piece of paper.

'Checkpoint,' he whispered. 'Stay silent.'

Alex strained to see beyond the dazzle as the truck ground to a halt. Two armoured cars, parked across the road in a wedge formation, blocked the way. Several British soldiers appeared.

Abu Khamsin proffered his pass. 'Good evening, sir,' he said, shielding his eyes from the flashlight one of the soldiers shone into the cab. 'I have the usual consignment – and I have brought my dear wife for company on the long journey ahead.'

The soldier briefly studied the paper and handed it back. He glanced at Alex. She felt his eyes on her but dared not move, staring resolutely at a small chip in the truck's dirty windscreen. She gulped, her throat dry.

Risking a look in the passenger wing mirror, she could make out one of the soldiers climbing on to the back of the truck. He moved with the nimbleness of youth, hopping on to the sturdy rear mudguard and quickly hoisting himself on top. She heard him cursing as he struggled to untie one of the tarpaulin's anchor ropes.

Pulling the cover back a touch, the soldier suddenly shrieked. 'Holy Mother of God,' he shouted, quickly leaping to the ground. He hurried into the darkness, retching loudly.

'That'll teach you to be too nosey,' the officer in charge shouted, laughing. He turned to Abu Khamsin, shaking his head. 'It's his first night on roadwatch – never seen the likes before.'

Barking an order into his radio, the soldier stood back. Seconds later, one of the armoured cars roared into life, reversing off the road on to the verge.

'Mind how you go,' the soldier nodded, waving them through.

Alex let out a deep breath as they set off, only realising then how tense her body had become. She took out her cell phone, wondering whether to switch it on. Not yet, she told herself, best to conserve the battery. She pulled the niqab down from her face, turned to look at Abu Khamsin, his features set in grim concentration.

'I guess our cargo's not a pretty sight – it must be hard,' she said.

Abu Khamsin remained silent for a minute, eventually clearing his throat. 'At first it was difficult. I used to have nightmares. Then. . . ' His voice trailed off.

'Then?' Alex persisted.

'I became used to seeing the dead, to handling the bodies.' He sighed, the sigh of a man weary of life itself, despair in his very existence. 'It is the facing of their loved ones that is now the nightmare. They gather outside the mortuary, crying and wailing. The noise is pitiful and never leaves you, even after they go away. I pray to God it will all end soon.'

Alex was lost for words. She felt tempted to sympathise, to tell him of her own nightmare, one that had tormented her relentlessly since Kandahar, but she felt the gesture inadequate. Instead, she focussed on the road ahead as they motored into the countryside, the wind whipping up occasional showers of sand that rattled on the windscreen like the roll of a snare drum.

* * *

In the car from the airport to the Pentagon, Gene Kowolski brooded. He'd been unable to make contact with Alex, trying her number a dozen times since his plane landed. His gloom intensified still not knowing where McDermott was or what he was up to and, because of it, what sort of reception he would receive when he got to his office.

He was surprised to see Carl Whittingham waiting for him when he arrived. Kowolski hadn't seen him since that day outside the Abu Ghraib palace when he'd first mentioned the name of Matt McDermott and the plot that would ensue. To Kowolski, it all seemed an age ago.

'What gives, Carl?' Kowolski said, putting his briefcase down on a chair.

Whittingham rubbed his chin. 'This McDermott stuff – it's causing a pail-full of fucking grief.'

'Tell me about it,' Kowolski said, puffing out his cheeks. 'Your idea though, wasn't it?'

Whittingham looked at him, sheepishly. 'I had to spill. It's gone right to the top.'

'Yeah, well it wasn't my idea either, as much as I'd have liked the credit if it hadn't turned out this way,' Kowolski said, loosening his tie. He was about to take off his jacket when Whittingham, agitated, glanced at his watch.

'There's a meeting in the boardroom.'

'When?'

'Now.'

Kowolski sighed and set about making himself presentable. 'Lead the way, Carl.'

The bespectacled figure standing with his hands behind his back gazing out of the window was instantly recognisable. He didn't flinch as Kowolski and Whittingham entered the room.

'Sit, gentlemen,' the man said, maintaining his posture. Several moments passed before he spoke again. 'The colours are quite remarkable at this time of year, don't you think?'

Whittingham shifted in his seat. Kowolski smiled inwardly. He knew the routine. Rank meant power. And power meant the subservience of others. Without wishing to appear hostile, deep down Kowolski no longer gave a fig for the game.

The man eventually moved away from the window, sitting at

242

the head of the large table. He pursed his lips, leant back, putting his hands behind his head. 'Well, Gene, this soldier business has gone way off beam.'

'Sadly, yes. You might call it an unknown unknown,' Kowolski countered.

The man stared at him over the top of his glasses. Kowolski stared back, hoping his expression was as neutral as he intended.

'Well, it's over as far as you're concerned. The whole idea emanated out of Langley – I've tossed it back in their court.'

Kowolski tried not to smile even though a sense of relief swept over him. Inside, he felt himself laughing. He stroked his chin, took a laboured breath. 'If that's what you think best, chief.'

The man stood up to signal the meeting was over. 'You're doing a good job over there, Gene. No doubt you'll be anxious to get back.'

Smiling meekly, Kowolski watched him leave the room. He resolved immediately that his resignation letter would be on the appropriate desk within the next twenty-four hours. The guy had done him a great favour. If people wanted to think he was quitting in a huff over the McDermott issue, then that was fine. The subject was bound to come out in the usual office gossip. In reality, he was off the hook and now joyously free to pursue his other plans. Wouldn't those who knew him get a shock when he turned poacher and began seeking out the truth for a change?

* * *

Abu Khamsin brought the lorry to a gradual halt and cut the headlights. The road ahead should have been clear all the way to their rendezvous point. But he was sure he had just seen the flash of a light at some point in the distance.

'What is it?' Alex said.

'You're going to have to get in the back, quick,' he said, the tension rising in his voice.

Alex turned round. There was no back of the cab, just a solid wall of metal behind her seat.

'Not...' she said, the realisation dawning. He was asking her to hide in the back, under the tarpaulin, among their deathly cargo.

'No choice, be quick,' he demanded, his fear palpable.

Opening the driver's door, he leapt to the ground. Alex shivered, the cold chill of the strong wind compounding the alarm that suddenly struck her.

'Take this, wrap it round you,' he said, handing her a blanket.

She wanted to protest but realised it was futile. Within seconds, Abu Khamsin undid a section of the tarpaulin. He held out his hand and pulled her up, creating a space just big enough for Alex to scramble inside. Hurrying back to the cab, he selected low gear and moved slowly forward.

The darkness consumed her. She gagged at the smell, a stinking mass of bodies in various stages of putrefaction. Trying desperately to close her mind, she screwed her eyes so tight they hurt. At the same time, she pulled the blanket around her trying to take short breaths through her mouth. But she could feel the panic rising, claustrophobia taking charge. She was sure she wasn't getting enough air. A dull heavy ache settled on her chest, slowly crushing as she sunk lower into the morass. Visions of her Kandahar nightmare flashed into her head.

Ahead, the lights became brighter. Abu Khamsin prayed it would be another British army roadblock. Someone was standing in the middle of the road waving a lamp. His headlights picked out a small group of men, rifles pointing straight at him. The realisation they were not soldiers sent trickles of sweat down his neck. For a split second, he thought of putting his foot down, running the gauntlet. But he realised it would be useless in such a ponderous vehicle. He had no choice but to bring the lorry to a stop, his eyes wide, hands trembling on the wheel.

The noise of the air brakes being released was just audible

above the shrieking wind as Alex lay agonisingly still, heart thudding. She heard muffled voices, Arabic. A small gap in the tarpaulin allowed a burst of wind to blow in. Alex felt the coolness of the welcome draught. Lifting her head to gasp at the precious chill, her body shifted. Suddenly, an arm fell across her throat. She tried to push it away but, in such a confined space, her hands could find no leverage. The weight of the arm began choking what little breath she had left. She opened her eyes and saw only blackness. Kicking out in a fit of terror only worsened the situation.

Her Kandahar nightmare, now a shocking reality, pounded unmercifully at her brain. Unable to move, and on the verge of blacking out, she summoned one final burst of will and did the only thing she was capable of doing.

With all the strength she could muster and as loudly as she could, Alex screamed.

* * *

Alerted to the shrieks, two of the men rushed forward. One of them, no more than a teenager, quickly untied the tarpaulin, pulling it back. For a moment, both men appeared stunned as Alex struggled to push herself free. They grabbed hold of her, dragging her towards the rear of the truck. At the edge of the tailboard, she shrugged free and jumped to the ground, sprawling in a heap. The men towered over her, laughing, their outlines made more menacing in the dim light of a small floodlamp. Abu Khamsin stepped forward to help her. As he did so, another of the group, a youth, raised his rifle and struck him with the butt on the back of the neck. Alex watched in horror as Abu Khamsin slunk to his knees.

The men gathered round Alex, shouting, jabbering, pushing in one direction then another, impatient for a response. She was forced to the ground, her back against the front wheel of the truck. She watched as Abu Khamsin was hauled to his feet.

Scared, her knees weak, she felt defiance suddenly rise within her. She wanted to kick out, fight, to tell whoever these people were to go to hell. But she knew such bravado was to no avail. Instead, she played dumb, two of the men standing close by.

Abu Khamsin slowly drew himself up to his tall frame, aware that guns were trained on him. His neck hurt and his head swam. Though groggy, he knew he had to appear humble, mindful of appearing as subservient as possible. But he had made up his mind. He was about to play a huge gamble. In a measured, conciliatory tone, he turned and spoke.

'Brothers, this woman is the widow of one of the newly departed,' he said confidently, gesturing to the truck's cargo. 'Her life is now full of such grief that she has been struck dumb since the day the dogs of America killed her husband and her two young children. She is inconsolable and has insisted on accompanying their last remains until they are laid to rest in the loving arms of our beloved saint Ali ibn Abi Talib. We humbly ask that you let us free to continue our merciful journey to al-Najaf.'

Abu Khamsin stared at them, trying to catch each man's eye in the inky gloom. He and Alex had a chance if these men were followers of the cleric, Muqtada al-Sadr. Men from this southern Shia stronghold had flocked to join his Mahdi Army in the past few months, so disenchanted were they with the aftermath of the US-led occupation. Bolstered by al-Sadr's well-publicised July sermon in Najaf, thousands responded with a unanimous denunciation of the US and its provisional government. It was common knowledge that here in the south, al-Sadr's Mahdi Army had taken security into its own hands, patrols and roadblocks such as this becoming more prevalent.

He stole a glance at Alex, praying that she would not open her mouth. To do so would result in certain death for both of them – killed as spies once they heard her accent. It was a fate that was highly likely to be excruciatingly slow just for the fun of it.

Abu Khamsin had not been able to determine who was in

charge and so had pleaded with each of the men in turn. Now, another man shuffled forward, his head and face covered with a red-checked keffiyeh. He pulled down the scarf, letting it rest loosely on his stooped shoulders, and cleared his throat, spitting into the sand.

Abu Khamsin guessed the man was the leader of this rag-tag bunch. From the row of crooked and missing teeth, the manner of his dress, he surmised the man was a local, a poorly-educated farmer or such, probably illiterate. Maybe he was one of the few remaining Marsh Arabs of the area, a simple herdsman who once tended buffalo and chickens or grew wheat and barley and rice and hunted fish and wild boar as did thousands of his kinfolk. Perhaps he had escaped Saddam's brutal retribution against the failed Shia uprising following the Gulf War of 1991. Draining this area's vast marshes and turning it into bleak desert was the physical legacy of the pogrom.

Abu Khamsin knew it was as natural as their former way of life that the people here would harbour a hatred for America and a burning contempt for its leader. George Bush senior was the man who encouraged the uprising those years ago but did nothing to help. A quarter of a million people simply left to Saddam's merciless onslaught. Those who couldn't get away to become refugees in Iran were killed. Bush junior was from the same tainted stock.

'You are also of the al-Ahwar?' Abu Khamsin said, his voice dropping a notch.

The man stared at him, slowly nodding. 'I am of the Ma'adan,' he said.

Abu Khamsin sighed. 'My late parents also. They died in exile, driven out. Some of my family had no way of escaping. Cousins, aunts, uncles – they all had their throats cut by Saddam's pigs.'

The old man eyed him, suspicious. Abu Khamsin knew he must try for some sort of rapport with the man. It was their only chance.

'I am a builder of things, a civil engineer. It is my dearest wish that when the American pack of dogs has gone, I can return here and help rebuild this wondrous place.'

The old man looked up into the sky for what seemed an age. Then he stared at Abu Khamsin, moving closer. 'Do you think you can do it?' he whispered.

'With the help of Allah, I'm sure we can,' Abu Khamsin said, spreading his arms out wide as if taking in the whole of the landscape. 'This glorious land will be returned to its rightful state and I will help the kingfishers to come back.'

Alex had no idea what was being said. She kept her gaze on Abu Khamsin, vainly trying to decipher the mood of their plight. One of her guards turned to watch the conversation. An AK-47 hung limply from his shoulder. She was sure she could reach it, take him off balance. But the younger man standing over her had a knife, which he kept running over the palm of his hand, glancing at her with a leering smile. She held her eyes steady, refusing to give him the satisfaction of seeing her fear. But, behind the niqab, her bottom jaw trembled uncontrollably.

If one of them should search her...

* * *

The group's leader fumbled in a pocket, pulled out a mobile phone. He stared at it for several seconds, hesitant as if it would blow up in his hands, his body crouched over to protect it from the wind.

With ponderous deliberation, his stubby fingers jabbed at the buttons. He pulled one side of the keffiyeh free and lifted the phone to his ear. It was a full minute before someone answered and the man began shouting excitedly into the mouthpiece.

Abu Khamsin cast a nervous glance at Alex. The man was describing the patrol's catch. It was obvious he was talking to someone more senior, seeking advice as to their next move.

But no one except the older man could hear the response of the sleepy voice on the other end of the line.

'Let them go – or kill them. I'll leave it up to you,' it said.

24

Slowly, the old man put the phone back in his pocket. He gazed hard, past his two captives and into the inky distance. The wind was now increasing, occasionally howling over the bleak landscape like a tormented animal. Everyone eyed the old man as he stood motionless, their concentration broken by the constant flapping of a loose corner of the lorry's tarpaulin, slapping against the tailgate.

Finally, the man turned, raising his rifle and pointing it directly at Abu Khamsin, his hands trembling. Sensing some sort of action, his compatriots sprang to attention. Alex shifted, the tenseness in her body agonising. She could feel the truck's wheel bolts digging into her, yet she couldn't stop herself pressing back further.

The youth with the knife darted forward, lunging and slashing at thin air like he was in a macabre and sadistic solo dance, as if in practise for what he hoped was to come.

'Stop,' the old man shouted, at once raising his arm. 'Stop. I have decided. Our brother and sister are to be allowed to continue their merciful journey in peace with Allah's blessing.'

With a wave of his rifle, he quickly gestured for them to get into the truck. Abu Khamsin spoke sharply in Arabic to Alex, indicating with a nod of his head and his outstretched hand that she should climb into the cab. His motioning needed no translation. She stepped on to the footplate and allowed him to push her aboard, quickly sliding to the passenger side.

Abu Khamsin joined her, starting the engine. 'Inshallah, inshallah, thank you,' he blurted through the open window.

The old man raised a hand in acknowledgement. 'Please God

249

that I live long enough to see your kingfishers return,' he shouted as they moved off and were quickly on their way.

'Jesus Christ,' Alex blurted, her body still shaking, the relief overwhelming. 'I don't know what the hell you said back there but it worked. Thank you for saving my life, Abu Khamsin.'

She leaned over and kissed him on the cheek. He exhaled sharply. 'I think it was close, very close. Some of them I think would have liked to kill us both, maybe after they had some amusement first. I had to tell the old man a fanciful story. Thank God it worked.'

Alex shuddered, slumping back in her seat and closing her eyes. She shook her head as if to rid it of the petrifying thoughts that had tormented her during their ordeal. But the sense of shock proved too strong, hitting the pit of her stomach like a sledgehammer. Quickly, she wound down the window and threw up into the night.

* * *

Alex awoke with a start. Pale pink streaks of daylight were just visible on the horizon and the wind seemed to have picked up strength. She glanced at Abu Khamsin. 'Sorry, I must have dozed off,' she said, rubbing her eyes. 'How are we doing?'

'Be there in twenty minutes,' he said. 'I hope our man's still waiting.'

It suddenly struck Alex that, without transport, she had no hope of finding McDermott. Their delay might have cost them dear. She could only pray the lure of a 500-dollar deal for what was likely to be a clapped-out vehicle would prove too strong a bait.

Abu Khamsin cleared his throat, preparing to speak. 'My dear cousin Farrah told me to tell you something only when we were about to part, but I think there will be no harm in telling you now,' he said, glancing at her.

Alex looked at him quizzically.

'She said to say that Aban's secret is safe with her and that she intends to put it to good use. You remember you liked a particular wrap she wore?'

'Yes, I do.'

'Well, Farrah said she hid whatever it is she's talking about in the lining of the wrap when she fled to Jordan. That's all I know.'

Alex's eyes widened. A memory stick. It just had to be – with Aban's explosive information on it. The incriminating file he died for. Her thoughts turned to the extensive list of corrupt companies all with their snouts in Saddam's trough. She'd conceded Northwood had tricked her out of the only remaining copy and, with it, the inherent worldwide publicity the story would attract. Her heart leapt.

Abu Khamsin looked across at her. 'It is good news, yes?'

Alex laughed. 'Good news? It's absolutely fantastic.'

* * *

The friend of Abu Khamsin was waiting at the crossroad as promised. Alex saw the small open-topped vehicle through a cloud of dust as though it had been speeding and just come to an abrupt halt.

'This is George,' Abu Khamsin said, helping Alex from the cab. 'He is like the Beatle, yes?'

Alex stared at the young man, incredulous. His hair was shoulder length, and he wore a moustache that drooped down the sides of his mouth and a gold-braided turquoise tunic that looked as if it had come straight from a hippie music festival. He looked just like the late George Harrison in his psychedelic days, an image she remembered from the cover of a CD amongst her collection.

'We were at university together – everyone there called him George,' said Abu Khamsin, hugging his friend in a warm embrace.

'Hope he can play the guitar,' Alex said, laughing.

'Alas, no longer,' George said, grinning. To Alex's horror he held up his right arm revealing only a hook where his hand should have been.

'Oh my God,' Alex said with a gasp.

'Shrapnel in the invasion,' he said. 'But your dollars will hopefully give me a new hand. Then at least I play something again.'

Flustered, Alex stepped forward, offered George his roll of dollar bills. He nodded, a generous smile on his lips. He gestured to the vehicle. 'She is not much to look at but at least she drives okay. I was late for your arrival – sometimes there are British tanks on patrol and it is still the curfew.'

Alex examined the vehicle, a type of small jeep. A badge on the rear proclaimed it was an Austin Mini Moke, left-hand drive, no doors. Where it wasn't dented or scraped, the paintwork was a jumble of green stripes and brown zigzags resembling the camouflage of a military vehicle. George started the engine. 'You are planning to go far?'

Withdrawing a hand-held GPS from beneath her abayah, Alex pressed a button and got a reading. 'Should be only four or five miles west to where I need to be,' she said, shielding her eyes from the wind.

George looked up into the lightening sky, a frown on his face. 'You must hurry,' he said, without explanation.

Alex clambered into the driver's seat, fiddled with the gear shift. 'Which way's reverse?' George asked her to put her foot on the clutch then jerked the shift up and away. She nodded. 'Seat belts?'

George held out his arms in a hopeless gesture, smiled and shrugged.

'I guess I'm off then,' Alex shouted. 'Wish me luck. Thank you Abu Khamsin – I'll never forget what you've done.'

Had daybreak finally dawned, she would have seen Abu Khamsin blush. She turned and waved, selected a gear and roared off.

They watched her until she was out of sight. Abu Khamsin

turned to George, shaking his head. 'That, my good friend, is one crazy American woman.'

* * *

After thirty minutes' travel, Alex reckoned she had less than a half-mile further to be slap bang at the centre of her GPS co-ordinates. She squinted, scouring the immediate landscape. Nothing but scrubland, parched and bare, the taste of salt on the wind. A deep water-filled gulley ran parallel to the road, beyond which she could just make out the ruins of a house, dotting the horizon.

She had turned off the main road, her GPS guiding her on to a rough sand track pitted with the occasional large stone boulder which had made progress painstakingly slow. Suddenly, the vehicle's engine began to splutter. Her heart sank. 'Not now, *please*,' she urged. But the jeep soon rolled to a stop, an obstinate camel digging in its heels.

She leant forward, fumbling under the dashboard for the hood release catch, found a lever and pulled while praying it was the correct one. Jumping out, she only then realised how strong the wind had become as she fought her way to the front of the vehicle and lifted the hood. She was greeted by a strong smell of fuel. The engine compartment was as foreign as a page of Arabic. A feeling of dread descended as she stared helplessly at the cables, wires and parts that meant absolutely nothing.

It was only then that she heard the noise; faint at first somewhere in the distance. She glanced south, surveying the sky. Emerging daylight had brought with it a cluster of white billowing clouds, scurrying against the palest blue as if in flight. Turning backwards and shielding her eyes from the dust, her mouth dropped. A great menacing shroud of darkness moving at speed towards her. Angry coils of wind, whipping up loops of sand, shrieked like banshees, howling and wailing across the landscape like mini tornadoes. A sandstorm. Closing fast. Alex felt panic setting in. To be caught here in such a ferocious storm would be perilous. Her open vehicle would provide little protection and the onslaught could last for hours.

Frantically, she began running her fingers along the wires and rubber pipes of the engine bay, checking connections but hardly knowing what she was doing. Before long, she found a narrow piece of thick tubing that had obviously come loose, its end dangling. She sniffed it – petrol. Looking to where the tube might go, she traced it to the nozzle end of a dull metal casting. A mechanic would have told her it was the carburettor and what she held was the fuel pipe whose clip had come undone. She grunted, hopefully pushing the end into place, jamming and twisting the tube until her fingers and arms ached and it would go no further.

* * *

Alex drove forward at a snail's pace, half expecting the engine to splutter and die at any second. What little daylight remained was rapidly draining in the frightening gloom. She found a headlight switch but all the beam did was to reflect the particles of whirling sand, each one a shiny blinding mirror. Her GPS indicated she should turn northwest. Was there a way over the gulley? Even with the wind behind her, it was difficult to see any distance. Then, she brightened. Up ahead, only a matter of metres, she could make out a crossing, a short stretch of stout wooden transoms strung both sides of the clay-baked banks of the gulley. She gunned the motor and made it to the other side, turning into the wind to follow a track running alongside the waterway.

Visibility was soon down to a matter of yards, the storm now battering down hard. Squinting, one hand shielding her eyes, and with only one hand on the wheel, she eased down on the accelerator. The little vehicle picked up speed but it only increased her anxiety as it rattled over the bumps and hollows in the track. She knew that time was running out. The fog of the storm was slowly swallowing her, like a gigantic beast toying with its prey.

A short distance further on, the track evened out to run parallel with the low embankment of the waterway. Using the barrier as a guide gave her the confidence to increase her speed. But she realised the vehicle was still in too low a gear and the engine squealed as if in protest, its small wheels spinning over debris and sending Alex bouncing and jiggling as she grasped the wheel, knuckles draining. Changing up a gear, she pressed on. She hit a small rock that skewed the jeep into a slide and she fought to regain control, just managing to get the vehicle straight.

Desperate now, her head bent low against the ferocious stinging assault, Alex cried out into the wind. She'd always been sure that God did not exist, ever since she'd been old enough to think for herself, to reason. But, for a split second, the ludicrous thought entered her head that it was Him throwing down this challenge, almost as an invite to test the limits of her intrepidity; flagrant and teasing and daring her to resist.

Her whole body ached and she could feel the strength draining from her. But she fathomed there was no alternative but to grind her teeth and continue. She pressed the accelerator to the floor but had travelled no more than another 50 yards when the jeep smashed into a large boulder half-buried in the mud. The collision ripped off the front section of the exhaust with an almighty crash sending the vehicle skywards. The impact was so sudden, so severe, that Alex was flung sideways out of her seat. Time seemed suspended as she reached the point of no return, her hands clawing at the air in a futile attempt to stay aboard.

She landed in a scrub of sand, rolling over several times to take the brunt of the impact. Looking up through the haze, she was just in time to see the jeep careering up the embankment and disappearing over its crest into the waterway.

* * *

Stunned, Alex checked herself over, first flexing her arms. She could feel grazes on her elbows, which stung. Slowly pushing up into a sitting position, she yelped. Her right ankle suddenly screamed at her, a sharp painful stab that made her grimace. Gingerly, she eased it one way, then the other. Movement was slow and deliberate but, although she gasped in recoil, she was satisfied it wasn't broken. Desperate to escape the sniping torrent around her, a chill of fear struck at her like a snake. For the first time, she doubted whether she could summon the strength from her rapidly-draining reserves to battle on.

Her body, tired and weak, wanted her to lay back and give in, to collapse into the cool grit beneath her and simply succumb. Turning her head away from the incessant driving wind, she made an effort to stand but managed only a few steps before collapsing to the ground.

The sand was everywhere; in her eyes, her ears, her mouth. She pulled the niqab tighter across her face, a tingling burning sensation tormenting her cheeks.

Lying prostrate, she could feel the cell phone in her pocket digging into her thigh. Shifting position seemed to require an enormous amount of effort and she flopped down, now hardly able to catch her breath. As she lay there an unfathomable feeling swept over her. She started laughing, a small chuckle at first, then loud chortling belly laughs that racked her frame and competed with the howling storm. How would Kowolski spin her death? 'Another journo wasted. Paid the price of her independence. Should have been embedded.'

Moments later the laughing turned to coughing which shook her violently and made her wretch. Her fingers pulled frantically to rip the niqab from her mouth and she raised herself on all fours hawking mouthfuls of spit and sand from her throat until her eyes watered and she slunk back groaning with the effort.

* * *

She didn't know how long she'd been lying there and she was halfway to delirium when it happened – almost as if in a dream. Alex felt herself being lifted, pulled effortlessly from the ground. Allowing herself to be carried like a baby, she looked up to try and see her rescuer's face but it was covered with a keffiyeh. The man's head was slanted away from her, tilted against the gale as he took large steady strides, never stumbling, over the rough uphill terrain.

They reached the wall of an abandoned building, which momentarily gave them shelter. It was only then that he turned and looked at her. Instantly she recognised those eyes.

Lieutenant Matt McDermott's were the darkest of dark brown.

* * *

Neither of them spoke as he gently laid her down in a corner of the ruined house. He fetched a blanket and joined her, covering both of them with it and pulling it over their heads. Alex nestled against the warmth of his body. So tired, she knew the talking could wait. Within minutes she was fast asleep.

25

Richard Northwood stretched his arms high above his head and did his best to stifle an involuntary yawn. His office clock signalled a little after 4.00 a.m. and while his mind was racing, his body needed sleep. The present flux was making him more unsettled by the minute. He'd had one false alarm when he thought Alex had made her rendezvous. But, just as he was about to call everyone to action, the red dot on his screen had started moving again.

Now he stared at the monitor watching the dot that hadn't budged in over an hour. This had to be it, he told himself. He picked up the phone and called the airbase at Ali al-Salem.

'I'm sure we've got a definite this time,' he said to the colonel at the ground control station. 'You set to go?'

The colonel hated to sound uncooperative. But what could he do about the weather north of the border? The Predator drone had been on standby for several hours. He could see it standing in the baking heat on the tarmac, the sun throwing shards of piercing brilliance off its silver fuselage. He had his two best combat systems officers itching to send their baby airborne.

'Negative, I'm afraid, sir,' the colonel almost sighed. 'We've got one helluva sandstorm blowing north of Basra. We wouldn't see a thing up there even with infra red. These babies tend to be a little fragile.'

'Shit.' Northwood clenched his fist. 'Colonel, you'd better monitor the situation every fifteen minutes and let me know the moment we get a green light.'

He glanced across the room at Carl Whittingham from the Pentagon. The guy was practically asleep in his chair. Northwood eyed him contemptuously. He knew Whittingham had been sent to keep tabs on him. But he was out of his depth. This was a CIA operation – his operation – and he was resolute to the point of obsession that nothing would stand in his way. He'd long since put aside any self-recriminations over the McDermott exercise that had gone so horribly wrong. It was now up to him to solve the problem and he didn't want some pen-pushing poodle getting in his way, someone who might prove squeamish in the end game.

The President needed to be protected at all costs.

'Say, Carl,' Northwood cooed, tapping him gently on the shoulder. 'You can bed down in my secretary's office down the corridor. I'll let you know if we get any action.'

Whittingham leant forward rubbing his eyes. He nodded and stumbled out of the room. Northwood closed the door after him, breathing a sigh of relief. Then he locked it. There was no margin for complications in what he'd planned. Whittingham wasn't the type who would like it when they started playing hardball and Northwood hadn't told him the drone was armed.

Glancing round his office, Northwood surveyed the dual screens that would beam pictures in real time when the drone was airborne. UAVs might be military hardware, but their surreptitious capabilities meant they were eminently suited to CIA control. With an eye to the future, he had already written a paper pressing for the agency to train its own drone pilots, thereby adding another dimension to its undercover work. Northwood's section had relied on army or air force personnel to fly them in the past. Much better, though, if all aspects of an operation could be kept in-house.

Still, this was the first time he planned on using one that had a Hellfire tucked under each wing and with him giving the orders.

* * *

The kid sat at the mess hall table staring blankly at his plate of food, clicking both thumbs against the two nearest fingers of each hand in a non-stop nervous rhythm. Kit Finkelstein was known on the airbase as Fingers, but not because he was always clicking them. At the age of twenty-two, his lonely obsessive childhood as a computer games nut had paid dividends by landing him the position of a combat systems officer with the US Air Force.

Forgotten were the nightly admonishments from his mother to 'quit the Devil's own game and come down for your supper'. Now, she was so proud of her 'pilot' son that she glowed whenever she talked about him to anybody willing to listen at the local thrift store where she worked, even though she didn't understand what a drone did.

Many a meal went cold while he sat mesmerised by the screen, his fingers flitting manically over the controls of some latest craze, ignoring his mother's pleas. And here he was, about to bestow the same fate on another dish. Only, this time a heady mixture of excitement and fear was to blame.

'Hey Fingers, you lost your appetite?' Steve Lewis sat down beside the kid, noting the untouched food with a frown. They'd often sat together chatting, Steve considering himself almost a fatherly figure. 'You've gotta put oil in the engine or you'll seize, man.'

Fingers looked up, giving his dining companion a hapless grin. 'I'm on standby with the bird and she's armed. Just a bit nervous that something big's going down.'

Steve forced a piece of pancake into his mouth. He wasn't that hungry himself. A hollow gnawing sensation had kept him awake for most of the night, worrying if Alex was all right. He'd left messages on her cell phone since first thing without reply.

'How big?' he said, chewing laboriously.

The kid looked about him, lowered his voice. 'Top stuff from DC an' all. An op over the border.' Fingers pushed his plate away and stood up ready to go. He leaned in closer to Steve's ear. 'AQI at thirty-one and change, forty-seven and change – that's all I know.'

Fingers was out of the door before the shock hit Steve so hard he almost choked. The kid was talking co-ordinates. He couldn't be absolutely sure, but they sounded ominously like the numbers Alex had given him and made him write down. Al-Qaeda at large there? He suddenly went into a cold sweat, panic immediately gripping his insides, churning and nauseating.

Rushing to the exit, there was only one way he could be certain. He had the co-ordinates written down in his quarters. His dorm was half a mile away on the edge of the camp in a recently-installed prefabricated building with plywood walls. Outside the mess, he wasn't concentrating and let a half-empty camp bus sail past. He cursed, deciding he'd have to jog the distance. He was soon lathered in sweat, his mind in a whirl. Trying her cell phone again, there was still no reply so he left a message he said was urgent.

Inside his room, he opened his bedside desk drawer. His heart sank. The co-ordinates were the same. He stood for a minute, chest heaving, trying to think of the best course of action. Alex was in danger – but from al-Qaeda? Maybe the area was home to another group of insurgents the CIA had been keeping tabs on. Maybe the agency labelled any enemy as al-Qaeda. Fingers had been quite specific: AQI he had said: al-Qaeda in Iraq.

He rooted in the drawer, found the business card he wanted and, with a trembling hand, dialled the number. It rang for ages before a sleepy voice answered.

'Gene Kowolski.'

'Sorry to wake you, Mr Kowolski. It's about Alex… she could be in a life-threatening situation in Iraq.'

Steve rattled off all he knew, hardly pausing for breath. A couple of times Kowolski interjected, probing further.

'AQI – you sure?'

'That's what the kid said. And that it was an operation run from Washington.'

Kowolski was silent for a while, his mind working overtime. 'Might be the Pentagon, although drones are increasingly under

CIA control. But they don't send up a UAV lightly so there must be some hostile activity in the same area. Whichever way, it doesn't look good. If Alex has found McDermott, they need to be gotten out of there and fast.'

'Well, AQI or no AQI, I'm going to get her,' Steve said, ending the call.

For a few seconds he stood rooted to the spot, a chill fear racking his frame despite the searing midday heat. Should he explain the situation to the ground control station commander? He had no proof Alex was even in the area, or that she'd even found McDermott. He reckoned he'd only be losing precious time. If al-Qaeda had been spotted, he needed to act fast.

His mind in a crazy state of turmoil, a sudden familiar sound garnered his senses. Some of the men on camp called it the lawnmower because of the noise of its loud whining engine, particularly on take-off. He turned to see the Predator drone rushing along a distant runway, the unmistakable four-cylinder turbo urging the rear propeller on to its 72 mph take-off speed.

He watched it climbing until it became a speck against the steel-blue sky, disappearing a few seconds later. Without thinking further, Steve Lewis wheeled about and bolted for his own machine.

Only one thing galvanised his thoughts. He had to try and save Alex, the most important person in the world to him.

* * *

Alex opened her eyes and forced a smile, hoping the shock at his appearance didn't show. McDermott stood before her looking slightly ridiculous in a loose-fitting white kaftan that had gold embroidery on the front.

She set about flipping sand from the blanket that had covered them, glancing at him between shakes. The lieutenant looked a shadow of the man she knew. Face gaunt and with several days' growth of beard, it was his eyes that struck her the most.

Sunken into sockets grey and hollow, they held a dead, faraway look as though he was someplace else.

'Why did you come here?' he asked in a monotone.

'Because I needed to find you, to take you back home,' Alex said, standing up and brushing herself down. 'No more media, no parades, jamborees, whistles. We'll go back, somewhere quiet, forget about all the bullshit and the hype. Maybe rest up with your folks a while.'

'No,' he said, taking a step backwards. Alex could see he was clearly agitated, continuously ringing his hands, his body stooped.

'But you can't stay here.' She cast her eyes around the wreck of the building. The storm had almost stopped, but flurries of sand eddied through the openings that once served as windows, settling in haphazard patterns on the clay floor. A gust of wind ripped through the space where the double doorway once stood, two giant columns of dense wood supporting a heavy wooden lintel twice their size.

McDermott held out his hand. 'Come, I want to show you the Garden of Eden.'

She followed him as he stumbled towards the building's entrance. When he turned to check she was behind him, she saw a smile on his lips. McDermott turned to face the glorious vista, the one he had viewed only a short time ago.

'God, no, it can't be,' he cried, his face immediately draining.

Alex looked out at the desolate landscape; brush and scrub as far as the eye could see, a dead tree nearby, its branches twisted grotesquely as if in agony. Everything was covered in fine layers of sand and grit and dust that gave the desert a foreboding bleakness.

McDermott shook his head as if to rid himself of the vision. 'It can't be,' he repeated softly in disbelief. 'It was so beautiful before – my Garden of Eden.'

He turned towards her, tears in his eyes. She opened her arms and he fell into them, burying his head on her shoulder as he had once before. Soon, his body shook as he fought for air between his deep, mournful sobs.

Alex could sense his utter despair. His burden was unremitting and was destroying him. She had to get both of them out of this place and to safety. McDermott stood motionless, lost in his own world. She guided him to the corner where they'd slept and made him comfortable with the blanket.

Returning to the entrance, she got out her cell phone and made to switch it on. But it was already on, the battery dangerously low. She stared at it in horror, the sickening realisation dawning that it must have switched on accidentally when she fell from the jeep and she hadn't heard its start-up chime above the noise of the storm.

The signal was weak, but at least it was working. She saw there was a series of messages. She decided to open the latest one, a voicemail sent by Steve half an hour ago. The message was garbled but she understood he was saying something about insurgents in the vicinity and that she was in danger. He told her to stay where she was until help arrived.

Shoulders slumped, her heart suddenly pounding, Alex immediately switched the phone off to conserve its energy. The message had certainly spooked her. Gingerly, she stood back from the entrance, peering one way then the other. Nothing moved. But it did little to allay the feeling that someone might be watching them. She bit her lip, all at once feeling alarmingly vulnerable. She turned to look at McDermott. Should she tell him? Was he in a state to even care?

The lieutenant was sitting with his knees drawn up, the blanket discarded, reading his Bible and rocking to and fro.

* * *

The Predator UAV has a cruising speed of a little over 80 miles per hour. The helicopter Steve Lewis used was an OH-58 Kiowa that could do half as much again. As he took off heading north towards the co-ordinates near the small town of al-Qurnah, he estimated his flight time at forty-five minutes. The drone had a twenty-minute start on him so his quick calculation told him they should arrive at roughly the same time. He was hoping they could help each other.

A multitude of visions filled his mind. His Kiowa, an army scout machine, wasn't armed so could not be used offensively. And if he had to get in very low, which he imagined, there was considerable risk of attack from a shoulder-launched surface-to-air missile, or a rocket propelled grenade, even small arms fire. All he had was his service revolver. He knew it was madness.

Would he discover the insurgents on open ground or a camouflaged lair? Would the drone be able to flush them out? What if the insurgents had already got to Alex? He just couldn't bear the thought and banished it from his mind.

Checking his bearings, he pressed on, maintaining radio silence. He resolved to face the music when the show was finally over.

* * *

Kowolski could not get back to sleep. Something did not feel right. The words AQI kept spinning in his mind. He was convinced al-Qaeda in Iraq was an illusion, another bogeyman others dreamt up and which he had spread, now regretfully, into virtual reality.

He paced his hotel room and called down for a pot of coffee. Although he had no concrete confirmation, he had to assume that Alex had found McDermott and was bringing him in. So why the drone at those exact co-ordinates? And armed? And likely controlled by the CIA? A sudden chill nipped him in the pit of his stomach. Anything that pointed to Richard Northwood had to be viewed suspiciously. After all, he was the instigator of the whole McDermott fiasco. But to what lengths would he go to round off the affair?

Twenty-five minutes later, when he was on his third cup of

coffee and still ruminating, he received a call from Carl Whittingham.

'Gene, sorry to wake you.'

'I'm wide awake, Carl, shoot.'

'I don't know if you know but the boss sent me to Langley to sort of monitor how the agency was going to tackle this McDermott thing.'

Kowolski laughed. 'You? Spy on Northwood, the master spy?'

'Something like that,' Whittingham said. 'The guy's hyped up over this. He thought I was asleep in his office but I could see he was manic. He's had all this equipment installed – large screens, headphones and all. While he went to the John, I peeked at his desk. There was a pad with lots of scribble on it – doodling, that sort of thing.'

'Go on,' Kowolski urged.

'Well, he'd written the name of McDermott and next to it the letters KIA with a question mark.'

'Christ,' Kowolski blurted. 'Killed in action?' He thought for a few moments. 'Carl, the more I hear the more I don't like. Maybe he'd want McDermott KIAd to put a neatly-tied ribbon round his whole fucking package. Wouldn't that be just cup-cakes and ice-cream?'

'What should I do?'

'You'll have to keep him monitored and hope he won't do anything stupid while you're around.'

Kowolski clicked off, straight away dialling Alex's cell phone for the fourth time since Steve's early call. Still no reply. He paced the room deep in thought. There was only one conclusion he could reach: Richard Northwood was out to kill McDermott – and if Alex got in the way, her as well.

26

Gazing at the blank UAV picture screen so hard that his eyes hurt, Richard Northwood suddenly turned up the volume on his headset as a picture burst into view. The nervous voice of Fingers Finkelstein came through to tell him the drone's powerful camera and sensor images were now transmitting in real time.

'Sir, we've been scouring the area without success but we found this place just shy of those co-ordinates. You should be able to see the ruined building – it's the only place around.'

'I see it,' Northwood said.

'And then you get this, sir.'

Northwood's mouth dropped as the camera closed in and the heat-seeking infra red sensor revealed two figures inside the building.

'What you been seeing?' Northwood said, his voice rising. His eyes flicked to the pulsing red dot on his computer screen. It told him it was Alex inside the building – the other figure had to be McDermott.

'Sir, two people in there. One person keeps going to the building's entrance, kind of tip-toeing slowly, then peering out.'

'The other?'

'Seems to be huddled in the corner, sir.'

'The bomb-maker,' Northwood hissed.

'Could be,' Finkelstein said.

'The al-Qaeda bomb-maker busy preparing his IED, and the other's the lookout. We've got to stop them.'

Finkelstein gasped. So far his duties had consisted of a couple of surveillance sorties, a remote, passive third-party, participation. Now his fingers trembled on the controls, knowing he was one button away from unleashing a devastating onslaught on some unsuspecting target.

'Shouldn't we wait and check them out a while longer, sir?'

'No,' Northwood spat. 'They must be dealt with – you think these murdering bastards would give us time to fanny about?'

There was a moment's silence before Finkelstein spoke. 'It's your call then, sir.'

'Right,' Northwood said sharply, sitting down at his desk, his eyes not wavering from the screen.

'Prepare to fire. And count me down,' Northwood said, frantic.

Finkelstein wiped the perspiration from his hands and reached for the missile control button. Eventually, he said, 'Target locked on, sir. Preparing to fire... and four, and three and two... Holy shit! '

The helicopter swooped as if from nowhere, its image immediately filling the screen as it hovered close to the building.

'What the fuck... ' Northwood shouted, his mouth gaped open.

'Firing aborted, sir,' Finkelstein said. 'That bird's one of ours.'

Northwood watched, aghast, as the drone's camera pulled back revealing the chopper only yards from the building.

If there was another talent the young operator possessed, it was that there were few flying machines currently in service that he couldn't recognise.

'It's US Army – a Kiowa, definitely ours,' Finkelstein said, his voice now shrill.

Within seconds, the pictures were lost in a dense swathe of sand and dust debris thrown up by the helicopter's rotors.

'Keep that target building locked on. Do not, I repeat, do not waver,' Northwood screamed.

He picked up the phone, an open line to the colonel in the control centre. 'Colonel, you'd better tell me I'm seeing a fucking mirage.'

268

'No, I'm afraid you're not. She's one of ours and not authorised to be anywhere near the place.'

* * *

The noise inside the ruin was thunderous, the staccato beat reverberating off the walls like a machine gun, making it almost impossible for Alex to think straight. Was it friend or foe? Her mind was numb. Gripped in fear, she fumbled for her phone, almost dropping it, switched it on. The swirling sand blew in all directions, attacking the open doorway and windows and blasting her face so she could hardly breathe.

Backing up against a wall, she thrust the phone underneath her abaya, pulling the garment away from her body and peering down to see the phone's display screen. She needed to call someone, anyone. Steve, Kowolski, who? A new message flashed up. She opened it. Her eyes widened in shock as the words, in capital letters, screamed out at her.

'GET OUT OF THERE NOW.'

She glanced around for McDermott. He emerged from the murk, stumbling towards the window where the helicopter hovered, one hand shielding his eyes from the onslaught. Alex shrieked, at once horror-struck. McDermott had withdrawn his service revolver and was waving it menacingly at the helicopter like a madman. He laughed, a deranged faraway look in his eyes as he brought the pistol level, about to fire.

Alex cried out but her warning was lost in the cacophony. Gritting her teeth, her senses suddenly bristled with rage. The helicopter might be their only hope of escape. And here was the lieutenant, acting like a maniac and threatening their very survival.

She darted forward, her foot slipping on the sandy floor almost causing her to lose balance.

'No!' she screamed, lashing out with a frantic high kick. Her aim was true, focussed through fear and adrenalin. The gun flew from McDermott's grasp, clattering into the corner. He stood, stunned, not fully comprehending what had happened.

Now, she had to be the leader, she the rescuer. Alex grabbed hold of his arm, half pushing, half pulling him towards the far end of the room away from the helicopter. 'We have to get out of here. Do you understand?'

Hoisting herself up on to the window ledge, she grimaced as the rough jagged stone scraped her knees. She held out her hand for him to follow but he was reluctant, standing stock still, dazed, in his own world.

'Lieutenant. Come with me – that's an order,' she shouted as loud as she could. He stared at her, a look of recognition suddenly in his eyes. Straightening his body, he reached up, took her outstretched hand and clambered up on to the ledge.

Together they prepared to leap from the window.

* * *

Northwood thumped his desk in frustration. The screen was a fog. And now someone was hammering at his door. He glanced round. The door handle was being twisted and turned. Carl Whittingham was trying to get in.

Finkelstein's excited voice suddenly erupted into his headphones. 'The picture's beginning to clear, sir.'

Northwood squinted, his heart leaping. Sure enough, the faint outline of the building came into view. And the helicopter was no longer there. Wherever it had gone it was no longer in the line of fire.

'Prepare to fire,' Northwood said, rubbing his eyes and blinking at the screen.

But Finkelstein could not discern any figures in the building. He zoomed the drone's camera out, then in again. Nothing.

A louder crash at Northwood's door distracted him. It sounded like Whittingham was using something as a battering ram because he could see the hinges starting to give way. He rushed to the door, dragging a chair with him and wedging it against the handle.

'Fire when ready,' Northwood yelled into his mouthpiece, no longer looking at the screen.

'But... ' Finkelstein protested.

'Fire that goddamn missile.'

'Firing now, sir.'

Northwood glanced back at the screen just in time to see the bright flash as the Hellfire was released. An instant later, a smile spread across his lips as the building was pulverised.

* * *

They'd landed in a heap, knocking each other over. The helicopter had changed position and Alex could now hear it some way above them.

'Quick, come on,' she shouted as they scrambled to their feet.

'My Bible,' McDermott said, frantically looking around.

'There, there it is, quick,' Alex said, spotting it just a few feet away where it had fallen from his waistband, her urgency at fever pitch.

They were halfway down the hill when the missile struck the building. The air turned a yellow-orange colour and the deafening blast from the explosion sent them sprawling. Rocks and debris rained down, stinging like needles, covering them in a shroud of grey dust. Alex felt herself lifted into the air in a helpless, uncontrollable spin. Twelve inches either way and she would have had a soft landing. But she couldn't prevent herself crashing into a boulder jutting out of the sand, landing head first with a sickening thud.

She wasn't sure if she'd been knocked unconscious but when she finally opened her eyes, everything was surreal and nothing made sense. Her face was wet and she could see blood on the ground. Her mind in turmoil, she fought for logic, some sort of perspective, and lost. At first, she thought she was staring at someone else's blood. But, now finding herself on all fours, she could see it dripping from her nose and her chin, staining the bleached white rock crimson.

Trying to raise her head, the sun was dazzling. The beat of the helicopter sounded high above. She tried to find it, but couldn't lift her head enough. She'd been wrong, she thought. The helicopter had not come to save them. It must have fired the rocket that nearly destroyed them. And now what? Is this when it closed in for the kill? Did the pilot shout or sing or swear when he hit the button or was the exultation silent, maybe with a touch of sombre reflection? She turned slowly, the pain in her neck almost unbearable, and that was when she saw the lieutenant. McDermott, his clothes torn and bloodstained, was staggering towards the wreck of the building. The walls were no longer standing, now just a mound of rubble. But the wooden pillars and the giant wooden lintel were still there, leaning crazily, on fire and blazing like a gateway to hell.

She watched the lieutenant reach the conflagration, pause for a couple of seconds. Then, his head low as if reading from the open Bible in his hands, he marched forward. Alex tried to cry out but no sound came from her lips.

McDermott disappeared into the flames and was gone.

The blood stung her eyes and her head pounded mercilessly. She could hear herself groaning, deep mournful whimpers that shook her body but seemed to come from someplace else. The helicopter sounded closer now, its thud, thud, deafening. So the helicopter was the foe. It had blasted the building and now it was coming for her. Soon it would open up with its 30 mm automatic cannon, ripping her to shreds. Would death be instantaneous, or would there be a split second when the first round hit the torso and the senses screamed in pain?

It was only a moment after these garbled thoughts had teased her brain that she passed out.

* * *

Richard Northwood turned the key in his office door and opened it. 'Carl,' he smiled. 'What's going down, man?'

Whittingham stood there, feeling foolish. 'I... I was trying to get in.'

'Well, old buddie, you should have just knocked.'

Then he returned to his chair, put his feet up on the desk and leaned back, hands behind his head.

'Anyway it's all over. You missed a great show,' he said contentedly.

27

Steve Lewis watched intensely as the small drops of propofol entered the intravenous catheter attached to Alex's arm. The effect on him was almost trance-like. He had never seen so many tubes and wires attached to one person. Never seen anyone lying so still and looking so vulnerable.

The Kuwaiti doctor he had met several times over the past week entered the room. A monitoring nurse sitting in the corner stood up and smiled at him. The doctor nodded his acknowledgement and strode to Alex's bed, unclipped a chart from the bed-frame and began studying it.

'Good,' he murmured, 'very good.' He flicked over a page of her notes. 'How long is it now? Nine days,' he answered himself. 'I think tomorrow we will have her back in the land of the living.'

'Fabulous,' Steve said, the relief on his face palpable. 'I wanted to be here when she came round of course, but time's getting pretty tight back at the base.'

'Well, I hope to see you tomorrow, then,' the doctor said, leaving.

Steve sat down again, held Alex's hand. 'You hear that, baby? Tomorrow you can open those lovely big eyes of yours and say hello again.'

He puffed out his cheeks, ran a hand through his hair. In a longer spell of conversation with the doctor, Steve had been told the salient aspects of her treatment. The intravenous drip contained the anaesthetic that would keep her in the induced coma for as long as was necessary to allow the swelling on her brain to subside. This would reduce the metabolic rate of brain tissue and slow the cerebral blood flow. The rest of the

274

apparatus surrounding the bed was monitoring her heart rate, blood pressure, temperature and gases.

Steve went out into the corridor. Hospital habit had drilled him with the need for change for the coffee machine and he fished in his pocket for the right coins. Taking a sip from the steaming carton, he found a bench, pulled out his phone and hit a speed key.

'Hi Kowolski. The doc says tomorrow.'

'Wow, that's great news, Steve.'

'Where are you?'

'I'm here in Kuwait – arrived last night.'

'You all done now, the business finished?'

'Yeah,' Kowolski sighed. 'Hated every minute of it, every goddamn lying word I had to write.'

'I saw it on the news. So the lieutenant was killed in combat on a special mission to flush out al-Qaeda. Needed to be done, though?'

'What we put the poor guy through, it was no wonder he cracked. But he was still a hero, Steve, deserved to be buried like one – full military honours an' all.'

'Watched it on television in Alex's room. She sure as hell won't be happy.'

'Tell me about it. The President's rating's gone sky high since he appeared at the funeral. Did you see him put his arms around McDermott's mom and pop? Jeesh, I almost puked.'

'I caught a glimpse of Northwood, too.'

'You know what? People like him seem blessed to sail through every event with a following tail-wind. But, sooner or later, he'll be forced to meet the hurricane head on. I, for one, want to be around when he does.'

'Will I see you tomorrow, then?'

'Sure thing. I feel it would be better for me to explain things to Alex if she's up to it.'

* * *

Kowolski arrived at Alex's bedside with a couple of minutes to spare. Steve greeted him, worry etched on his face. He gestured for Kowolski to stand the same side of the bed as him. Opposite, the doctor nodded to one of the two nurses present and watched her turn off the intravenous drip.

'Now we wait, but not long,' the doctor smiled.

Kowolski shifted nervously. He felt like cutting through the tension with a light-hearted remark, but thought better of it. He swallowed hard, his throat suddenly dry. He was used to being in control, directing things the way he wanted. But this situation was out of his hands and he felt uncomfortable because of it.

Moments later, Alex opened her eyes, blinking. She saw Kowolski and Steve, felt Steve holding her hand. For a fleeting moment she thought she was in her apartment in New York and wondered what these other people were doing there. Slowly, the realisation dawned.

A nurse helped her to sit up, held a glass of water to her lips. Her throat hurt when she swallowed. Her mind swam with a blunted awareness that was vague and surreal.

'I've been in a very strange, dark place,' she said, her voice weak and shaky. 'It was horrible.'

'You're okay now, babe,' Steve said squeezing her hand. 'So how're you feeling?'

'Weird, but okay I guess.'

Suddenly her eyes narrowed, a frown appearing. 'McDermott...' she tailed off.

Kowolski moved closer, felt the need to rub his chin, a self-conscious gesture to shield the bare-faced reality of the answer he didn't want to utter. He glanced at Steve, the seriousness in his face told its own story. Then he turned to Alex, could see her eyes pleading for a reply. He simply shook his head.

Alex closed her eyes. She could see flames, bright and dancing, McDermott stumbling towards the conflagration. It was like she was hanging by her fingernails from a cliff edge, straining to hold on to the picture that flashed tantalizingly into her head. But the vision then slipped from her mind just as if she'd lost her grip.

'I'll bust their goddamned asses,' Alex said, her shoulders shaking with anger. 'Everyone should be told what happened, what they did to him.'

Kowolski grimaced. 'It's too late to turn over stones, Alex. He's been buried as a fine soldier. We have to let it be. Think of his folks.'

Alex slumped back, sinking into her pillow.

'From now on, Alex, there'll be no more lies from me – only the truth. And I want you to join me in spreading the right word. What do you say?'

But Alex said nothing. Her eyes were already closed.

* * *

A little over three months later, 25 January 2004, the Iraqi daily newspaper *Al Mada* broke the story on the UN's oil for food kickbacks scandal. The news quickly made headlines throughout the world. In New York, a new website, Freedom is Truth, joined calls for a full-scale inquiry into the affair, starting with Congress. The website's founders were listed as Gene Kowolski and Alexandra Stead.

—